Something
to
Crow About

Something

to

Crow About

Another P.J. Benson Mystery

MARIS SOULE

Something to Crow About
Copyright © 2021 by Maris Soule
First Tier Press

ISBN 13-978-1-7326493-2-3

Cover design by Christopher Wait
High Pines Creative, Inc
www.highpinescreative.com
Cover images © Getty Images

MYSTERIES BY MARIS SOULE

The Crows
As the Crow Flies
Eat Crow and Die
Eye of the Crow

A Killer Past

Echoes of Terror

ROMANTIC SUSPENSE

Haunted
Chase the Dream

Dedicated to P.J. Benson's fans who begged
for one more book.

Chapter One

"He caught me," a female voice said from the other side of a stall door. "I didn't even know he was in the store. I was at the computer looking at the pictures I'd taken when he came up behind me. I barely had time to disconnect from the USB port and get out of there."

I stopped where I was, still holding open the door to the women's bathroom. All I could see was a pair of snow boots under one of the two stalls and an Out of Order sign on the other. I didn't want to eavesdrop on the woman's conversation, but with this baby pressing against my bladder, I was lucky to have made it this far without peeing my pants.

"Yes. These pictures show everything you need," Snow Boots continued. "The hidden compartments, origins of the shipments, everything. If I can get to a computer, I'll send you the pictures."

The woman's voice reminded me of a former coworker's, and I might not be one to eavesdrop, but Snow Boots now had me wondering where those hidden compartments were located and what was being shipped. It didn't sound like legitimate merchandise if having those pictures meant she had to get away as fast as she could.

Slipping into the other stall and listening in on the conversation wouldn't have been a problem if there hadn't been that "Out of Order" sign on the stall door. I debated what to do next. The church had an upstairs bathroom, but I wasn't sure it would be unlocked, or if I could make it up there without losing control.

"No, I'm not home," Snow Boots said. "He threatened me and came after me, so I didn't want to go there. I'm at the church near the brewery where we met last week. I'm pretty sure I gave him the slip, but you and I gotta meet. You promised you'd take care of me. Well, these people don't play around, so take care of me."

I let the entry door close behind me and cleared my throat. Loudly.

"Oh, shit. There's someone in here with me."

"Just a pregnant woman who needs to pee," I said. "Really, really needs to pee."

"Yeah, yeah. Just give me a minute," she answered, and then said, "I'm in the church's bathroom. There's some sort of meeting going on down here."

One I was supposed to be attending. I squeezed my thighs together. "Please hurry," I begged.

"Keep your pants on," she snapped back.

Keep your pants on? That did sound familiar. More than once Brenda Cox had said that to me when I wanted a set of figures for a tax form.

"I don't care," Snow Boots continued, "I ain't got no family. Just put me somewhere where they can't find me."

"Brenda, is that you?" I asked.

For a moment my question was followed by silence, then a hesitant, "Who's out there?"

"P.J.," I said. "P.J. Benson."

"P.J.?" she repeated, then, "Oh my gosh. I . . . Look . . . I'll be done in a minute."

I hoped it wouldn't be a long minute. With pressure building, I glanced at the stall with the "Out of Order" sign.

Brenda went back to talking to the person on the phone. "It's a friend," she said. "Someone I've known a long time. Yeah, she's safe. Listen, you've gotta meet me. At the brewery. Okay?"

Come on, Brenda, finish up, I mentally urged.

"What do you mean you've got to get this approved?"

I closed my eyes and clenched my thighs.

"Okay. Ten minutes."

I sighed in relief when I heard her flush the toilet.

"Yeah, that's a good idea," she said over the rush of water. "Maybe I'll pray this all works out."

Brenda was slipping her cell phone into her purse when she stepped out of the stall. Although it had been over a year since I'd last seen her, she looked the same. Fifteen years my senior, Brenda took me under her wing when I first started working at Quick Sums, and we quickly became close work friends.

Physically, we were totally opposite. Her burnished brown skin was a stark contrast to my pale coloring, she was five-feet-seven in bare feet, and she used makeup like a fashion model. I, on the other hand, barely made it to five-feet-two and rarely put on anything more than lipstick. We did both have curly hair that we would alternate between calling a blessing and a bane, and we both had brown eyes, though hers were so dark they looked almost black.

Seeing her now, I felt guilty for letting so long go by without reconnecting with her. Of course, I'd been busy during that time, first finding a body in my dining room, then being accused of murder and having my life threatened. I'd also been busy doing other things.

"What the hell have you been up to?" Brenda said, her gaze locked on my nine-month swollen belly. "Weren't you the one who said you were never getting pregnant?"

"Yeah, well, I've learned not to depend on birth control pills."

"An 'oops' huh? Do you know who the father is?"

"Yes." Just like Brenda to ask. She was the one who used to talk about the men she dated and slept with. She used to tease me about my lack of dates. "I married him. And—"

Brenda cut me off. "Whoa, that's something else you said you'd never do." She glanced toward the exit door, then back at me. "Look, I've gotta meet someone, but seeing you gives me an idea. When you left Quick Sums, you moved, didn't you? Started your own accounting business?"

"Yeah, I have a home-based office. If you're in trouble, my husband might—"

Again, she didn't let me finish. "You got a business card or something?"

"Yes, but . . ." I was going to ask her to wait until after I used the toilet, but as edgy as she seemed, I decided it would be just as fast if I gave her a card, especially since she now blocked my way to the toilet. I quickly dug into my over-sized purse.

Brenda took the card I handed her and nodded. "Yeah, that's it. Zenith, Michigan. Small town, right? Hard to find?"

"It's small," I agreed, then grimaced, my bladder once again reminding me why I was in the bathroom. "Look, I really need to pee," I said, trying to edge around her as she slipped my business card into her purse. "But I couldn't help overhearing what you were saying. I don't know who you're meeting, but if your life is in danger, you need to call 9-1-1."

"I'll be fine," she said and grinned. "But give me a hug, girl."

I didn't have a chance to refuse. Brenda wrapped an arm around my shoulders and jerked me close. Her hug was awkward, primarily because of the size of my belly, the differences in our heights, and my bulky cross-body purse.

"I can't begin to tell you how good it is to see you," she said close to my ear. "Running into you here is perfect. Absolutely perfect."

"Right," I said, hoping she wouldn't squeeze me too tight. "Call me. Okay?"

To my relief, she stepped to the side, and I rushed into the vacated stall. I barely heard her say, "See you soon."

Chapter Two

As I left the bathroom and headed down the hall to the meeting room, I thought about my encounter with Brenda. What I'd overheard sounded like a scene from a spy movie. *These people don't play around,* she'd said.

Who were *these* people? What exactly did the pictures show? And who was she meeting?

I could almost hear Wade saying, "Don't get involved, P.J."

Well, my husband wouldn't have to worry about me this time. I was two weeks from my due date and could barely get from one bathroom to the next. All I wanted was an easy delivery and a healthy baby. As much as I liked Brenda, this baby was my priority. I wasn't going to get involved in her problems, but I would tell Wade what I'd overheard.

As quietly as I could, I entered the classroom.

The Mothers-to-Be group appropriately met in the church's downstairs preschoolers' classroom. Two windows on the outside wall allowed natural light into the room but were set too high to cause a distraction to toddlers. On the walls, next to religious posters showing Jesus as a baby, were childish crayon drawings. It was a cheerful room with a decorated toy box, a colorful rug where children could play, low shelves with children's books, a variety of stuffed animals, and chairs sized for preschoolers. Thankfully, the room also had adult-sized chairs, six of them now placed in a circle near the door—two of them empty.

"I am so tired of always having to go pee," Sarah said as I slid into the nearest empty chair. "There are times I'm not sure I'm going to make it."

I just barely did, I could have added.

Sarah is the youngest member of the Mothers-To-Be group. Barely out of high school and unmarried, she talks about her boyfriend as if he were her husband and acts as though being pregnant is a fun adventure. She has purple hair and colorful tattoos, and I've found it hard to identify with her. Actually, I've found it hard to identify with any of the women in the group.

Connie Ryder, the founder of the Mothers-to-Be group, is in her early fifties, a widow with two grown sons. She'd been an OB/GYN nurse for twenty-five years. Two years ago she'd retired to become a midwife. She told us Michigan had one of the highest infant mortality rates in the nation—especially for Black and Hispanic infants—and, even though the Kalamazoo area's infant death rate wasn't as high as Detroit's, in her opinion any death that could be prevented was one too many. That was why she created the Mothers-to-Be group. This was her effort to save as many babies as she could by preparing first-time mothers.

Being white, thirty, and in relatively good physical shape, I don't really fit the "at risk" criteria; however, my doctor highly recommended I join this group. She's worried about my mental state, and so am I. So, for the last two months, starting right after the first week in January, I've been coming twice a week to meet with Connie and four other pregnant women: Sarah Fry, Tamara Trulain, Maria Gonzales, and Anna Carr.

My guess is Sarah is in the group because of her age and obvious immaturity, and Tamara is here because she is thirty-five and has had two miscarriages. She is eight months pregnant and so far everything seems to be going well for her, but she is very nervous. Maria, on the other hand, comes across as angry. More than once she's said she didn't want to join the group and only did so because she was ordered to. By whom she won't say. Considering how often she badmouths her husband I don't think he's the one who gave the order.

Anna is the member I feel the closest to. Although she's a self-proclaimed lesbian and Black, she also graduated from Western Michigan University with a major in business and a minor in accounting. Numbers are important to both of us. In fact, since she's only four years older than I am, there's a good chance we had accounting classes together, though I don't remember her.

Once settled in my seat, I saw the other missing member was Maria, but before I had a chance to wonder if Connie had said why Maria wasn't there, the door opened, and she entered the room, frowning and shaking her head. "Sorry," she said. "Husband call. Big problem." She sat beside me and gave an irritated grunt. "He iz an idiot. He can do nothing right."

"You're a newlywed," Tamara said. "Give him time. He'll learn."

Maria shook her head. "He make more mistakes like this, he not live long enough to learn."

"Oh-ho," Connie said, frowning. "That's pretty harsh. You want to talk about it, Maria?"

"No," Maria snapped, then looked around at the rest of us. She must have realized how angry she sounded, because she finally smiled and said, "Iz okay. All will be okay."

Personally, I doubted that. This wasn't the first time Maria had sounded off about her husband's intellect, or lack of. The day I met her, she told me she'd only recently moved to Michigan and that things were done different in Mexico, where she had lived all of her life. Although she is twenty-seven-years-old, Hispanic, and probably Catholic, I'm guessing she was forced to marry the guy. It didn't take a master's degree in accounting to figure being eight-and-a-half months pregnant but only married for six months indicated some hanky-panky went on before the wedding.

Connie waited for Maria to say more, but Maria said nothing. The blare of a car horn outside of the church broke the silence, and Connie turned to Anna. "Last time we met you said you were having leg cramps. How are you doing?"

"Better. Those leg stretches helped, but I sure would like to see my feet again."

"Me, too," I echoed. Anna's even shorter than I am, and last month she and I laughed about the size of our bellies and the loss of our feet. The closer I was getting to my due date, the less funny that was becoming.

Connie's focus turned to me. "How about you, P.J.? Any swelling? Legs? Ankles? Feet?"

"No, no swelling, but by the end of the day, my legs are really tired. And," I patted my belly, "some days I feel like my skin has been stretched to its limit."

"Use the lotion I gave you last week. That should keep your skin supple. As for your legs, tonight when you get home, sit down, put your feet up, and let your husband fix dinner."

The idea sounded great, but not possible. "Actually, the three of us—Wade, Jason, and I—were planning on coming into town together and going out for pizza after this meeting. But Wade got an emergency call just before we were about to leave."

"Jason's your stepson, right?" Tamara said. "Do you just leave him home alone when you and your husband are gone?"

"Oh, no," I assured her. I didn't want her thinking I'd leave a seven-year-old alone by himself for several hours. "Today I dropped him off at my grandmother's house before coming here. I'll pick him up from there, and we'll go have pizza."

"Emergency call?" Maria made the idea sound questionable. "Iz Friday. Date night. Maybe his girlfriend want him to spend evening with her, not you and his son."

I turned to face her. "My husband does not have a girlfriend. This afternoon he's investigating a possible murder."

"You sure no girlfriend?" Maria smirked. "Last week you say he keep getting calls from some woman. It make you really upset."

"I was upset with her, not him." Though the fact that he took Marge's calls and went into the other room to talk to her, did bother me. "I was overly tired that night, and she called at a bad time."

"Hey, I'd be upset if some woman had the hots for Tommy," Sarah said. "I told him if I ever caught him seeing another woman behind my back, he'd be out the door."

"Wade doesn't need to see this woman behind my back," I said. "She's the sheriff's department's forensic photographer. They work together."

"Well, I'm glad I don't have your problem," Tamara said. "My husband owns several businesses and often has to be away, traveling. If I thought Alan was being unfaithful . . ." She shook her head.

"I *am* sure my husband is not being unfaithful," I said firmly.

"Okay, enough about husbands," Connie said, "I want—"

The loud wail of an emergency vehicle siren pierced the air, followed by the grinding of brakes. Connie stopped talking, and we all looked toward the windows. I couldn't tell if it was a fire engine or an ambulance, but it had stopped right outside of the church.

"I want to see what's going on." Tamara left our group and went over to the windows.

"What do you see?" Connie asked and stood.

Tamara looked through one window, then the other. "I see a Kalamazoo Safety Patrol car parked in the church's driveway and a fire engine on the street."

Connie headed for the windows, then Maria and Sarah. Finally, Anna and I got up and went over, though I wasn't sure why we bothered. Even standing on our toes, the two of us couldn't see out. The bane of being short.

Connie became our eyes. "There are two patrol cars now. Lots of people milling around. Oh, oh. Whatever happened, it can't be good. Here comes an ambulance."

I heard the ambulance's siren. Heard the siren turn off right outside of the church. Connie said something about going up to see if she could help, then talked herself out of it. "Nothing I could do that the paramedics can't," she said.

Since I couldn't see anything, I drifted back to my chair. The others soon followed. We were all subdued after that. To my relief, Wade's fidelity or infidelity was forgotten, and Connie demonstrated a new exercise that she assured us would help us when we went into labor. We tried it, but with little enthusiasm. I think we were all bothered by what was going on outside. Connie ended the session earlier than usual.

When I came out the back door to the parking lot, I was hit by a cold blast of air. Two Kalamazoo Public Safety vehicles were now parked by the side of the church, blocking that exit from the lot. For a second I thought about walking up to the street and asking one of the officers what had happened, then decided against the idea. Picking up Jason so we could go out for pizza was more important than being a gawker. I was halfway to my car when Anna called from behind, "P.J., wait."

I paused.

"I need some professional advice," she said the moment she caught up with me. "I think a well-known, well-liked woman in this community is embezzling, but before I report it to anyone, I'd like a second opinion."

.

Chapter Three

"Embezzling?" I repeated.

"Yes." Anna waited until Sarah walked by, then went on. "I'm on the board of the charity: Homes4Homeless. That's written as one word with the numeral four. It's fairly new."

"Actually, I've heard of it. Some of my clients have donated to the charity."

"Okay. Good." She smiled. "Well, anyway, having been homeless myself when I was younger, I'm all for the idea of finding homes for the homeless. So, a couple years ago when a friend asked if I'd be on the board, I agreed. Since then, I've even volunteered at some of the charity's money-raising events and I've gotten to know many of the regulars." Anna paused and lowered her voice. "Have you heard of Madeline Welkum?"

"Yes." The woman's name often appeared in the *Kalamazoo Gazette*, usually in connection with social events, and recently had been mentioned as a possible candidate for the state senate. "Is she connected to Homes4Homeless?"

"Connected? She created the charity."

That I hadn't heard.

"Yes. She's the CEO and director. And if you've ever seen her on TV or met her in person, she's rather imposing." Anna laughed. "She reminds me of Maleficent from Disney's *Sleeping Beauty*."

I had seen the woman on TV and agreed, in part. Madeline Welkum was tall, slender, and had a haughty, almost regal, way of holding herself. On the other hand, I'd never pictured her as a villainess. "You think she's evil?"

"Oh, no," Anna said. "At least, I hope she isn't. The problem is—"

"I talked to the police out front," Connie said, coming up beside us. "They wouldn't say much about what happened, just that the driveway by the church was going to be blocked for hours."

"Must have been a bad accident," Anna said.

"Which means, from what my husband has told me, the evidence gathering will take hours." I glanced at the street that ran behind the church. "Thank goodness this lot had has two exits.

"I'm sure it helps with the traffic situation Sunday mornings." Connie gave a shiver and gathered her jacket close around her body. "Aren't you two getting cold standing out here? You don't want to catch a cold before the baby's born. There's nothing worse than being all stuffed up and having a difficult time breathing while in labor. Trust me, I know."

I was starting to feel cold, but I hadn't wanted to interrupt Anna.

"You're right, Connie," Anna said. "Let's go get a cup of coffee, P.J."

"No can do." Although the smell of coffee no longer made me throw up, as it did the first three months of my pregnancy, I didn't have the time. "As I said earlier, I have to pick up my stepson and take him out for a pizza." I dug into my purse, pulled out a business card, and handed it to Anna. "Give me a call. You can either tell me more over the phone or we can figure out a time and place to meet."

Anna took the card and frowned. "P.J. Benson? I thought you said your last name was Kingsley."

"That's my married name. I decided to keep my maiden name as my business name."

"You and Maria," Connie said.

It took me a moment to understand what Connie meant, then I remembered Maria had said she could barely pronounce her husband's last name, much less spell it, so she'd kept her family name. "The difference is," I said, "I use Wade's last name for everything else."

"If I were ever to marry," Anna said, "I would keep my last name. I like Carr. It's easy to spell, easy to remember." She slipped my business card into her jacket pocket then clicked open her car door. "Tomorrow a good time to call?"

"Far as I know. I'll probably be home with Jason."

I said goodbye and started toward my car. Connie walked with me. "So has your stepson accepted the idea that he's going to have a sister soon?"

"I think so. Wade and I have talked to him, told him this baby won't change how we feel about him, but I really wish this wasn't happening so soon after the death of his mother. I know he's still mourning the loss of her."

"You said you've taken him to a therapist. Right?"

I nodded. "She said we need to keep Jason involved in the pregnancy so he feels a part of the process, which is why we let him pick a name for the baby. He came up with Paige." I still had to smile, remembering Jason's enthusiasm for the name. "Turns out there's a girl in his class that he really likes, and her name is Paige. Joy is Wade's mother's name, so our baby will be Paige Joy Kingsley."

"Paige Joy," Connie repeated and then chuckled. "Another P.J. It's perfect."

I agreed. "The therapist also thinks having the baby at home will help."

"I'll make sure he feels like he's a part of the experience." Connie patted my shoulder. "It's all going to work out fine, P.J. You'll see.

Relax and enjoy these last few days when you don't have a baby demanding your full attention."

Relax. I wished I could. The closer I got to my due date, the more nervous I felt.

At her car, Connie and I said our goodbyes, and I walked on to mine. I'd just gotten in when my cell phone chimed. The call was from Ken Paget, the computer whiz who had helped me several times over the last twelve months. Ken and I have become friends, but I was usually the one who called him—when I was having computer problems—not the other way around.

I pressed accept, but before I even had a chance to say hello, I heard a whispered, "Did they get there in time?"

"Get where? Who is this?" I didn't recognize the voice.

"It's me, Ken."

"Uh-huh." I wasn't convinced. The caller might be using Ken's phone, but Ken usually called me Pajama Girl.

He must have sensed my doubt. "It is me, Pajama Girl. I . . ." he stammered. "I did something really stupid."

"Stupid like what?"

"Is your husband home?"

"I don't know. I'm not home; I'm in Kalamazoo."

"Do . . . Do you know where he is?"

Ken sounded nervous, his voice cracking as well as the whispering. Something was wrong. "Wade left the house before I did," I said. "Some sort of an emergency. Why? What's the problem, Ken?"

"An emergency in Zenith?"

"He did say it was at the trailer park." And Zenith did have a mobile home park just past the grocery store, about a half mile from the one and only blinking stoplight at the center of the village. "Why?" I repeated.

"He's homicide, isn't he? They wouldn't call him unless someone was dead, right?"

Wade was a homicide detective and did investigate murders. "What is going on, Ken? Why do you want to know where Wade is, and why are you whispering?"

"I'm whispering because I'm at a meeting. I found Jer—" He didn't finish, but immediately, in a loud voice, yelled to someone, "I'll be there in a minute." He was whispering again when he came back to me. "I'm sorry, P.J., I shouldn't have called you. It's just . . . Damn, I really screwed up this time."

He hung up before I had a chance to ask how he'd screwed up, and for a second I simply stared at my phone, my thoughts in a jumble. As much as I liked Ken and respected his computer abilities—I was the one who recommended him when the Zenith Township Office needed a part-time IT person—Wade doesn't think highly of Ken. Mostly, I believe, because Ken was arrested last summer for marijuana possession. He and his friend, Jerry, were found with a lot more of the weed than is legal. It was Ken's first offense, and he was given a slap on the wrist, but his friend took off for parts unknown.

"I found Jer—." Did he mean his friend Jerry?

I put away my phone and started the car, but I kept wondering what was going on. Had he found Jerry and wanted to turn him in? Did something go wrong? How did Ken screw up?

I just didn't know.

Chapter Four

Grandma Carter was standing outside her front door, smoking. I have noticed she doesn't smoke around Jason. Much as I love her, I wish she hadn't smoked around me when I lived with her. I've had years of being exposed to secondhand smoke.

Grandma isn't a big woman—I think I got my short height from her—but she has more energy in her seventies than I've ever had. I also inherited my curly brown hair from her, though her hair is now a salt-and-pepper gray.

"Sorry I'm late," I said when I reached her. "There was some sort of an accident in front of the church where we meet. Police cars everywhere. I had to take side streets to get around the area they had blocked off."

"No problem," she said and gave me a quick hug.

I glanced at the door in front of me. "Jason inside?"

"He's mopping my kitchen floor and dusting in the living room." She chuckled. "That will teach him to bet he could beat me at checkers."

"I warned him about you."

She grinned. "Took you a while before you learned not to challenge the Pro. Also, I think something's bothering him."

"Like what?"

"He wouldn't say, but while we were making cookies, he sighed a lot."

"Sighed a lot?"

"Yeah, sighed and seemed distracted. Maybe it's nothing, but I figured you should know." She shrugged. "So, how'd your baby meeting go?"

"All right. Pretty much the usual. Complaints about lack of sleep and having to run to the john every half hour. A lecture about the benefit of staying physically active, and that we shouldn't be afraid about giving birth."

"What about you? Are you still afraid? Still worried that you'll end up like your mother?"

I shrugged, but I couldn't deny it.

"You realize she started showing signs way before she actually gave birth to you. Had delusions. Some paranoia."

"You're not making me feel better, Grandma. Just last week I couldn't find my wallet and went paranoid. I accused Jason of taking it. Even blamed a neighbor who'd stopped by to talk to Wade. And then I found it, behind the recliner, Baraka's tooth marks and doggy slobber clearly marking him as the thief. Oh, and delusional? Wade's still giving me a bad time for waking him out of a sound sleep to kill the monster spider in the shower."

"Yes, but in your case, I'll bet there really was a spider in the shower. Your mother saw things that weren't there."

"I hate spiders," I said, a shiver running down my spine as I remembered the one in the shower. "And it was really big." Maybe not monstrous, but big. "For the rest of the day, I felt as if spiders were crawling through my hair and up and down my arms."

"You've always been afraid of spiders, P.J., so stop worrying about becoming schizophrenic."

"How can I not worry?" I said. "I just turned thirty, a common age for schizophrenia to show up in women."

"So, if it happens, it happens. There's nothing you can do to prevent it. What you need to do is start enjoying your pregnancy."

I patted the large lump that protruded beneath my breasts. "I guess for the most part I have been, but it's a little hard to enjoy something that kicks my sides, gives me heartburn, and presses against my bladder. Which reminds me, may I use the bathroom?"

"Sure." Grandma laughed, snuffed out her cigarette, and followed me into the house.

* * *

I let Jason choose where we should go for pizza, and I let him choose what he wanted on the pizza, so I was a little surprised when he only ate half a slice. "Too many cookies?" I asked when he sat back in the booth and stared out the window.

"Yeah, I guess."

"They are good." I'd had one before we left Grandma's house. She'd kept a few for herself and sent the rest home with me. "Should I freeze them so you can take them to school on Saint Patrick's Day?"

Jason looked at me. "Will they still be good?"

"They should be. It's less than two weeks away. We can put green frosting on them."

He shrugged and looked back out the window. "Okay. Maybe they'll help."

"Help?" That wasn't a response I expected. "Help with what?"

"Nuttun'."

"Come on, Jason. What's up? Why do you need help at school?" His last report card had indicated he was doing well. His second-grade teacher had even written positive comments about his work ethic.

"There's just a couple of kids. They don't like me. So maybe . . ."

"How do you know they don't like you?"

Again, he shrugged. "I just know."

Since he still wouldn't look at me, I had a feeling it was more than that. "How? How do you know?"

"They . . ."

He clenched his lips and squeezed his eyes closed, but I still saw a tear slide down his cheek. "Honey, what is it?" I asked as I scooted out of my side of the booth—the edge of the table rubbing the top of my extended belly—and moved over next to Jason.

"Nuttun'." He repeated as I put an arm around his shoulders and drew him closer.

"It's more than nothing," I said. "Now, tell me what's up. What do these kids do that makes you think they don't like you?"

"They push me. At least one does. And he calls me names. The others just laugh."

"And why does the one push you?"

"I don't know," Jason mumbled into my side.

"What kind of names does he call you?"

"Piglet." Jason did look up at me. "He said, since my dad is a pig, I must be a piglet. And he called your house a pigsty."

I would admit I'm not the neatest person around, but I certainly wouldn't classify my house as a pig pen. "And what do you do when he says these things?"

Jason again lowered his head, his words barely above a whisper. "Daddy said I shouldn't fight."

"Hmm." I wasn't sure how to respond. I'm the stepmother, the figure portrayed as evil in so many children's stories. Should I give him advice? I don't want to contradict anything Wade has said.

"I think we need to talk to your dad," I said. "Shall we box up this pizza and head home? Maybe your dad will be back."

Chapter Five

Wade didn't get home until Jason was already upstairs in bed. I had planned on watching the eleven o'clock news. I thought there might be something about the accident in front of the church, but I fell asleep in the lounge chair in the living room sometime around the middle of my ten o'clock show. It was my dog, Baraka, rising from where he'd been lying next to the chair that woke me. Wade had pulled into the driveway.

I was waiting in the kitchen, Baraka by my side, when Wade came into the house. A giddy sensation stirred within me. From the first time I met him, Wade has had that effect on me. It's not just his looks, though he does remind me of Nicolas Cage, with maybe a bit of Tom Cruise mixed in. A tall Tom Cruise.

No, it's more than his physical appearance. It's the self-assured way he carries himself, his subtle sense of humor, and his devotion to his family. Although I haven't been around his parents much, I love the way he spars with his sister, Ginny, and acts with his son. It was breaking Wade's heart when he thought his ex would move to California and take Jason with her. Although I'm not glad she's dead, I am glad things turned out as they have.

Wade and I should not have ended up as lovers, and I'm sure we broke all sorts of law enforcement policies, but hormones ruled. As I told Brenda, I never planned on getting married. Now I can't imagine life without Wade, and I worry every time he leaves for work that he might not come back alive.

Tonight, he returned looking exhausted. "Rough one?" I asked.

He nodded. "Is there anything to eat? I'm starving."

"Pizza," I said, "I'll warm it for you."

I also got him a beer. As he ate, seated at the old wooden table in the dining room, I sat across from him and silently tried to think of the best way to bring up what Jason had told me. Wade had finished one slice of pizza and half of the beer when I decided it would be a good time to talk to him about Jason being bullied. "I had an interesting talk with—"

Wade interrupted me. "When did you last talk to your buddy Ken?"

His question surprised me. "Ken?"

"Yes, Ken Paget, your computer guy."

"Today." Ken's call still confused me. Wade asking about Ken confused me even more. "Why?"

"He's in trouble. Big trouble."

Wade leaned back in his chair. He was looking at me with his you-will-tell-me-everything detective look. "What did he say?"

I didn't see any reason not to tell him about the call, so I did. "He said he'd screwed up, but he didn't say how. And, he kept whispering, except when he told someone he'd be just a minute."

"That's all he said, that he'd screwed up?"

"No. First he wanted to know if you were here, at home, then, when I said you'd been called to an emergency, he wanted to know if it was in Zenith and if you were homicide, if you investigated murders."

"What else?"

"That was about it." I tried to remember exactly what I'd said and what Ken had said. "I did tell him you'd been called to a trailer park. That's when he said he really screwed up and hung up."

"Nothing else?"

22

"No, nothing more. So, was the trailer park the one in Zenith? Was someone murdered?"

"It was an overdose. Another friend of yours. Jerold Herman."

I shook my head. "If you mean Ken's friend Jerry, he's no friend of mine. I've never met him. All I know is he's a musician and last June he was the one who figured out how to bypass a password on the cell phone I found."

"The cell phone you were supposed to turn over to Kalamazoo Public Safety."

I smiled. Wade wasn't going to let me forget that.

"You say he died of an overdose?"

Wade nodded. "Paramedics said Herman was already dead when they arrived. Interesting part is the trailer is owned by a Mister Kenneth Paget."

That surprised me. "I thought Ken had a place in Kalamazoo."

"Neighbor said Paget bought the trailer a few months ago, but only stays there occasionally."

"That's weird." Ken wasn't married, so he probably wasn't using it for a rendezvous with another woman.

"The paramedics found an empty nasal spray bottle beside the body. We're assuming it was Paget who administered the NARCAN and called 9-1-1."

"Isn't NARCAN supposed to revive a person?"

"Depends on when it's used. It may have worked for a short time, but then Herman may have had a second episode. We only found the one bottle."

"Ken wasn't there when the paramedics arrived?"

"The door was propped open, but he was gone." Wade shrugged and once again picked up the second slice of pizza.

"Is Ken now a wanted man?" That would explain why he'd sounded so nervous when he called me.

"At the moment he's simply a 'Person of Interest,' but we did find a bag of white powder with his name on it. If it's—" He stopped himself. "If you hear from him again, you tell him to contact me."

I didn't know what to say, so I said nothing. Wade's view of law enforcement was pretty much black and white. Break the law, you pay. Smoking weed might not be illegal nowadays, but leaving the scene of a crime was, and if that white powder turned out to be a narcotic, Ken was right. He'd screwed up.

Wade finished the pizza and gave a satisfied sigh. "That was good. Thanks for taking Jason out for pizza."

"My pleasure, but there's a problem."

Wade frowned. "Why? What happened? Did he act up?"

"No, he was fine, but evidently he's having trouble at school. Some of the boys are picking on him. One in particular, I gathered. They're calling him a piglet. Saying you're a pig, so he must be a piglet."

"Did he tell you the boy's name?"

"No, and when I asked him what he did when the boy said that, Jason said he did nothing, that you'd told him no fighting. I think you need to talk to him."

"He's in bed, I assume."

"He went upstairs around nine."

"I'll talk to him in the morning." Wade downed the rest of his beer and stood. "I'm beat. I'm going to take a shower and go to bed. You ready?"

* * *

I was in bed, waiting for Wade, when his phone rang. He was naked when he came out of the bathroom and into the bedroom, cell phone to his ear. "Yes, it was an overdose," he said. "I'll tell you all about it tomorrow, okay?"

Wade looked my way, raised his eyebrows, then shook his head. "Yes, I'm home. In fact, I'm about to crawl into bed."

The caller evidently said something, and Wade looked at me and smiled. "Yes, with P.J."

I didn't know what was said next, but his, "Goodnight, Marge," had a harsh edge.

I tried not to smile.

The first time I met Marge was last year when she came to my house to photograph the body in my dining room. I could tell she liked Wade. That day she was acting so sweet and sexy when she asked him to drive her back to the station. It was nauseating, and I was so glad when my dog peed on her shoe. He got an extra treat that night.

More than once Wade has told me Marge means nothing to him, that she is just a friend, but I've seen a couple of the notes she's given him. That woman's looking for more than friendship. I think she's hoping he'll realize he's made a mistake and will divorce me once this baby is born.

Wade turned off the lights and crawled into bed with me. "Doesn't she realize what time it is?" I asked as he snuggled up against me.

"She was curious."

"So, she wasn't at the trailer park today?"

"No. Now, go to sleep, P.J."

"Yes, sir." Secretly, I was feeling pleased. When Wade was talking to Marge, I didn't see any physical reaction on his part. But then, again, maybe it was just too cold in the bedroom.

As Wade wrapped his arms around me and snuggled even closer, I could tell I wasn't sexually stimulating him, either. I sighed. What did I expect? I looked like a blimp.

"I love you," I whispered.

The soft rumble of a snore was his response.

Chapter Six

Saturday I woke to the smell of coffee. Thank goodness my negative reaction to coffee ended soon after Wade and I were married. Wade loves his coffee in the morning. It usually took two cups before he was ready to talk to anyone. He must have been on his third cup because by the time I came out of the bathroom, I found both Wade and Jason at the dining room table having what looked like a serious conversation.

I listened in as I fixed myself a cup of tea.

"You can't let what others call you bother you," Wade said.

"I try not to." Jason's answer was accompanied with a sniff. "But they keep pushing me. And one of them tripped me."

"Have you said anything to the teacher?"

Jason hung his head. "They said I'd better not or they'd make things really bad for me."

Wade simply nodded. "Are all of them mean? Or is one of them like a leader?"

"Danny." Jason looked up. "He's the leader. He's the meanest. He's the one who calls me piglet."

"What's Danny's last name?"

"Heart. Or something like that. One of the other kids called him a lover, and Danny hit him and said not that kind of heart."

"And Danny's in your class?"

Jason nodded, but then his expression changed. "You're not going to say anything to him, are you? Or to the teacher?"

I heard the panic in the boy's voice and wondered what Wade would do.

"No, not yet. I'd rather you deal with this yourself."

"How?" Jason looked as scared by that idea as by the thought of his dad stepping in.

"What you need to do is stop looking scared."

As Wade talked Jason through ways to appear confident and avoid the boys, I went into the kitchen and scrambled a couple eggs. By the time I'd finished my breakfast, Wade had Jason practicing how to walk so he would look confident. "Head high, back straight," Wade instructed. "Look around, but don't look like you're ready for a fight. Stay aware of what's going on around you. That way you will notice if your bully and his friends are approaching."

"What do I do if they do come after me?" Jason asked.

I wondered the same thing.

"Let's say this Danny grabs you, like this." Wade grabbed Jason's pajama top and pulled him closer. "Or starts pushing you." He flattened his hand and gently pushed Jason backwards. "There's an easy way to stop him."

Wade let go of Jason's top.

"There is?"

"Grab a finger." Again, Wade put his hand against Jason's chest. "Just one finger. . . or two." He waited as Jason reached up and tentatively touched the back of Wade's hand.

"Any finger will work. Just quickly grab it and push it back."

I watched Jason fumble at first and then wrap his hand around Wade's middle finger and try to push the finger back.

"You don't need to use your whole hand," Wade said. "In fact, it's better if you just use two or three of your fingers. Maybe your thumb and middle finger."

Jason corrected his hold and pushed. Wade gave a yelp and immediately stepped back.

"That's it," he said, freeing his hand from Jason's hold. "Now, do it again."

This time, Wade placed his hand flat against Jason's top. Jason grabbed a finger with more confidence and bent it backwards. Again, Wade gave a yelp and moved his hand. Next Wade grabbed Jason's arm. Jason repeated the procedure. Same when Wade grabbed Jason's shoulder. Wade then turned Jason around and wrapped his arms around Jason's waist, Wade's hands across Jason's stomach. Jason reacted immediately.

Over and over Wade grabbed, pushed, or hugged Jason until the boy was laughing as he freed himself from Wade's efforts. That was when Wade added, "Now, yell 'Help' as you get loose. 'Help! Get the teacher!' "

I had just fixed myself a second cup of tea when Wade told Jason, since he had the finger release down perfect, to go upstairs and practice walking with confidence. "Yell for help. Make it good and loud, so we can hear you down here."

Once Jason was upstairs, Wade came over and sat down next to me. "I probably shouldn't have shown him that hand release. Next we'll be getting a call from the school that Jason has broken a kid's finger."

"At least you've given him something he can do to protect himself."

"I'd rather just go grab that Danny kid by the throat and tell him to leave my son alone."

I could tell from Wade's expression he meant it. "Being a parent isn't easy, is it?"

"Not one bit." He leaned close and patted my bulging abdomen. "How's my little girl doing?"

"Punching and kicking my sides," I said. "I think she wants out." A thumping noise sounded above us, and I chuckled. "Well, he does sound confident."

Wade glanced up at the ceiling. "Stomping wasn't what I had in mind."

Shouts of "Help" now accompanied the thumping of feet, but the shouts weren't very loud. I could barely hear them. Wade shook his head, and then looked back at me, at my belly. "What's that midwife-nurse person say about your condition? Everything all right?"

"She says my blood pressure's good and everything looks fine. She thinks I'll deliver in a couple weeks."

"You still want to have the baby here? At home?"

"I think so." I looked around the room. "Except . . ."

Our house was once my grandparents' house—my dad's parents'. It is an old two-story farmhouse—kitchen, dining room, living room, bathroom and one bedroom downstairs and two bedrooms, a bathroom and attic upstairs The kitchen is old-fashioned, the linoleum needs to be torn up and replaced, the walls need painting, and both the plumbing and electricity need updating. Connie would not be impressed, especially not by our small bedroom, where clothes that didn't fit in the armoire were piled on a chair in the corner, boxes of Wade's things still sat on the floor, and the top of the dresser was covered with anything and everything that didn't fit in the drawers.

"Except what? Are you getting nervous?"

"Sort of. I'm not sure there's enough room in that bedroom for delivering a baby, and I'm a terrible housekeeper, and—"

Wade interrupted. "I meant about giving birth. Linda worried that Jason might not be perfect and if having him would ruin her figure."

I laughed at that. "She worried about her figure; I worry about my brain." I looked at Wade. "Be honest, doesn't it worry you that I'll turn out like my mother?"

"A little." He took my hand. "But just a little."

He leaned closer, his lips brushing my forehead, and I barely heard his, "I love you." Barely, but it sent a sensation of warmth spiraling through me.

For a moment neither of us said anything, the only sounds in the house Baraka's doggy snores from the living room and Jason's stomping above our heads. Then Wade got up and went over to the bottom of the stairs. "Yell louder," he shouted. "And don't stomp your feet. Simply walk with confidence."

Jason's next "Help" was a bit louder, but it still didn't sound forceful, and I couldn't hear any difference in the way Jason was walking. It still sounded like stomping.

Wade chuckled and slowly walked back toward me.

"At least he's trying," I said.

"That he is." Wade sat back down beside me. "About your friend Ken."

So, we were back to Ken. "Yes?"

"Last night I told you to tell him to call me. I changed my mind. You need to call him and tell him to come by the station."

That sounded like an order. "And turn himself in?"

"Yes. He needs to talk to us."

"I had no idea he was doing drugs."

"We know he smoked marijuana. A couple of the other trailer owners confirmed that. Personally, I think he's into a lot more. I told you we found white powder in a bag with his name on it. I'm guessing it's heroin, but we'll wait for the lab report on that. We also found a bag of pills on the floor near Mr. Herman, pills marked M30."

"M30?" I didn't know what that meant.

"They're oxycodone pills. Take too many and your brain stops sending messages to your vital organs, which is probably why Mr. Herman is dead."

"Stupid, stupid, stupid," I said. Although over the phone Ken always sounded young, he had to be in his late thirties. Old enough to know better.

Wade said nothing, but I had a feeling he was thinking *I told you so.*

"Okay, so what happens to Ken?"

"That depends on what the lab tells us about that white powder, how he got the pills, and—"

A crash from above followed by a very loud, "Help!" stopped whatever Wade was going to say. Immediately, Wade bolted for the stairs, Baraka on his heels.

* * *

By the time I lugged myself up the stairs, Baraka was sniffing Jason and Wade was placing an empty bookcase back against the hall wall. The books that had been housed on the shelves were scattered across the hallway, along with a couple knickknacks that had amazingly survived unscathed. "Are you okay?" I asked as Jason pushed books and memorabilia to the side—along with Baraka— and scrambled to his feet.

"I didn't mean to knock it over," he said, looking at his dad and then me. "But there was a mouse. It ran right by me, and I jumped back and bumped into the bookcase, and—" Tears filled his eyes. "I'm sorry."

"Do you hurt anywhere?" Wade asked.

Jason rubbed his head, his neck, and his arms, and then shook his head.

"Good. By the way, that was a great 'Help' you yelled. Exactly the way you should."

I noticed Jason's tears switched to a smile. I also saw Wade run a hand over Jason's shoulders and down his back, checking for tender spots, I assumed. Once certain his son was all right, Wade continued.

"I think you need to pick up all of these books and things and put them back where they belong."

He then looked at me. "And I think I'd better buy some mouse traps."

"Or maybe a cat?" Jason said, looking hopeful.

"A cat?" Wade glanced over to where Baraka was sniffing near the upstairs bathroom door. "He would probably eat a cat. Remember, he was bred to hunt lions."

Jason turned to me. "You said they just chased the lions until the hunters caught up."

"Chased them and held them at bay until the hunters caught up." I didn't want to contradict Wade, but I also didn't want to give the Rhodesian Ridgebacks a bad rep. "If your Dad says you can have a cat, you'll have to help me teach Baraka not to chase it or eat it."

"Tell you what," Wade said, stepping back from Jason. "You get so you don't let any of the kids at school bully you, and I'll let you have a cat. Meanwhile, I need to get to work."

Chapter Seven

An hour later, Wade had showered and dressed and left for the station. Jason was in the living room, playing with his Xbox, and I was at the dining room table working on Lucy Applegate's taxes. When my landline rang, I hoped it wasn't the Yardleys calling about their taxes. I hadn't even looked at them.

"P.J., this is Anna," was the response when I answered. "Any chance you could come into Kalamazoo to meet with me today?"

Even though I knew Anna couldn't see me, I looked over at Jason and shook my head. "Wade's working, and I'm watching my stepson."

"Your husband works on Saturdays? I thought he was a detective or something."

"It's because he is a detective," I said. "When they're investigating a murder, they don't have regular hours."

"Ooh, a murder. That doesn't sound good. Well then, any chance I can come to your place?"

I glanced at the unfinished taxes spread out across my dining room table. "You can't tell me what's up over the phone?"

"I'd rather not, and I need to show you something."

"I live way out in the country," I warned her.

She didn't seem to care.

I gave her the address, and after hanging up, I shoved the dirty dishes into the dishwasher, had Jason pick up his things, then collected the paperwork I had on the table and took it back to the small office area I'd had built at the end of the living room. I estimated it would take Anna roughly forty minutes to drive out, which gave me enough time to take a shower and get dressed. I'd just stepped out of my bedroom when Baraka began to bark.

"Who's here?" Jason asked, putting down his game to look out the window.

"A lady who wants to talk to me about taxes." I knew that wouldn't interest him.

"Oh, okay." He went back to the couch and picked up his game.

Baraka by my side, I opened my front door the moment Anna reached the porch. As cold as it was outside, I expected her to step right inside. Instead, she stopped at the threshold, her gaze focused on Baraka's back. "I don't think your dog likes me."

"What?" I said, and then understood. People unfamiliar with the Rhodesian Ridgeback breed often think the raised hairs on Baraka's back indicate he's mean or aggressive. "The hairs grow that way," I told her, and ran a hand over his ridge, tracing the whorl of hairs that formed crowns at his shoulder blades to the narrow point at his hips. "A good ridge looks like a sword."

"So, he's not aggressive? He won't bite me?"

I was about to say, "Only if you try to attack me," but she looked so worried, I simply said, "No."

"I had a dog bite me once," Anna said, finally coming inside. "A little dog. Took me totally by surprise." She kept looking at Baraka. "He's big."

"Bigger than breed standards," I admitted, which had ended my original plan of using him as a show dog.

"He likes to play growly," Jason said, having left his video game to join us. "And sometimes he knocks me down."

"And that doesn't scare you?" Anna asked.

"Naw. Have you dropped?"

My stepson pointed at Anna's belly, and I cringed. "Jason, you don't say something like that to a complete stranger."

He looked up at me, "Yesterday Nonna said you dropped, and this lady looks like you do."

"And you're right," Anna said before I had a chance to respond. "My baby has dropped. Your mother and I will probably have our babies about the same time."

"She's not my mommy," Jason said. "My mommy died. She's in heaven now with Daddy Michael, so Daddy married P.J."

I could tell Anna didn't know what to say, so I spoke up. "Jason, if you're finished with your game, could you take Baraka upstairs? My friend is a little bit afraid of dogs and having him down here while we work might bother her."

"Oh, okay." He grabbed Baraka's collar and headed for the stairs.

"Tea or coffee?" I asked Anna as she shrugged out of her winter coat.

"Tea. Decaf, if you have it." She pulled out a chair and sat at my dining table. "He seems very blasé about his mother's death. How long ago did she die?"

"Just last August," I said and went into the kitchen to heat some water. "She and her new husband were on Wade's boat when it blew up. So was Jason." Kettle on, I stepped back into the dining room. "Jason and Wade were lucky. They had just gone to the bow of the boat to lower the anchor. The explosion threw them into the water."

"Oh my gosh." Anna glanced toward the stairs. "As I said, he seems very comfortable talking about it. Did you get him counseling or something?"

"We did." I had told Connie about the therapist, but not the group. "Basically, the counselor said to talk about it with him and encourage him to talk to us about his feelings. I think he's accepted that it wasn't his fault, that it just happened." I didn't want to go into any more detail than that, so I asked her, "Why do you think someone is embezzling the charity?"

Anna's attention came back to me. "I received a letter in the mail two weeks ago. Three of us on the Homes4Homeless board received the same letter. It said funds were missing, and we should double check the accounting. The letters weren't signed. One of the other board members asked Mrs. Welkum for a copy of the most recent audit. She gave him all sorts of excuses why one hadn't been done this year. That's when he decided one of us should look at the accounts." Anna grinned. "And guess who has a major in business and a minor in accounting?"

"So, you've been volunteered."

She nodded. "You know, when I agreed to being on the board, I was told it would be a simple task, a cushy job. Just attend a few meetings during the year and agree to whatever the director wants. Well, trust me, this director does not want me doing an audit. When I showed up at the office Monday, Mrs. Welkum just about exploded."

"But you're doing it?"

Again, Anna nodded. "And, I'm finding some things that simply don't make sense. Or, rather, it does look like someone has been stealing money from the charity."

"Someone?" Friday, Anna had indicated the thief was Madeline Welkum, which didn't make sense. Madeline Welkum was a wealthy widow, a society maven. Articles I'd read made her sound saintly. She volunteered at the food bank, had created several college scholarships for single mothers, and had started Homes4Homeless. Now she was thinking of running for the state senate. Being arrested on embezzlement charges would certainly hurt her political career. "Are you saying the thief is Madeline Welkum?"

"Maybe. Or maybe her daughter. I'm not sure."

The teakettle whistled, and I went back into the kitchen. Quickly I gathered an array of tea bags, two mugs, spoons, sugar, and the teakettle. "There's milk in the fridge if you want some," I said when I set the tray of fixings on the table in front of Anna. "I don't have any lemon, but I do have honey."

"Plain is fine," Anna said and fixed herself a mug of peppermint tea. After taking a cautious sip, she set her mug down and pulled a folder from her over-sized purse. "Look at these," she said and laid two sheets of paper on the table.

In front of me were two bank statements. Each was from the same bank, but one was addressed to Anna Carr and had her mailing address, the other was addressed to Homes4Homeless and was addressed to the charity's Kalamazoo office. "Do you see any differences?" she asked.

"They're two different accounts." That was obvious.

"Anything else that's different?"

Since she'd asked twice I assumed there must be something different, so I looked closer. The bank's logo seemed the same on each statement. Except for the specific account numbers, the accounting period and contact information, including hours of business, phone numbers, and customer service address looked identical. That section of the statement was separated from the balance summary by a line, under which the important data appeared: beginning balance, deposits, checks, deductions, charges, fees, and ending balance.

I looked from one statement to the other. Again, the glaring difference was they were statements for two different entities, had different account numbers, and different balances. That, I was sure wasn't what she wanted me to see. There had to be something else. I began to feel like I was doing one of those tests where the viewer is supposed to pick out the differences between two pictures. I was failing the test.

"I don't see it," I finally admitted.

"Look at how the numbers are lined up under the category headings," Anna said.

I did, and I finally did see a difference. "The numbers on your bank statement are aligned slightly different from the alignment on the charity's statement. But, it's not a very big difference. A slight difference. That's all." I looked up at her. "And you think that's proof that funds are being embezzled?" I didn't buy it.

"It's more than that, but first, let me show you something else. Note how the statements show the check numbers but not the payees' names. Since, in cases of embezzlement, checks are sometimes written to dummy or shell businesses, I looked at the account ledger. Everything balanced and, as far as I could tell, the checks were written to legitimate businesses for legitimate purchases. Rents paid, furniture purchased, food and clothing bought. As a double check, I looked at the actual checkbook. That's when I discovered both Mrs. Welkum and her daughter are authorized to sign the checks, and—" She paused dramatically. "—only one signature is required."

"Oh, not good." One thing we'd been taught in our business classes was to require two signatures on checks. It eliminates the possibility of one employee cashing checks without the other knowing. "The treasurer is her daughter, right?"

"Yes. Jewel Wiscoff. I've met her at a couple of the charity's money raising events. She's ah—" Anna hesitated. "A little weird. Laughs at things that aren't really funny. Makes faces behind her mother's back. She's on vacation right now, skiing in Idaho."

A trip paid for by the charity? I wondered. "Do you think some of those bills aren't legit, that the money has gone into a personal account?"

"Possibly, but even more puzzling is certain checks don't show up on the bank statement at all. The word 'Void' is written on the checkbook register for those check numbers."

"Which would explain why they aren't on the bank statement."

"Exactly," Anna said. "And I'm sure that's what our embezzler hopes people believe, that she makes mistakes, maybe messes up a payee's name or the amount, and voids the check. If I hadn't received that anonymous letter, I might have let it go at that. After all, you had trouble seeing the difference with that bank statement."

"You're smiling," I said. "Do you know who wrote those letters? Who your whistleblower is?"

"She hasn't admitted it," Anna said, then paused to take a sip of her tea before going on. "But Thursday mid-morning. I stopped by the charity's office. Not because of this, but because just two weeks ago Mrs. Welkum asked me to design a new plan for the guest bathroom in her house. She gave me pictures of how the bathroom looks now and asked for suggestions and a bid on how to modernize it. I stopped by the office with some designs to show her, but Laura—that's Laura Parks, the charity's receptionist and event planner—said Mrs. Welkum wasn't in, however, my timing was perfect. She said the current bank statement had arrived in the morning's mail and I might want to look at it. I thanked her, told her I was in a rush to see a client, but I would look at it later. I started to take the statement back to Jewel's office, but Laura stopped me and said I might want a copy of it, for my audit records. The way she said it, I decided to do just that. And here's why."

Anna pulled a third bank statement out of the folder. "Look at the beginning balance."

I did. I also looked at the period the statement covered. It followed the previous statement, the one I'd just been looking at. "Wow," was all I could say at first. I looked at the numbers twice to make sure I was reading them correctly. "This beginning balance is almost twenty thousand dollars less than last month's ending balance."

"And," Anna said, pointing at a check number near the bottom of the page, "remember those voided checks? That number matches one of those. I remember because the check number is my birthdate."

The check had cleared early February and was for five thousand dollars. I looked at Anna. "You need a copy of the check."

"I know." She looked worried. "but I don't think getting permission to go into the account is going to be easy. Mrs. Welkum called me Friday morning. At first she made it sound as if the call was about the designs I'd left for her. She went on and on about how much she liked my ideas and if everything went well, she'd have me redo her bathroom and then she would tell her friends, and I would have more business than I could handle. I was thrilled. With this baby coming, I need more clients, and her friends would be ones who commissioned big projects."

I could see where this was going and wasn't surprised when Anna said, "And then Mrs. Welkum asked if I'd seen the February bank statement."

"And you said?"

"I lied. I should have confronted her right then, asked what was up, but I said no, I hadn't seen it and asked if it was missing. She said, 'No' but that it had come in the mail Thursday and she thought I would want to see it. I told her I'd be in Monday afternoon and to leave it on Jewel's desk, that I'd look at it then."

"You think she believed you?"

"I don't know. If Laura is the whistleblower, I don't think she'll tell Mrs. Welkum I have a copy of the statement. But—" Anna shrugged. "I just don't know."

I wasn't sure what she wanted me to say or do. "So, what's next?"

"I could go to the board with what I have, but I'd like to see an image of the cancelled check, see who signed it and what it was for. I'd like to have a little more evidence, would like to know if it's Mrs. Welkum who's embezzling the charity or if it's her daughter. Maybe she doesn't know her daughter has been doctoring those bank statements. Maybe—" She stopped herself. "Damn, I wish they hadn't asked me to do this."

I understood Anna's concern. Like me, Anna was self-employed. We walked a fine line. Do a good job for your clients, they told others, and your business grew. Get on the wrong side of an influential client and it could really hurt your business. Madeline Welkum helped a lot of people and knew a lot of influential people. Even if she was proven a thief, the person who took her down might suffer. Nevertheless— "If she's taking money from the charity, she should be exposed. I mean, she's talking about running for the state senate. I don't want an embezzler elected."

"You're right." Anna gathered up the bank statements she'd shown me and slipped them back in the folder. "I think—" She paused, and I could tell she was pondering what to do. "I think," she finally said, "I'll go back to the charity office Monday afternoon after my last appointment and will gather as much evidence as I can. Once I have that, I'll take it to the board, and they can take action."

"Want help Monday?" I asked. "Moral support? I have some tax papers I need to deliver just outside of Kalamazoo. If you'd like, I could stop by the charity office while you're there." To be honest, I wanted to see inside the house. Back when I worked at Quick Sums, I used to drive by the place going to and from work. The house was old and had been getting pretty rundown. Then one day there was a "For Sale" sign out front and a month later it sold. Contractor trucks appeared. Workers were still there the day I quit my job at Quick Sums. I hadn't been by since.

"I won't be free until after four."

That worked for me.

Before leaving, Anna paused at the door. "By the way," she said, "did you see on TV why all those cops were out front of the church while we were meeting? Seems some woman was killed crossing the street."

"A woman was killed?"

"Yeah. A hit and run."

Chapter Eight

As soon as Anna left, I sat down at my computer. Every nerve on edge, I scanned for information about the hit and run. What I found was scanty. The websites of the two local TV channels identified the victim as an African-American, middle-aged woman, but that was all. The name was being withheld until notification of kin. As for the car that hit her, it was described as a black sedan. No make or license plate number. Channel 3 did have a video interview of a homeless man who had been sleeping on the bench in front of the church.

"Scared the (bleep) out of me," the man said. "I hear a thump, open my eyes, and see a car comin' at me. Almost hit me, too."

When asked, however, the man said. "Couldn't really see who was driving. Car's windows were too dark."

The local paper found another witness, a woman who said she'd just turned onto the street when a car pulled out of a parking spot in front of her, nearly hit another car, then swerved onto the sidewalk and hit the woman. "The car didn't stop," the witness reported. "Hit her, almost hit a guy sleeping on a bench, and took off."

The newspaper's headline was "Hit and Run Accident Near Brewery," and the reporter had gone on to list the number of DUIs in the area, adding Friday's as one more accident caused by drunk driving. Which was possible, I told myself.

As for the victim being Black, since the area was primarily populated by people of color, she could have been anyone from the neighborhood, maybe a parishioner of the church. But, if Brenda was the victim, this was no accident. In the church bathroom, she'd known her life was in danger. *"These people don't play around,"* she'd said. *"He threatened me."*

I'd been going to tell Wade what I'd overheard, but between Ken's phone call and Jason's problem, I'd totally forgotten. I should have made Brenda stay and talk to me. Should have asked her what was going on. If only I hadn't been in such a hurry to go to the bathroom.

If only. Life was full of those moments.

Emotionally drained, I thought back on the years Brenda and I worked at Quick Sums. She wasn't the best accountant they'd hired, but she was steadfast and reliable. As far as I could recall, Brenda never missed a day of work. The same couldn't have been said about me. I was always having to take time off when my mother had one of her spells. More than once Brenda covered for me, finished projects so I didn't miss deadlines. She even sat with me in the hospital waiting room the night we thought Grandma had had a heart attack. It was Brenda's optimism that kept me from falling apart. "That lady's too damn stubborn to have a heart attack," Brenda had insisted, and she'd been right. "Muscle spasms," the doctor had said. "She needs to slow down, relax a little, and stop smoking."

Grandma hasn't stopped smoking, but Brenda helped Grandma find a way to slow down and relax. It was Brenda's suggestion that led Grandma to the schizophrenia caregivers' support group. Grandma calls that group a lifesaver.

"Please, don't let it be you, Brenda," I said and closed the newspaper's online article about the hit-and-run. When Wade returned, I would ask him to find out the identity of the woman who was killed. The Kalamazoo Sheriff's Department and Kalamazoo Public Safety were separate entities, but they did have a good working relationship and often shared information. If the victim was Brenda, what I'd heard in the bathroom might be important.

That decision made, I decided I'd better get back to work. Since leaving my job at Quick Sums, the P.J. Benson L.L.C. was doing fairly well; however, that would change if I didn't keep my clients happy.

I'd barely started inserting figures in my computerized tax program when Jason and Baraka came back downstairs. "She gone?" Jason asked.

"She's gone." I glanced at the clock and realized it was nearly noon. "You hungry?"

"Starving."

I turned on the television before going into the kitchen to heat some chicken noodle soup and fix sliced turkey sandwiches for both of us. I hoped the noon news might give the name of the hit-and-run victim, but if the police knew the woman's name, they weren't releasing it. After lunch, I let Baraka out and told Jason, "I'll give you a quarter if you'll pick up the twigs and branches that blew into the yard yesterday."

Jason looked out the door and then back at me. "Dad always gives me a dollar to clean the lawn."

"Okay, a dollar." I knew I was being manipulated; however, I needed time to work. "But that yard better be clean."

"Sure sure." He grinned and grabbed his jacket and gloves.

As I finished Lucy Applegate's tax return, I occasionally checked on Jason and my dog. Watching the two made me laugh. Every time Jason added a branch to his pile, Baraka would grab it and run. Then Jason would run after Baraka, and the game was on.

I'd just clicked "Print" for the copy I would show Lucy when my cell phone chimed. I hoped it was Wade calling so I could ask him to see if they'd identified the hit-and-run victim, but the number showed it was Ken.

"You need to turn yourself in," I said before he spoke a word.

"And I love you, too."

"They're looking for you. The longer you wait, the—" I stopped myself. I was starting to sound like Wade. "What happened yesterday?"

"I screwed up, that's what happened." Ken half laughed. "Jerry showed up a couple weeks ago, said he'd found a job but was low on cash and needed a place to stay until he had enough money to rent something. He swore he was off drugs, that what happened to us last summer had made him turn his life around. He and I have been buds for years. I wanted to believe him, so I told him he could stay at the trailer until he found something better. Yesterday morning, just as I was getting ready to leave for a meeting in Zenith, he called me. He was rambling, said we'd be rich, that I needed to come to the trailer and see what he had."

"What did he find?"

"He wouldn't say over the phone. He was singing some song and slurring words. I figured he was either drunk or back on drugs. Last summer, when he was playing in the bars, he sometimes stayed up all night drinking."

I could hear Ken's sigh through the phone. "When I got to the trailer, I could tell Jerry wasn't simply drunk. He was pacing the floor, rambling. He kept telling me how hot it was, but he had all the windows open and it wasn't hot in the trailer, just the opposite. I saw some pills on the counter and asked him what he'd taken and how many. He just rambled on.

"I should have called 9-1-1 right then, but you know how gossip spreads in Zenith. I was afraid if word got out that I had a druggy living in my trailer, I'd lose my job with the village, that no one would hire me to work on their computers. I thought I could get him to the hospital, and no one would know."

He paused, but I could hear him breathing. Shaky breaths. "Ken?" I said, not sure what to say or ask.

Finally, he continued, his words slow and measured. "I told Jerry we needed to leave, but he wouldn't listen to reason. Said he wanted to show me what he'd found. He wouldn't budge when I tried to get him to the door. And then he started stripping off his clothes, ranting about how hot it was. I tried to stop him, but I couldn't. And then, he collapsed. Fell on the floor half-naked. I thought he was dead."

"So that's when you used the NARCAN spray? Wade said there was an empty container by the body."

"Yes. And within a few seconds Jer seemed to be back to his normal self. I was thanking my lucky stars that I'd had that one dose of naloxone and that we'd had a demonstration at one of the village meetings on how to use it. We were each given one four-ounce spray bottle, and told, if we were smart, we should have several on hand. Well, I wasn't smart. That was all I had, and, when Jerry started convulsing again—"

I finished for him. "You finally called 9-1-1."

"Yes, and they were there in seconds."

The trailer park was close to the fire station, so that made sense. "But you weren't there. You didn't stay with him." That was what I couldn't understand. "If he was your friend, why didn't you stay with him?"

"I panicked," Ken confessed. "I lucked out last summer when Jer and I were arrested. I was given probation and had to attend some classes on drug addiction, but that was it. If I was connected with this . . . If the Village Council found out I was . . . That he . . ." Ken's voice sounded shaky, and I realized he was crying. "I should have stayed, P.J. He was my friend. I should have stayed with him."

Before I could think of how to respond, he went on.

"But what could I have done if I'd stayed? I had hoped the paramedics would be able to revive him, but I didn't want to be there if they couldn't."

"You need to turn yourself in, Ken. You're wanted as a person of interest."

"I know. I know." He sniffed and hiccupped.

"Where are you now?"

"Down the road from your place. I thought if Wade was home, I'd turn myself into him."

"I'm not sure where he is," I said. "What you need to do is go to the Kalamazoo County Sheriff's Office." I didn't want him coming to the house. "Do you know where it is?"

"Uh huh," he mumbled, then cleared his throat. "I shouldn't have let him stay in the trailer. When he took off last summer, I swore I would not get involved with him again. Since we were kids, he's gotten me into trouble. He plays the 'Poor me' card and I fall for it. I shouldn't have let him stay in the trailer."

He was right, but I didn't say so. "Why do you even have a trailer in that park? I thought you lived in Kalamazoo?"

"I do. I have an apartment just a short way from my shop. I bought the trailer as a fixer-upper to resell. I stay in it the nights I have to attend Village meetings or work late at the Village office."

His answer sounded reasonable, and I wanted to believe his being involved with Jerry's drug use and death was purely circumstantial, but Wade has told me not to believe what anyone involved with drugs says. Ken might be my favorite computer guru, but he was no choir boy. Wade had said they found a paper bag in the trailer with Ken's name written on the outside. A bag filled with an unknown white power.

"What was in the paper bag?" I asked.

"What paper bag?"

"The brown paper bag. The one with your name on it."

"I didn't see a bag with my name on it."

"Wade said it was filled with a powder. A white powder."

"Heroin?" He sounded surprised. "If it is, it's not mine. I don't do that stuff. Never have. Honest, I don't know anything about a paper bag."

Was he telling me the truth?

I wasn't sure.

"You need to turn yourself in, Ken," I repeated, unwilling to get involved in his situation

Chapter Nine

That evening, I was debating what to fix for dinner, and if it would be a meal for two or three, when Wade arrived home. "Your buddy showed up at the station," he said the moment he removed his jacket. "Told me you talked him into it. So, you called him?"

"No, he called me. This afternoon. Is he under arrest?"

"Not at the moment. We could have arrested him for harboring a known criminal, but he swore he didn't know a warrant was still out for Herman's arrest, and he insisted the counterfeit pills we found on Herman weren't his. He said he didn't know Herman was doing drugs. Seems he didn't know a lot of things about his friend."

"Being friends doesn't mean you know everything about each other. I think he wanted to trust Jerry, was giving him the benefit of the doubt. Ken said they'd been friends for a long time."

The look Wade gave me said I was too gullible. And maybe I am. "Ken's a nice guy," I argued. "Helpful. He doesn't know much about me, but he's helped me a couple times."

"Yeah, well, that's because you're adorable. And your buddy's not off the hook. We're still waiting to hear what that white powder is."

"He said he didn't know what it was."

"Uh-huh. And you believed him?"

I was about to tell him where he could take his sarcasm when Jason came bounding down the stairs from his bedroom.

"Daddy, P.J. had to pay me a dollar." He raced to his father's side, Baraka right behind. "I cleaned up all the twigs and branches that blew off the trees. And Baraka helped."

Jason patted Baraka's head, and I smiled, remembering how my dog had helped.

"You made P.J. pay you?" Wade said, scowling at his son. "I thought we agreed you would help around the house."

"Yeah, but this was outside." Jason looked at me for confirmation.

"He did a good job, Wade. I was glad to pay him. But what about your room, Jason? Did you get that cleaned up?"

"Ah, well, sorta." He backed away from us, avoiding eye contact.

"Upstairs and get that room clean," Wade ordered with a wave of his hand.

I'd wanted Jason upstairs for a reason. I needed to talk to Wade uninterrupted. As he headed toward the refrigerator, I said, "I have a favor to ask. Could you find out the name of the woman killed in a hit-and-run yesterday? The one that happened in Kalamazoo in front of the church I was at."

Wade paused, hand on the door handle. "Why? Did you see it happen?"

"No, but I think I know the woman, and if it is her, I talked with her not long before she died."

"And?"

"And she sounded like she was in trouble. Her life had been threatened."

"She told you that?"

"Not directly. I overheard her talking to someone on the phone." I held up my hands to stop his questions. "Wade, just find out who was killed. Okay? I'm hoping it wasn't her." I prayed it wasn't. "While you do that, I'll start dinner, and then I'll tell you everything I overheard."

I sensed he was about to say something more, but he didn't. Instead he opened the refrigerator and pulled out a bottle of beer. I waited, watching him as he flipped off the bottle cap and took a long draught. I know he doesn't like me getting involved in police matters. He's told me that often enough. And I certainly did not plan on getting involved. Having our baby is my priority; however, that doesn't mean I shouldn't relay what I'd heard Brenda say yesterday.

Wade kept looking at me, but I didn't say anything. I'd asked. Now it was up to him.

Finally, he set the bottle of beer down on the table and pulled out his cell phone. The moment I heard him ask for Detective Ferrell, I knew he'd called Kalamazoo's Public Safety's number. I'd met Detective Ferrell last summer when I brought an elderly woman with dementia to the police station.

I held my breath as Wade questioned Ferrell about the hit-and-run. I didn't want the victim to be Brenda, yet deep down I was sure it was. I felt the baby kick and had a feeling I was relaying my tension to her. *Relax*, I told myself. *Breathe*. But as I watched Wade wander over to the buffet and grab the pen and pad of paper I kept there, breathing became difficult. He continually said, "Uh-huh." I wanted words. Finally, he started writing, and I moved to his side. Seeing Brenda's name brought a lump to my throat and tears to my eyes. Wade must have sensed my distress. He put down the pen and slipped an arm around my shoulders, drawing me closer.

He finally thanked Detective Ferrell and hung up.

"You okay?" he asked.

"No."

Our baby gave a kick, or maybe a punch, that Wade must have felt. He put a hand on my abdomen. "Doesn't that hurt?"

It did, but I was more concerned about what Wade had discovered. "Let me sit down," I said and moved over to the nearest chair. "I think she'll calm down."

"You're not ready to, ah . . .?"

"No, not yet." At least I hoped not. I wasn't ready. I pointed toward the notepad. "Brenda is the woman I talked to."

As I summarized what I'd heard, Wade sat near me, and made notes. Occasionally he asked a question: Was I sure that was what she said? Did she mention a name?

"No name," I told him. "Just that she'd been at her computer looking at pictures she'd taken when her boss came up behind her and saw what she was doing." Saying that triggered a thought. "Hey, you can find out where she works, and that will tell us—"

"*Us*, P.J.?" Wade sat back and looked at me. "There is no *us*. *We* are not getting involved," he said firmly. "*You* are not getting involved."

"I know, I know," I said, "I'm not going to, but Detective Ferrell needs to know what Brenda said. Right?"

"Did she tell you what the pictures showed?"

"Not exactly. Just that they showed hidden compartments and origins of shipments. That information must have been important because she said her boss threatened her and came after her."

"You said she was going to meet the person she was talking to at the brewery, that this person had promised to take care of her. Did she say how?"

I shook my head. "No, but she said she didn't have any family." I knew that. "And she wanted to be put somewhere where they— whoever 'they' were—couldn't find her."

"You're thinking witness protection?"

"I don't know. Maybe. What I do know is Brenda sounded scared. She said, 'These people don't play around.' She was afraid for her life."

Wade said nothing for a second, then asked, "Did she ask you for help?"

"No." I sighed. "But I don't think she realized her life was in immediate danger. I think she thought this person she was talking to would take care of her."

"You do know that this sounds like something out of a spy movie."

"Maybe so, but this is real. Brenda's dead."

Wade shook his head. "Detective Ferrell thinks she was simply crossing that street at the wrong time. He said they've had several close calls in that area. Rear-enders. Parked cars being hit. Kids speeding. Most are DUIs."

"The paper said she was on the sidewalk when she was hit, and the car drove right into her."

"Run down by someone who saw her go into the church and waited around for her to come back outside?" The lift of Wade's eyebrows said he wasn't buying that idea. "Doesn't that church have a back entrance as well as a front entrance? If this driver was specifically targeting your friend, how would he know which door she would exit from? If she thought she was being followed, to evade being seen, she might have gone in the front and out the back."

"I think she parked in front of the church. Where did they find her car?"

"I don't know. Ferrell didn't say."

"She was going to meet the person on the phone at the microbrewery just down the street," I said, but I could tell from Wade's look that he didn't understand. "She probably parked her car there. The person following her might have seen it and—"

"That's a Black neighborhood," Wade said, as if that made a difference.

"And Brenda's Black. Didn't Ferrell mention that?"

"No he didn't, but I think you're trying to make this into something it isn't. The 'might have' is that someone who'd had too much beer got into his car, took off at a fast speed, went onto the sidewalk, and hit your friend. She was simply in the wrong place at the wrong time,"

"No!" I insisted, irritated with his simplistic explanation. "Don't you understand? She was afraid this would happen."

Wade said nothing for a moment, probably waiting for me to calm down. That, or he was trying to think of what to say that wouldn't make me angry, angrier than I was already. Finally, he asked, "Did you know her well?"

"Yes. I won't say we were best friends—" A best friend wouldn't ignore her buddy for over a year, would know where her friend was working and if she was in trouble. "—but we were close. She helped me when Grandma Carter had her pseudo heart attack. Helped me at work. Helped me . . ." A lump filled my throat, and I couldn't go on. "I should have helped her."

Wade slipped an arm around my shoulders and drew me closer. "I'm sorry, Honey."

For a minute—maybe two—he said nothing, and I appreciated his support as I tried to control my emotions. But then he stood and said, "So what's for dinner?"

"What's for dinner?" I glared up at him. He evidently thought he'd answered all of my questions. Well, he hadn't. I also stood and faced him. "What about the driver of the car that hit her? Have they found him? Found—"

Wade stopped me. "P.J., your friend was hit within the city limits. That's the Kalamazoo Department of Public Safety's jurisdiction, not mine."

"I know. But as you said, they think it was just an accident. They don't know that she died less than an hour after I heard her telling someone she was afraid she'd been followed, killed by someone driving a car that no one seems able to find."

"Actually, they found the car," Wade said. "Detective Ferrell said it was abandoned in a wooded area outside of town."

I raised my eyebrows and waited for him to go on.

He worked his upper lip for a moment, then went over and grabbed the paper he'd taken notes on. Finally, he looked at me. "It had been stolen. There were no fingerprints."

That was all I needed to hear. "Don't you think Detective Ferrell should know what I overheard?"

He sighed. "Okay, I'll check into it, but you stay out of it. I do not want you getting involved."

I raised my eyebrows.

"Please," he added softly. "I don't want anything to happen to you."

Since I didn't want anything to happen to me, or our baby, either, I nodded my agreement and headed for the kitchen.

Chapter Ten

March is always an unpredictable month in Michigan. One day it might be warm and sunny, giving everyone hope that spring is on the way; the next day might take us right back into winter. Sunday the weather was beautiful, not a cloud in the sky and the weatherman predicted the temperature would reach the mid-sixties. Even the air smelled like spring.

After so many cold, cloudy days, I wasn't about to argue when Wade suggested I forget about doing taxes, and, instead, the three of us go to Meijer Gardens in Grand Rapids to see the butterfly exhibit. I remembered my dad taking me there once when I was a child. It had been an amazing experience, stepping into the conservatory and seeing thousands of free flying tropical butterflies with different colors and patterns on their wings.

We were just about to leave the house when I received a call from Detective Ferrell on the land line. Wade had called the detective back yesterday, given him the number, and said I might have some information regarding the Brenda Cox case. Now that Ferrell had called, I didn't want to put him off, so I motioned for Wade to take Jason to the car while I gave Ferrell the information I had.

I still felt guilty that I hadn't done anything to help Brenda on Friday, but by the time I finished telling Detective Ferrell what I'd overheard in the bathroom, I didn't feel I'd done much to help her this time, either. His response was simply, "Thank you."

That was it, just, "Thank you."

Well, that wasn't enough for me, so I started asking him questions. I got the feeling he didn't like that, but he answered a couple simple ones. I might have kept going, but I heard the sound of the Jeep's horn. My men were getting antsy. "Thank you, Detective Farrell," I finally said and ended the call.

Again, the Jeep's horn summoned me. I grabbed my purse, gave Baraka a quick pat on the head, and told him, "You be good."

I left through the kitchen door, waddled down the cement steps, and hurried around to the passenger's side of the car. Jason was snuggly strapped into his booster seat in the back. The way he was growing, he wouldn't need that much longer.

"Happy now?" Wade asked once I was in the Jeep and had my seatbelt fastened.

"I don't know. He didn't sound very impressed with what I had to say, but he did answer a couple questions. Not that his answers cleared anything up."

"What did you ask him?" Wade started the Jeep and backed out of the yard.

"If they'd found her car. They have. It was parked at the McDonalds by the train station. Why would she park there? That's several blocks from the church."

"Did he have an answer?"

"No. He also didn't know why his officers didn't find Brenda's purse Friday, but found it Saturday, in a spot they swore they'd searched Friday."

"Someone at the scene of the accident probably took it," Wade said, his attention on the road ahead. "You said there was a homeless man outside of the church when the accident occurred."

"Okay, then explain why her purse shows up the next day."

"Was her wallet still in it? Money and credit cards?"

"Credit cards yes. Money no."

"Makes sense. Credit cards can be traced. You know that church isn't in the best neighborhood." He slowed the Jeep and glanced my way as we passed the speed limit sign outside of Zenith. "Which is why I wasn't wild when you said you'd be going there for those meetings."

"We haven't had any problems."

"Which I am glad to hear." Wade stopped at Zenith's one and only blinking stop light and looked at me. "Anything else you learned?"

"No, not really."

"Then let Ferrell do his job. He'll find out what happened." Pulling forward, he said, "Anyone ready to see some butterflies?"

"Yeah!" Jason shouted from the back seat. "Butterflies!"

"Butterflies," I repeated and smiled. Time to put thoughts of Brenda aside. We were off for the hour and a half drive to Grand Rapids. Off for a family outing.

* * *

We arrived back home late in the afternoon, all three of us exhausted. Nevertheless, the trip had been worth it. Jason seemed to have as much fun with his dad as I'd had with mine years before. Most of all, I loved spending the day as a family.

"What a perfect day," I said as we pulled into our driveway.

And then I saw Baraka sitting by the back door.

"How'd he get out?" I looked at Wade.

"Don't ask me, you were the last one out."

"I pulled the door closed behind me." I was sure I had. "I wouldn't have left it open." Wade knew how I worried about Baraka getting out the back and going around to the road. Cars and trucks went by too fast. Soon after I inherited my grandparents' house, I'd had the front yard fenced in to keep my dog safe. That was his free zone. The only time he was allowed out the back door was if he was with Wade or me.

When Baraka didn't come bounding down the cement steps to greet us, I knew something really was wrong. "Wade?" I said, opening my car door as my dog limped over to the car. "He's hurt."

"Close your car door, P.J.," Wade ordered, cracking his own door open. "Stay in the car." He glanced toward the back seat. "And Jason, you stay in, too."

"Why?" Jason asked.

"Just do as I say."

I couldn't close my door, not with Baraka's head now blocking me from shutting it, and I wasn't about to push my injured dog away, but I kept my hand on the handle as I watched Wade ease out from the driver's side. He touched the side of his jacket beneath which I knew his ever-present Glock was holstered. Slowly he worked his way toward the steps.

A chill ran through me as I watched his progress.

"What's wrong?" Jason asked from the back seat.

"I don't know." One handed, I dug in my purse for my cell phone.

My stomach in a knot, I watched Wade hesitate outside the kitchen door, listening. He reached over and turned the knob, gave the door a slight push, waited, and then pushed it all the way open.

My breathing stopped when he disappeared inside. I wanted to get out of the car so I could hear better, so I would know if there was any yelling, so I could call for help. I also wanted to check Baraka, see why he was limping, look for wounds.

I clutched my phone but didn't move.

My baby pushed against my sides. Jason grumbled. I could feel my heartbeat, and let out my breath, and then held it again. Waiting.

The crows in the trees around the house loudly cawed their warnings, telling others that we were home, or maybe something more. I wished they could tell me what was going on. The moment reminded me of last spring when my house was repeatedly broken into. Back then, Wade had accused me of imagining things, had questioned my assertion that someone had broken in. Less than a year ago, I'd feared for my life. Today, I feared for Wade's.

That fear didn't go away until Wade stepped back outside and waved us in. Jason raced up the steps and past his dad. I took my time, first checking Baraka's body and paws. He moved away from my hand when I pressed against his left side, and the pad of his left forepaw had a cut. It looked like there was something in it, but I couldn't pull it out.

He limped by my side to the back door, and I saw spots of blood on the steps. I immediately felt responsible for Baraka's cut paw. I still hadn't cleared out all of the junk my grandfather had dumped behind the house and in the woods. Running loose, Baraka could have stepped on broken glass or a ragged piece of metal. "Poor baby," I said. "I'm sorry."

He looked at me with those big brown eyes of his, his injured paw raised, and I gave him an awkward hug.

Before I entered the house, I checked to see if the lock had been jimmied. As far as I could tell, there were no chisel or pry bar marks. Thinking back, I couldn't remember locking the door.

When I lived in Kalamazoo, with my grandmother and on my own, I always locked my doors. It was second habit. A necessity. But when I moved into my grandparents' house, neighbors told me, "You don't need to. This isn't like the city."

And, in a way, it wasn't. Locking my doors didn't stop the break-ins last spring, and during the summer not having anyone living close by allowed a burglar to gain entrance by breaking a window. Maybe I didn't lock the back door, but did I rush out of the house without making sure the door was fully closed?

If so, Baraka could have nudged it open. We hadn't replaced the storm door from when the sheriff's department took it last April. One more item put off until after the baby was born.

As soon as I stepped into the kitchen, I stopped Baraka from moving forward. I didn't need blood tracked from room to room. "Wade, could you get me some tweezers, cotton balls, and antiseptic?" I called.

It took him a couple minutes to find the tweezers, and he was the one who removed a piece of glass lodged in Baraka's pad while I kept petting my dog, telling him what a good boy he was for not going out on the road and getting killed. "He does seem a little touchy on his left side," I said as Wade applied an antiseptic to the wound. "Do you think he could have been hit by a car?"

"As fast as those cars fly by here, he would be more than touchy if he was hit by one." Wade pressed against Baraka's side, then shook his head when Baraka merely licked his cheek. "I don't think there's any internal damage. We'll probably never know what he got into while we were gone."

"I should have put him in his crate." But I hadn't been crating him for months. Hadn't needed to.

Once Baraka's paw was medicated and wrapped, I tried to remember exactly what I'd done after I finished talking with Detective Ferrell. "I am sure I closed the door," I told Wade, "but I don't think I locked it."

"My fault for honking the horn and urging you to hurry," Wade said. "All's well that ends well, or something like that."

I wished I could pass it off at that, but I couldn't shake the feeling that something wasn't right. I wandered into the dining area. Earlier, when Wade suggested we go see the butterflies, I'd been gathering the tax papers for Sporbach's Nursery so they'd be ready to take into Kalamazoo on Monday. I'd left those papers in a neat stack on the table, next to the envelope with their name on it. Once more checking to make sure I had everything and they would go into the envelope. Now those papers were fanned out.

"Did you do that?" I asked Wade, and then Jason.

"Nope," each said.

"Dog must have bumped the table and dislodged them," Wade said.

I didn't think so. The position the papers were in was too neat.

Room by room I went through the house. Nothing was obviously out of place, yet several things didn't seem quite right. An upholstered chair in the living room was at a different angle. A picture on my dresser had been knocked over. The door to the office at the end of the living room was half open.

Standing in the living room, I stared at that door. Had someone been in the house or was I simply suffering from "baby brain?" Connie had mentioned the term during one of our sessions. She'd said it referred to a proven relationship between pregnancy and brain changes and that four out of five pregnant women reported increased forgetfulness and mental fogginess. Both Anna and Maria had laughed and confessed to having it. As tired as I was, maybe I was making too much over a few things that seemed out of place. Did I fan out those pages? Move the chair? Not completely close my office door?

Wade had turned on the TV and stretched out in his favorite easy chair. "You okay?" he asked, looking up at me.

"I'm not sure," I admitted. "It's just that something doesn't feel right."

He pushed himself up, out of the chair and came over to my side. "Not right like?"

"Like not right." I couldn't explain and wandered into our bedroom, pulling dresser drawers open and pushing the underwear and tops aside.

"Are you missing anything?"

On top of the dresser, the birthing kit bag Connie had told me to purchase was open. I couldn't remember if I'd left it unzipped or not, but as far as I could tell everything was there. Not that I could imagine a burglar wanting to steal plastic backed paper sheets, OB pads, or a peritoneal bottle. Next to the kit I had a loose change jar. It was three-fourths full; about what I remembered.

I shook my head. "Nope. Nothing's missing."

"So . . .?"

"So, it must be my imagination," I admitted and went over and gave him a hug. "Thanks for being my hero and checking the place out when we first arrived. I was scared for you. And thanks for taking care of Baraka's paw."

"No problem, he said, and for a moment we just stood there, our arms around each other.

* * *

Later that night I discovered what wasn't right. While Wade was watching TV and Jason was in bed, I did the final check of Sporbach's tax papers, gathered them in a neat stack, and slipped them into the prepared envelope. Friday, when I had called and told them I would have their taxes done over the weekend and would just need their signatures to electronically file, they'd asked if I could drive into town. They said they had something they wanted to show me. Curious, I'd agreed. At the time I'd figured it would give me a chance to visit with Grandma Carter without Jason around. Now the trip was going to work out because of Anna.

Envelope in hand, I went to my office to check my email and do my nightly backup. That was when I discovered the problem. I couldn't do a backup.

No thumb drive.

Not in the USB port or on the desk next to my computer. Not in the plastic cup filled with pens and pencils off to the side of my computer. No thumb drive in my desk drawers, on the floor, or in the waste basket. No thumb drive anywhere in my office area or around the dining room table, where I often did paperwork, but never took the thumb drive.

Wade stopped me on my fifth time walking between him and the television set. "What are you doing?"

"Looking for the thumb drive I back my files up on."

"It's not where you usually keep it?"

"I usually keep it plugged into my computer."

"And?"

"No, it's not there. It's not anywhere." I plopped down on the couch next to his chair. "I don't understand. I don't remember pulling it out of the computer or putting it anywhere. I wouldn't do that. Not until tax season was over. Then I'd put it in the safe."

"Have you checked your purse?"

"I did." I'd dumped everything out on the bed, found a lipstick I'd forgotten I had, a pen I don't even remember picking up, but no thumb drive.

"You don't have any other thumb drives?"

"I have personal ones, but when I'm doing taxes, to make sure I don't forget and mix my clients files with my personal files, I put those backup thumb drives in a box in the file cabinet."

"And none of those are missing?"

"No." I had looked. "They're all there."

"So, it's just the one with your clients' files that you can't find. Does that mean you've lost all of that information?"

"No, I still have everything on my hard drive. The missing thumb drive is a backup, in case something happens to my hard drive."

And this was a good lesson on why I should have signed up and paid the money to save files in the cloud. I'd thought about it, looked into the idea, but I hadn't made a decision. After tax season I'd told myself. After the baby was born.

"Maybe Jason has it." Wade moved over from his chair to the couch and snuggled me close. "We can ask him in the morning. Meanwhile, relax. As long as you have everything you need on your computer, you can buy another thumb drive when you're in town."

"I can, but . . ."

"But nothing." He brushed a kiss against my forehead. "It's after ten. We've had a busy day. You've got to be beat."

I was tired. My back ached and my feet were sore from all of the walking at Meijer's Gardens. I leaned my head against Wade's shoulder, half-closed my eyes, and listened to the science program he was watching.

The next thing I remembered was Wade telling me it was time for bed, helping me from the couch, and leading me into the bedroom. I guess he undressed me. I woke Monday morning only wearing my underwear

Chapter Eleven

Jason swore he didn't take the thumb drive, which, in my mind, left one possibility. "Whoever broke in here yesterday took it."

"You're still sure someone broke in here?" Wade's tone indicated his doubts. "Did you find anything else missing beside that thumb drive?"

"No," I admitted.

"Did you have anything besides the actual tax returns on that thumb drive?"

"Notes. I make notes of anything a client tells me. That way, if there's ever an audit, I don't have to depend on my memory."

"Have any of your clients told you anything that might be worth stealing?"

"You mean something that could be used to blackmail them?" I laughed at the idea. "No."

My clientele primarily consisted of farmers, small business owners, and retired residents around Zenith. Even the few clients who followed me after I left Quick Sums were ones who led fairly uneventful lives. "Nothing salacious, but a thief might consider my clients' personal information valuable. Those files have social security numbers and bank account information." I shook my head at my own stupidity. "And I've been giving out business cards, letting anyone and everyone know I do taxes. Those business cards have this address on them. Wade, I've led the burglar here, straight to this house. Given someone an easy way to make money. Instead of being electronically hacked I've been physically hacked."

"It's a possibility, I guess." Wade looked toward my office area and computer. "What about your original files? Any deleted?"

I understood what he was asking, and I'd had the same thought earlier, that maybe the burglar had wiped a file off my computer as well as taking the thumb drive. A someone who didn't want a particular tax record to remain in my possession. But that wasn't the case. "Everything I've done this year is exactly as it should be. I checked."

"And you're sure you didn't put the thumb drive somewhere?"

That he asked again angered me. "Yes, Wade, I am sure. And I didn't leave the kitchen door open so Baraka could get out."

I was pretty sure about that.

Well, sort of sure.

"Wade, I don't know what's going on, but something's not right."

"I believe you," he said and hugged me. "We'll figure it out. Meanwhile, are you going to be all right? I do need to go in to work."

I wasn't sure Wade really did believe me, but until I could prove I was right, I wasn't going to argue with him. "You don't need to stay, but will you be back by the time Jason gets home from school? I promised the Sporbachs I'd stop by today; they have something they want to show me. I think it's a new greenhouse, one with all sorts of electronic gadgets that are supposed to improve production. And, of course, I want to give them their tax papers so we get paid." Every little bit helped, and Sporbach's check would be substantial.

"I also promised to meet up with Anna, from the Mothers-to-Be group. She's on the Homes4Homeless board, and it looks like the charity's bank statements have been doctored."

His eyebrows rose. "Doctored bank statements?"

"I'll tell you more after I look at the books."

"You say someone's embezzling the charity?" At my nod, he went on. "I should be home by two. I need to get those ribs in the oven by three."

"They'd better be as good as the last time you made them." I licked my lips, remembering that meal.

I loved when Wade cooked. Soon after our wedding, we decided I would cook four nights a week, Wade would cook two, and we would go out on the seventh night. We varied the nights, our work schedules often making the determination. When Wade was investigating a homicide, he might not be home for meals for a couple days. And, when I was working on taxes, I tended to forget the time. At first Wade's dinners were mundane, a can of tomato soup, toasted cheese sandwiches, and potato chips. Lately he'd been coming up with some really good meals. So far my favorite was oven-baked barbeque ribs.

* * *

It was actually closer to two-thirty before Wade arrived home. We kissed, I reminded him of where I would be in Kalamazoo and when I expected to be back. He reminded me that oven-baked ribs waited for no one.

The drive into Kalamazoo was uneventful. Although the sunshine from the day before had been replaced by heavy, gray clouds and the outside temperature had dropped to the mid-thirties, my car heater kept me warm, and I had time to mull over the disappearance of my thumb drive.

Not that thinking about its disappearance helped me figure out what had happened to it. Mainly, I kept telling myself I wasn't going crazy, that I hadn't put the thumb drive somewhere and forgotten, and I wasn't being paranoid thinking someone had been in my house while we were gone. By the time I pulled into the parking lot at Sporbach's Nursery, I'd almost convinced myself I was as sane as anyone else.

Almost.

Sporbach's Nursery was one of my first clients when I worked at Quick Sums, and Carol and Mike Sporbach were good natured, hard-working people. Even though the Internet has made communicating and filing taxes easy, because they stayed with me when I left Quick Sums and started my own business, I've always taken time for a more personal interaction with them.

As I'd suspected, what they wanted to show me was their new greenhouse. They took me on a tour, pointing out the automatic temperature and watering devices along with the specialized lighting. I took dozens of pictures and promised to email them copies. They also peppered me with questions about Paige Joy's impending birth and why I was using a midwife. Only after I'd explained my reasons did they tell me their daughter was expecting and thinking of using a midwife. And then, to my surprise, in addition to my fee for preparing the nursery's taxes, they gave me a generous check to be used for whatever I wanted to buy for the baby. My thank you was heartfelt.

I left the nursery later than I'd planned, so I called Anna to let her know I was on my way. When I arrived at the Homes4Homeless charity's offices, she was standing on the sidewalk in front of the house. She pointed toward the paved lot next door, and I recognized one of the two cars parked there as Anna's. I pulled up next to hers, grabbed my purse, and got out.

"Laura's inside," Anna said as I walked toward her. "She's working on plans for a benefit next month. I'll introduce you." Her voice dropped to almost a whisper when I reached her. "She doesn't think Mrs. Welkum will be stopping by this evening, but when I told her what we planned on doing, she suggested, if necessary, I should say the board wanted a registered CPA to stop by and make sure I was doing this right."

"She told you to say that?"

"Yes." Anna walked with me up the steps to the porch. "She also said to be careful."

At the front door, I paused. "Do you think Mrs. Welkum is dangerous?"

Anna didn't answer immediately which bothered me. I've been known to get into dangerous situations, but at those times I only had myself to worry about. Now there was the baby. I didn't want to put her in any danger.

"I don't think she's dangerous in a physical way," Anna finally said. "I think all Laura meant was let's keep this quiet, not force a confrontation until we're ready."

I hoped that was all she meant.

A sign on the front door gave the office hours—technically it was closed now—and a phone number to call for help. The door wasn't locked, and I stepped inside, followed by Anna. The work on the exterior of the two-story house had been primarily upkeep: new siding, a new roof, and repairs to the windows and porch. Once inside, however, I saw several changes had been made to convert the house into a functional workplace.

The room in front of me, which may have originally been a living room, had been sectioned off from the rest of the downstairs to act as a reception area and waiting room. Its walls were almost totally covered with photographs of people standing in front of various houses. Success stories, I supposed. Homes that the charity had found for the homeless.

To my left I could see a staircase leading up to the second floor, and on my right were two well-worn upholstered chairs and a three-cushion sofa. A desk sat directly opposite the front entrance door, and beside that desk was a closed door. A slender woman, whom I assumed to be Laura Parks—receptionist, event planner, and probably whistleblower—sat behind the desk. She looked to be in her late fifties or early sixties. What I noticed most, besides the

Rolling Stone's T-shirt and jeans she had on, was the streak of neon green running through her light brown hair, and that she was looking directly at me—at my midsection.

Her first comment after Anna made introductions was, "You two look like twins. Did you plan your pregnancies so you'd give birth at the same time?"

"Just happened by chance," Anna said. "We'll be in Jewel's office. You staying much longer?"

"No." Laura began gathering the papers she'd been working on. "I don't want to be around while you're doing your job. I'll lock up, that way no one should disturb you. Simply pull the door shut behind you when you leave."

We said our goodbyes, and I followed Anna as she went through the doorway by Laura's desk. On the other side of the wall the floor plan had been modified so what had once been a huge dining area and kitchen was now divided into a kitchenette—with barely enough room for a card table and two chairs—and two offices, one considerably larger than the other.

"Bathroom's there," Anna said and pointed to a doorway next to the kitchenette. "Door next to it goes to the cellar stairs." She wrinkled her nose. "I was down there once. Creepy place full of spiders."

I cringed at the thought.

"This is Madeline Welkum's office." She indicated the door to a larger walled-off space. "And this is Jewel's." Anna opened the door to a closet-size room.

Once inside the small office, I took off my winter coat, and dropped my purse on the floor. The room was warm and a little stuffy, so I left the door open. Anna removed a folder from the top drawer of a three-drawer file cabinet and handed it to me. "Here are the bank statements from last year and the start of this year."

In addition to the file cabinet, a desk and two chairs filled the room. A computer, printer and an in-and-out box took up most of the desk's surface. I cleared an area and opened the folder. The January statement was on top. "Any idea when they started doctoring the statements? When they started changing the deposits and withdrawals?"

Anna nodded. "I think it started last summer, back when Mrs. Welkum's daughter started working here."

"Ah-ha, so maybe we have our culprit." I slowly thumbed through the bank statements, going back in time to last summer. I stopped at July's, returned to August's, and then went back to July's. "Yep, it started here." I handed Anna the two statements. "If we hadn't talked about this before, I might not have noticed, but August is definitely when the statements start looking a little different." I placed the August statement next to the July statement. "It's like you showed me Saturday, like the difference between your bank statement and the charity's. The numbers under the different column headings simply don't line up right. The spacing is close, but not exact." I pulled out the June statement and the October statement. "June and July match. August and September match. But June and September show the difference."

"But if you weren't looking for it, would you have caught it?" Anna asked.

"I'm not sure. The doctored ones do look like the real ones."

"How did she do that?"

How? One thought came to mind. Not an answer to the question but a person who could tell me "how." I dug in my purse and found my cell phone. Ken answered on the third ring. "What's up, Pajama Girl?"

"How can someone duplicate a bank statement so it looks real?"

"What are you up to now?" he asked. "Doctoring bank statements can get you into big trouble."

"I want to know so I can get someone else in big trouble."

He chuckled. "Now, that's nasty."

He then told me how to figure out the font being used and how to create a template identical to the original. "That's how scammers can make it look like the letter really is from Social Security or Publishers Clearing House," he said. "All a good scammer needs is a good scanner and computer program."

I looked at the printer on the desk. It printed, copied, and scanned. "Thanks, Ken." I usually always followed with "Stay out of trouble" but it seemed a bit late to be saying that, so I finished with, "Keep in touch."

I looked at the computer on the desk. "Is that password protected or can we get into it?"

Anna smiled. "Password protected, but Laura gave me the password."

"Let's see what we can find." I sat down at the computer, and as soon as Anna told me the password and I was in, I began investigating the programs and files. "She uses Quick Books and Word," I told Anna. "Do you have the password for Quick Books?"

"No." She glanced the direction of the reception area. The door was now closed. "Laura's probably gone, but I can try calling her."

"No. Wait for now. We may need more than one password." I looked up at Anna. "Meanwhile, the February statement isn't in this folder. I'd like to see that again."

"I have the copy I made." Anna pulled that from her purse and placed it on the desk. "The original should be—" She moved the top piece of paper in the in-box and smiled. "The original should be here. Take a look."

She handed me what looked like the February statement from the bank, except it didn't look exactly like the statement Anna had copied last Thursday. They were almost the same, but not exactly.

On the one she'd pulled out of the in-box, the opening balance now matched January's closing balance. "It's been changed."

"Damn!" I studied the new statement and then went back to the computer. "There's got to be a template or something in here."

To my surprise, finding the template wasn't difficult. Jewel had named the file "Bank Statements." The most recent entries included February and March. The February file was what we had on the desk. The March file was the template. It showed the bank logo, address, account number and charity's address. The date hadn't been entered, and below the line all of the repetitive column headings were in place with no actual amounts except for the Beginning balance. That amount was the same as the Ending balance on the doctored February statement.

"She creates this for each month, types in the data she wants to keep and leaves out any she doesn't want to appear. The closing balance is the adjusted amount."

I pressed Print and the printer next to me came alive. Once I had a copy of the March statement, with its open areas, I placed it on the desk with the January statement, the February statement that Anna had copied on Thursday, and the February statement we'd found in the in-box. I then took a group picture and individual pictures with my phone. I also took a picture of the computer screen showing the March statement. That was when the Low Battery message flashed on my phone.

Time to recharge.

I slipped my phone back in my purse. "I should have enough pictures for Wade to tell us what to do next."

"Send those to me," Anna said, "I want—"

"Hello," a strident female voice called out from the front area of the house. "Who's here?"

I sucked in a breath, and Anna stiffened, her eyes widening. Her gaze snapped to the door between the reception area and where we were, then down to the papers spread out on the desk. "It's me, Mrs. Welkum," she yelled, all the while grabbing the statements spread across the desk. "Anna Carr. I'm in Jewel's office."

I moved over to the computer, clicked the file on the screen closed, and as soon as it was gone, clicked to shut down the computer. I expected the screen to go black. Instead, a message appeared stating not to shut down while Windows was updating.

The door between the reception area and the office area opened, and Madeline Welkum stepped into our section of the house. She stopped and stared at us. "What the hell are you two doing?"

I'd seen the woman on television and pictures of her in the newspaper, but I'd never met her in person. Tall, well dressed, and not a flaw in her makeup or hairdo, Madeline Welkum presented an imposing figure and I could see why Anna said the woman reminded her of Maleficent from Disney's *Sleeping Beauty*. Right now, as Madeline Welkum glared at us, I could picture her as a villainess.

"Well?" she said.

Her voice weakened the image. Its high pitch had irritated me even when I heard her on TV just the week before, and I'd told Wade then that I thought the woman's voice alone would keep her from being elected to the state senate.

"I'm," Anna began, closing the folder with the bank statements. "That is, we—" She took in a deep breath, smiled, and looked directly at Madeline Welkum. "We're working on the audit the board asked me to do."

I was impressed. My legs were shaking, but Anna sounded assured and calm.

Mrs. Welkum looked at Anna, then me, and then back at Anna. I glanced toward the computer. Windows was still doing its update. *Shut down*, I mentally ordered.

"What is this, the pregnant duo?" Welkum came closer. "I told you I would give you the files you needed. You have no right to be here." She glared at me. "And who are you?"

"P.J. Benson, C.P.A.," I said. I wanted to sound like I was in control. To my ears, I didn't sound that confident. "Ms. Carr asked me to come with her to make sure she had the appropriate data for an audit."

"P.J.?" Mrs. Welkum repeated, practically spitting out the initials. "That's a nickname. I asked for your real name."

"That is my real name." Now *I* was irritated. "But you're right. P.J. Benson is my business name. My legal name is P.J. Kingsley. I'm married to Kalamazoo Sheriff's Deputy Wade Kingsley." I wasn't above using Wade's connection to law enforcement to stop the woman from trying to intimidate us.

For what seemed like forever, but probably wasn't more than a few seconds, Madeline Welkum said nothing, her gaze never leaving my face. I stared back at those cold, blue eyes, unwilling to look away first. Finally, she gave a harrumph and faced Anna. "Did you find the February bank statement in the in-box?"

"I did." Anna touched the folder on the desk. "It's now in here. Should I have left it out for your daughter to see when she returns?"

Madeline Welkum's gaze dropped to the folder. "Those are the bank statements?"

I held my breath and watched Anna. Would she say something about the doctored statements? If so, how would Madeline Welkum react?

"Yes, I wanted to check them against the ledger. The two balance."

"Good." Madeline Welkum looked at me. "And what do you think, Mrs. C.P.A.?"

"I think . . ." I paused, searching for the right words. "I think Ms. Carr is doing exactly as she should for this audit."

Welkum's eyes narrowed slightly and her nostrils flared. And then she smiled. A forced smile that stretched her lips but failed to reach her eyes. "Now, I think it's time for you two to leave. The office is closed."

I glanced at the computer. To my relief, it had finally shut down. Anna started to take the bank statement folder to the file cabinet, but Mrs. Welkum stopped her. "No, leave that there."

The way the woman was looking at us, I knew she meant "leave now." Anna set the folder back on the desk, and I grabbed my coat and purse. We inched our way past Mrs. Welkum and headed for the front door. Before we were out of the reception area, she called after us, "Make sure when you make your report to the board that you can verify everything. You wouldn't want to make a mistake. That might hurt your reputation—both of your reputations—and your business."

Chapter Twelve

Once outside, we stopped at the top of the steps. "Oh no." Anna looked back at the closed door. "The February statement. The copy I made of the real one. I left it in the folder. It's there with the doctored one."

"Well, there's nothing we can do about it." I certainly wasn't going back inside. "Besides, she knows we know. She just threatened us. Threatened our careers."

"But that would have been my proof to the board."

"We have proof." I tapped the side of my purse. "As soon as I get home, I'll send you the pictures I took. That's all the proof you're going to need."

"I guess." Anna sighed and looked toward our cars. "Speaking of home, we'd better get there soon. This weather is getting bad."

While we'd been inside, the wind had picked up, and it had started snowing again. We both hurried to our cars, being careful not to slip on the icy pavement. Tiny, needle-like flakes hit my face, stuck to my hair, and had frozen on the car's windshield. I got in and started the engine, but I had to use my scraper before I could see clear enough to drive.

Days were getting longer; nevertheless, it was almost dark by the time I pulled out of the parking lot. As soon as I made it through the downtown area, I merged onto I-94. I reasoned that the county salt trucks should make the freeway faster than taking back roads.

That assumption ended before I'd passed the Sprinkle Road off ramp. Ahead of me brakes were being applied. Traffic slowed, then nearly stopped. Both eastbound lanes had become a quasi-parking lot as we inched ahead. A police car, lights flashing and siren blaring, passed on the shoulder. Then another police car.

I took the Sprinkle Road off ramp.

That road wasn't bad, but as soon as I turned off Sprinkle and headed east toward Zenith, the driving became more treacherous. Below the snow, a thin layer of ice made the roads slippery, and I didn't dare go over thirty-five. Even at that speed every nerve in my body was on edge. My hands cramped from gripping the steering wheel and my back ached from leaning forward to peer through a windshield that my wipers were barely keeping clear.

A drive that normally took forty minutes had already stretched into an hour. All I could think about was being home. I was tired and hungry. I was going to be late for those slow-baked spareribs. I knew I should call Wade, but I didn't want to stop and didn't dare try to talk while driving.

Time and distance lost meaning. I was on the road that went past my house, but how close or far, I wasn't sure. Snow and darkness obliterated my usual reference points. I passed a group of trees, then an open field, but one wooded area looked the same as the next, and a harvested field of corn, now covered with snow, was no different looking from a harvested field of soy beans covered with snow. Was I close to the VanderMeld's farm? The Mullen's pig farm?

The monotonous beat of the windshield wipers began to hypnotize me, and I felt my eyelids closing. Shaking my head, I struggled to stay alert . . . and then, suddenly, I was wide awake. Straight ahead of me, on the road and barely discernible through the falling snow, I saw three huge shapes.

I stomped on the brake pedal. Fought the steering wheel as my car went into a skid. Tried to remember which way to turn the wheel. Saw a mailbox coming toward me.

I couldn't react fast enough.

Couldn't stop the momentum.

My body jerked forward, then back as the airbag slammed against me, and for a second a billowing pillow of white engulfed me, took my breath away. Then the airbag deflated. The car had stopped.

My first reaction was to place my hands on my belly. Was my baby all right? When I left Kalamazoo, I'd made sure my seatbelt was positioned above and below my abdomen. Only the pressure of the air bag had impacted my baby, but had that hurt her?

I held my breath, waiting. Praying.

A nudge against my palm gave me hope. Then a kick.

She wasn't happy, but as far as I could tell, Paige Joy was alive. Alive and angry.

For a moment I sighed in relief. Then I heard a noise outside my car door. A sucking sound on the other side of the window. I jerked my head that direction.

A dark shape was pressed against the glass.

Too scared to even scream, all I wanted to do was escape. Pushing myself away from the door, half leaning across the console, I searched for the release of my seatbelt. Eyes on the window, I pressed the latch and felt the belt loosen.

The shape on the other side of the window pulled back, giving me a better view of my attacker, and I stopped struggling to escape. Heart still thudding in my chest, I half laughed, half choked in a calming breath.

With a snort, my attacker turned away, and I watched as a sow— a very big sow—ambled off from my car to join two other very big sows.

"What?" I yelled through the window as I straightened up in my seat. "Is this payback for having ribs for dinner?"

The three pigs continued on down the road.

"Damn." I leaned back and closed my eyes. Slowly my heartbeat returned to normal.

Once I had my wits about me, I assessed my situation. My car was sitting in a shallow ditch, its left fender hugging a mailbox. From where I was seated, I couldn't tell how much hitting that mailbox had damaged the car, so I cracked open the car door. A blast of icy cold air hit me, and I quickly closed the door again. So much for checking for damage. I would simply drive home and look at the fender when it wasn't snowing.

That plan died when I put the car in reverse and tried to back up. The tires spun, the engine revved, but the Chevy didn't move. I was stuck. The only way I would be driving anywhere was if someone pulled my car out of the ditch and back onto the road.

With a sigh, I turned off the engine and reached for my purse. I wasn't far from home. It wouldn't take Wade long to get here.

I clicked on the phone. Nothing. Tried again. Still nothing. Not even a narrow red line.

That's when I remembered how low the battery was when I was taking pictures of those bank statements. Before leaving the parking lot, I should have connected my phone to the car's charger. But I hadn't, and now the battery was dead. Absolutely dead. I couldn't call anyone, and I was leery about running the car to charge the phone. If I'd gotten snow in the exhaust pipe . . . Well, I didn't want to become a statistic.

Waiting for a car or truck to come by and offer help was also an iffy proposition. I hadn't seen one vehicle on the road in the last ten minutes. There was no telling how long it would be for one to pass, or if the driver would even realize I was sitting in my car and needed help. In the few minutes since sliding off the road, snow had already covered my windshield, and I could barely see the name on the side of the mailbox I'd hit.

Hammon.

Although the Hammons' house was just a little over a mile from mine, I'd never met them. Nevertheless, if I were lucky, they'd be home and would let me use their phone to call Wade. Or maybe Mr. Hammon would offer to pull me out of the ditch.

This time I didn't let the cold air stop me from getting out of my car. I could only button the top two buttons of my coat, but I held the lower portion over as much of my abdomen as I could and began the trudge up the Hammons' long driveway. By the time I reached their front door, my feet were freezing and snow kept sliding off my hair and down the side of my face.

George and Ina Hammon were home and willing to help, but the moment I saw the oxygen tank George was using, I knew I shouldn't ask him to go out in this weather. And, Ina wasn't fairing much better, her hoarse voice, along with the lingering odor of stale smoke, hinted at too many years of cigarette use. She did fix me a cup of hot tea while I called Wade.

Never had a man's voice sounded so good as when he answered.

"I almost hit a pig," I told him. "I didn't, but my car's now in a ditch about a mile down the road. I tried to back it out, but it's stuck."

I assured him that I was fine and that the baby was fine, and five minutes later, he pulled his Jeep up behind my Chevy. I thanked the Hammons for their courtesy and went back outside to join Wade. The snow was still falling, and I could barely make out the footprints I'd made going to the Hammons' house. As I approached my car, I could see Wade frowning as he checked the front fender, then he walked around to the other side and back again.

Finally, he looked at me. "Are you sure you're okay?"

"I'm fine," I said stopping by his side. "We just got bounced around a bit. Damn pigs."

The way he looked at me, I knew he didn't understand. "There were three of them, in the middle of the road," I said. "I had to hit the brakes, or I would have run into them. The car went into a skid, and . . ." I motioned toward my car. "Here's where I ended up."

"Pigs," he repeated. "I thought you said something about pigs on the phone, but it didn't make sense."

"There were three of them. Probably from Mullen's pig farm."

His eyebrows rose. "Three pigs, huh?"

"Yes. Big ones. Very big ones. Honest. You can see their tracks." I pointed the direction the pigs had gone.

But there were no tracks. No pigs. Not a sow or a boar anywhere to be seen.

"Honest," I repeated, turning back to face Wade.

He nodded and smiled.

"They were there," I insisted, but I could understand his disbelief. There wasn't a sign of the animals.

"Maybe they flew away," he said, grinning as he gazed up at the clouds.

"Just pull my car out," I finally grumbled, suddenly unsure if I'd really seen them or not. "I'm tired and I'm hungry."

Chapter Thirteen

Wade's slow-baked barbeque ribs were delicious. As I ate, I told him about Mrs. Welkum catching Anna and me at the charity office and that someone—probably Madeline Welkum—was embezzling money from the charity. I'd plugged my cell phone in as soon as I arrived home, and I told Wade I'd show him the pictures after I ate, except I was so tired by then I forgot. I also forgot to show him the pictures the next morning, mostly because I was still tired. Tired and sore. I woke with a stiff neck, aching muscles, and a bruise across my chest where my seatbelt had been.

All night I'd worried about the baby, but as far as I could tell, she was fine. She still kicked my ribs from time to time, and I could almost see the impression of her fist against my belly. "She wants out," I told Wade. "And I'm sure ready."

Except I wasn't, really. I still had tax forms to complete for three clients as well as ours. I'd hoped to get the most complicated return finished that morning while Jason was in school and Wade was at work, but the weather was thwarting me. "They cancelled school," I told Wade when he stepped out of the bathroom, dressed in his suit and tie. "It's March. Almost spring." I handed him a cup of coffee. "When is it going to stop snowing?"

I knew Wade couldn't answer that. In Michigan, there were times when it snowed in May. But I was frustrated. "I need to get these taxes done before the baby arrives."

"I'd take Jason with me," Wade said, "but I have to be in court." He walked over to where Jason was seated at the table, finishing his breakfast. "You can keep busy while P.J. works, can't you? I'm sure you have some reading you could do for school. Some math. And I'm sure she'd like it if you would shovel off the back steps."

"Sure," Jason agreed, almost too quickly, I thought.

"And no playing video games all morning," Wade added.

Jason's smile turned to a pout.

* * *

As it turned out, Jason did no homework or chores, and I had no idea if he would be playing video games or not. A half hour after Wade drove off, my neighbor Sondra Sommers called and asked if Jason would like to come over and spend the morning with her four children. She even offered to pick him up and bring him back in the afternoon.

Once Jason was gone, I got to work. Celia Hyland's state and federal taxes were next on my list, and even though they always took a fair amount of time to prepare, I loved doing her taxes. The woman was amazing. At eighty-five, she owned several rental units, bought and sold stocks, and went to the casinos regularly, winning more often than not. What I loved most was the paperwork she gave me at tax time was well organized and complete. My job was to find ways she could avoid paying taxes. Nothing illegal, but her philosophy and mine was why pay more than you owe?

I was totally focused on the form I was filling out when Baraka rose from where he'd been sleeping near my feet and started barking. As he limped toward the front door, I quickly saved the file and stood to see what had alerted him. A black sedan sat in my driveway.

I watched a tall, willowy woman ease out of the driver's side, pause to slip a black trench coat over a tailored black pantsuit, grab a briefcase, and close her car door. *Salesperson?* I wondered. *Lawyer?*

I was at my front door, Baraka beside me, by the time she came up the steps to the porch.

"Yes, how can I help you?" I asked, keeping the door only partway open.

"You're P.J. Kingsley?" she asked and at my nod, said, "I'd like to ask you a few questions."

"And you are?"

"Agent Andrea Tailor." She pulled a black case from her pocket and flipped it open to show a badge and her ID.

"Customs and Border Protection?" That surprised me. "What's this about?"

"May I come in?" she asked, slipping the case back in her pocket.

For a moment, I didn't move.

I knew I should say yes. It was still snowing, though not as hard as the night before, and the wind was blowing. It wouldn't be polite to force her to stand outside in the cold and talk to me. On the other hand, old habits are hard to break. Because of my mother and her schizophrenic episodes, I'd learned as a child not to let law enforcement into my house without a warrant or to say anything to the police.

The irony of being married to a sheriff's deputy never failed to amuse me.

Finally, I shook off my stupor. "Come on in," I said and held Baraka back so the woman could enter.

As I led Agent Andrea Tailor into the living room, she asked the usual questions about Baraka and the ridge on his back. I gave my usual explanation of how the European dogs owned by the colonists who migrated to southern Africa interbred with the semi-domesticated native hunting dog that had a ridge. "Over time the men realized the pups in a litter that had a ridge grew up to make good family dogs and protectors," I told her, "as well as hunting dogs."

"He seems gentle," she said. Baraka had put his head on her leg the moment she sat on the couch.

"He can be aggressive," I told her, smiling when she began rubbing his head, which was exactly what he wanted. "But they're smart, and as long as you're not a threat, he'll be a sweety. By the way, you'll be taking part of him with you when you leave."

Her look was a mixture of disbelief and curiosity. "How's that?"

"You're wearing black. He sheds like crazy."

She looked down at pant legs that were already covered with reddish-brown dog hairs and shrugged. "Could be worse."

I made myself comfortable in my favorite upholstered chair and repeated my earlier question. "What is this visit about?"

"Brenda Cox," she said and stopped petting Baraka to open her briefcase and pull out a pen and notebook. "You called the police Saturday, asking about her."

"Technically, my husband called," I said. "At my request."

"Why?"

"Because I wanted to know if Brenda was the woman killed in that hit-and-run in front of a church. If it was, I'd talked to her not long before she was murdered."

"Murdered," Agent Tailor repeated. "You're saying you think she was purposefully hit, that it wasn't an accident?"

"That's what I'm saying."

"And why is that?"

Since I'd told my reasons to Detective Ferrell on Sunday, I didn't see a problem with repeating what I'd heard to Agent Tailor. "Because not long before she died, I overheard Brenda talking to someone on the phone. She said she'd been caught looking at some pictures on the computer, pictures she'd taken."

"Did she say what these pictures showed?"

"Hidden compartments."

"In what?"

I shook my head. "She didn't say. What she did say was her boss had threatened her and that he came after her. She thought she'd given him the slip, but I think he must have figured out where she was and ran her down when she left the church."

"Did she ask you to keep something for her?"

"Keep something?" Her question triggered my suspicions. "No, she gave me nothing. Tell me, Agent Tailor, why is Customs and Border Protection investigating a hit-and-run?"

She smiled but ignored my question and asked, "How long did you two talk?"

"Not long. I had to go to the bathroom and there was only one working toilet, the one she'd been using. Was she working for the CBP?"

Again, Agent Tailor ignored my question. "And that's it?" she said. "You heard her side of the conversation, she left, and you used the bathroom?"

If she was trying to make me feel guilty, she was succeeding. "We did talk for a few minutes before she left, and I told her if she was being followed she should call 9-1-1."

"What did you talk about?"

"Me. That I was pregnant. Married. Living here."

"That's all?" Agent Tailor frowned. "Nothing about her job or where she worked?"

"No. As I said, I needed to use the toilet. Badly. If she'd waited around, I would have asked."

"You've never visited her at the furniture store?"

"No. You're saying she worked at a furniture store?"

Agent Tailor didn't answer. Without a word, she put her notebook back in her briefcase and stood. "Thank you for your information, Mrs. Kingsley." She handed me a business card. "If you think of anything more, call me."

I wasn't ready for her to leave. "You still haven't told me why an agency involved with border protection is involved. If she'd given me something, what would it have been?"

"I'm not sure." Agent Tailor said. "I was hoping you could tell me."

She started for my front door, and I followed. "She was talking to you, wasn't she?" I realized. "On the phone. You were the one on the phone, the one who was supposed to meet her."

Agent Tailor paused at the door, her expression sad. "Yes, I was the one."

"Was she working undercover?"

Agent Tailor touched my arm. "When is your baby due, Mrs. Kingsley?"

"Soon. You're not answering my question."

"From what I've heard, you seem to get involved in some dangerous situations. In this case, you need to concentrate on having your baby. Let law enforcement deal with your friend's death."

I understood her message. It was the same thing Wade was always telling me: let law enforcement solve crimes. So why, as I watched Agent Tailor walk back to her car, was I already thinking of ways to find out where Brenda worked and what she might have discovered?

Chapter Fourteen

I should have gone back to work on Celia Hyland's taxes, but the moment I sat down at my computer, I brought up the Internet. Thanks to social media, in less than ten minutes I'd found Brenda Cox's marital status—divorced—her age—forty-six—and that she was employed as a bookkeeper at Patterson's Furniture.

Patterson's Furniture. The name sounded familiar, but I couldn't remember why. I knew I'd never shopped there.

I found the store's website. The Home Page opened to the name of the store and a wide-angle view of a furniture display. The photo showed several couples—young and old and from various ethnic groups—looking at sofas, beds, tables, and chairs. The picture was slightly out of focus, forcing me to lean closer to the monitor to see if one of the women might have been Brenda. Considering her height, I figured she'd be easy to spot.

I didn't see anyone, black, tan, or white, who looked like her.

The menu bar under the picture was divided into room types: living room, dining room, bedroom. I clicked on the page showing mattresses and box springs. I wanted a king-size, but I wasn't sure one would fit in our bedroom. Once I saw the measurements, I knew I'd have to be satisfied with a queen. But even that would be better than the double I'd inherited with the house.

Next, I went to the pages showing baby furniture. Until we added another bedroom—which we planned on doing in the summer—we had everything we needed for the baby: a bassinet for the first few weeks then a crib, along with a changing table. Patterson's Furniture had some nice pieces with brightly colored designs etched into the wood. *Made in Mexico by indigenous native craftsmen*, it said in one corner of the page. The designs did have an Aztec look, and there was an adorable child's rocking chair I would love to get, someday.

I scanned other pages: living room sets, dining rooms, and patios. From the looks of the website, Patterson's Furniture was a first-rate store. So, what had Brenda discovered while working there that had ultimately led to her death? What did the pictures she took show?

The store had received four and a half stars, and the reviews I read were mostly positive. Furniture was of good quality. Salesperson was knowledgeable and helpful. One review was mostly smiling memes, the comment "More than I expected." On the other hand, a one-star review said, "Poor quality product."

I finally closed the site. I checked out a couple other places where the store was mentioned but learned nothing. All the while I was online, I kept telling myself to stop looking for an answer. I could almost hear Wade saying, "You're going to have a baby, going to be a mother. You don't need to get involved in Brenda's death. Let the police handle the investigation."

And I knew he was right, but I kept thinking I should do something.

I was about to go off-line when I decided I should check my emails. The moment I saw one from Anna, I remembered my promise from the night before. My phone was still plugged in, and I saw I'd also missed a text from her. All it said was: PICTURES?

I opened the photo icon on my phone and sent her copies of the pictures I'd taken while we were at the charity's office Monday evening. In case she had trouble downloading the pictures from her phone, I also emailed them to me so I could save them on my computer. If she did have a problem, I would email them to her as attachments.

That done, I returned to Celia's tax form and was almost finished with her federal taxes when Baraka again rose from where he'd been sleeping and began barking. A welcoming bark rather than a warning, his tail wagging as he headed for the kitchen.

I followed my dog, not surprised when I saw Howard Lowe's blue Ford parked behind my Chevy. Howard was my closest neighbor, and in the year and five months that I'd been living in what was once my grandparents' home he had transformed from a grumpy old man who ignored my "no hunting" signs to my best friend and uncle substitute. I guess I transformed a little, too. I know Howard still hunts in my woods, but whenever I've caught him coming out with a dead rabbit, I've pretended to believe his stories about how his dog Jake got loose and by the time he found him, Jake had injured the rabbit and Howard had to kill it.

We both knew the truth.

Howard is also very curious and seems to know what's going on around Zenith the moment it happens. I wasn't surprised to see him bent forward, checking out my left front fender. Either the Hammons told Howard about my accident or the pigs did.

He straightened and looked toward the house. From inside, I waved and he waved back, and then headed for my back steps. I had the door open by the time he made it to the top step.

"Fender doesn't look too bad," he said as he entered the kitchen. "There's a guy in Zenith who can fix it, and it won't cost you an arm and a leg. Everything else run okay?"

"Seemed to," I said and headed for my dining room, "but the airbags will need to be replaced. You want some coffee?"

"Is the Pope Catholic?" he answered. "I can get it myself."

He walked over to the buffet where I kept the coffee pot and a tray of mugs. There was half a pot left from when Wade had made some that morning. It would probably be pretty strong by now, but

Howard seemed to like his coffee strong. "You want any?" Howard asked, glancing my way.

I shook my head and he poured some for himself, took it into the kitchen to heat in the microwave, and two minutes later was seated at the table across from me. "You okay?" he asked. "Neck? Back? Baby?"

"Neck's sore," I said. "Back's okay, and I think the baby is all right, too. So far everything seems normal."

"When do you see the doctor again?"

I could tell Howard was concerned. I smiled. He really was a dear. "Not until Monday, but I have another of those Mothers-to-Be meetings tomorrow. I'll have the nurse check me out."

Howard nodded his approval, then grinned. "Pigs, huh?"

"Yes, and don't give me a bad time about that. There really were three pigs on the road last night. Really."

"Uh-huh." His grin turned into a chuckle. "Mike Mullen had a heck of a time rounding those sows up. It's the second time they've gotten out. Said to tell you he's sorry and he'll cover your repair costs."

That was a nice surprise. "Thank him, for me, and let him know I'll forgive him if he'll tell my husband there really were three pigs on that road."

"Oh, I'm sure your husband believes you, but we men like to tease you women. It's fun to see you get all riled up."

"Maybe fun for you. Not for me." I doubted Howard realized how much I worried about seeing things that weren't really there. You needed to grow up with a schizophrenic mother to worry about things as I did.

I still didn't know what happened to my thumb drive or if someone was in the house Sunday, and that bothered me. "Howard, you seem to know everything that goes on around here. Right?"

He shrugged. "It pays to keep informed."

"Did you see anything unusual around here Sunday?"

"Your husband stopped by yesterday and asked the same question. Wanted to know if any cars or trucks had been parked in the yard or near your place Sunday."

"He did?" Evidently Wade hadn't disregarded the possibility. That pleased me. "And what did you tell him?" If Howard had seen someone that would at least let me know I wasn't imaging things, hadn't misplaced my thumb drive, and hadn't left the back door open so Baraka could get out.

"Didn't see anything because I wasn't around Sunday. Drove to the VA hospital in Ann Arbor to visit an old buddy from the corp. He ain't doing well."

"That's too bad," I said, both because his buddy wasn't doing well and because Howard hadn't seen anyone Sunday.

"I did see a black car in your yard earlier today," he said.

"A CBP agent paid me a visit. A lady agent."

Howard's eyebrows rose. "That's Customs and Border Protection, isn't it?"

"Yes, she was looking for information about a woman I used to work with, the woman killed in a hit-and-run last Friday. Brenda Cox. I'd talked to Brenda not long before she was killed."

He nodded but said nothing. I knew he was waiting for me to say more. "That's basically it."

Again, Howard nodded, his brow furrowing. "A silver SUV went by your place several times yesterday. Know anything about it?"

"Silver SUV?" I shook my head.

"Older model Honda. Well kept up. I couldn't see the license number. Probably nothing to worry about but knowing you and how you keep finding ways to get in trouble, I thought I'd say something."

"I don't keep finding ways to get in trouble." Trouble found me, it seemed. "Ken Paget drove over here yesterday, looking for Wade."

"It wasn't your computer guru. He drives a Ford."

Leave it to Howard to not only know who Ken was, but also what kind of car he drove. "How do you get all this information?"

He grinned. "Crows tell me."

"That environmental agency you belong to or the birds?" Last spring it was the Civilian Resistance Opposing Wayward Science, otherwise known as CROWS, that helped solve the murder that brought Wade and me together.

"Come on, you know I never belonged to that group. I just contacted them when I saw a problem." Howard stood. "And no, the birds didn't tell me. However, they have trained some crows to talk." Coffee mug in hand, he started for the kitchen. "Actually, in the videos I've watched, the crows only say a few words. But they are smart, so maybe, with the right training, they could say more."

Howard was always telling me tidbits about crows. He loved those birds a lot more than I did. "Words might be better than the incessant cawing that starts as soon as I step out of the house," I said. Or maybe not. If crows talked as much as they cawed, it would probably drive me crazy.

Baraka and I followed Howard into the kitchen. He set his empty coffee mug in the sink, then faced me. "Another thing about crows is the juvenile birds are frequently seen bringing food to mom and dad, as well as feeding their younger siblings directly. You've got a juvenile living here. Make sure he helps you when the time comes."

"Don't worry. If nothing goes wrong and I have the baby here, Jason will be helping. Connie, my midwife, has a list of tasks lined up for him."

"Okay, I guess." Howard absently stroked Baraka's head. "But, if something happens, and you need someone to watch Jason when your time comes, don't forget I'm just down the road. I can be here in minutes. Seconds, if necessary."

"Thank you." I certainly hoped nothing went wrong, but it was reassuring to know Howard was willing to help.

"Any time," he said. "And, if I hear anything about Sunday, about someone breaking in here, I'll let you know."

He gave me a hug before he left. I smiled as he backed out of the yard. Maybe young crows help with parental duties, but I had an old crow ready to help me. He was a dear.

Chapter Fifteen

I finished Celia's federal and state taxes before Sondra brought Jason home. For fifteen minutes that boy talked constantly. He'd had a wonderful time. He'd helped the other boys feed the chickens and gather eggs, they'd chased the goats out of Sondra's vegetable garden—even though, Jason said, there were no vegetables in it yet, just weeds—and Mr. Sommers showed him how to milk a cow. "With my hands," Jason said, looking at his palms as if they'd changed into something miraculous.

Finally, he said he was going upstairs to change his clothes. Considering he smelled like a cow barn, I thoroughly approved of the idea; however, a half hour later, when Jason hadn't come back downstairs, and I hadn't heard any sounds from up there, I became curious.

I was huffing by the time I reached the top of the stairs. The door to Jason's room, which had been my father's room when he was a boy, was shut. Dad had told me about the time he tied bed sheets together and climbed out of the window. As cold as it was outside, I didn't think Jason would have done that, but I didn't hear any sounds from the other side of the door.

I turned the knob and slowly cracked the door open enough to see inside.

Almost immediately, Baraka pushed his muzzle into the open space, and I realized he'd gone up with Jason. On the floor behind Baraka, lay a pair of dirty jeans. Even from outside of the room, I could smell them. And on the bed, curled up in the fetal position, was Jason . . . sound asleep. "You want out?" I whispered to Baraka and opened the door farther.

My dog trotted past me and headed for the stairs. There he paused and looked back at me, as if to say, "Aren't you coming?"

I thought about simply closing the door again, then changed my mind. Heat rises, and the upstairs area was warm, but maybe not warm enough for a sleeping child. I went into the room and covered him with a plush throw. He made a small grunt but didn't move. He looked so innocent lying there.

Without thinking, I stroked my belly. Soon he would have a sister. Would they be friends? Seven years was a big span in ages. Would he become her protector? I had no brothers or sisters and growing up I'd envied those who had siblings. It would have been nice to have had an ally when I was dealing with Mom.

I sighed, picked up the smelly, dirty jeans, and holding them away from my body, quietly left the room.

I hoped neither Jason nor the baby in my womb would have to deal with a schizophrenic mother.

* * *

Jason was awake and downstairs by the time Wade came home. While I fixed dinner, Wade heard all about the chickens, goats, and cows. Jason kept talking during dinner, which was fine. I didn't want to say anything about my visitor in front of Jason. It wasn't until after dinner was over and I was putting dishes in the dishwasher that Wade and I had a chance to talk.

Wade spoke up first. "Your buddy's off the hook," he said as he opened another beer. "At least off the hook regarding the white power we found in his trailer. Turned out to be Epsom salt, some that our good neighbor Howard Lowe had dropped off for Ken to use for his plants."

"Epsom salt, not cocaine or heroin?" I grinned, knowing Wade had been sure Ken was using drugs. "Now, don't you feel like a fool?"

"Don't act so smug. An overdose of Epsom salt can lead to heart problems, coma, paralysis, and death."

"So, you think Epsom salt killed Jerry?" I wasn't sure I understood.

"No, but we couldn't rule it out. However, the medical examiner said, since Epsom salt is basically magnesium sulfate, Mr. Herman would have had to take a very large dose to cause death and using NARCAN wouldn't have revived him even for a short while. The quantity of powder we found does fit Mr. Paget's explanation about why the bag was in the trailer. Seems he has house plants at his apartment in Kalamazoo and misting once a month with a weak solution of Epsom salt helps produce greener leaves."

"Sounds like something I should try. That plant your mother gave me isn't doing well." Of course, if I remembered to water it regularly, that might also help. "Anyway, I'm glad to hear Ken isn't doing heroin or cocaine."

Wade simply grunted.

As I washed two plastic containers that couldn't go in the dishwasher, I said, "I had a visitor today. A Customs and Border Protection agent showed up around eleven thirty asking questions about Brenda Cox."

"A CBP agent?" Wade grabbed a dish towel and dried the two containers. "What did he want to know?"

"He was a she. Agent Andrea Tailor. She knew I'd talked to Detective Ferrell, and that I'd told him that Brenda had been threatened by her boss. She said Brenda worked at Patterson's Furniture, and she wanted to know if I'd been to that store."

"The agent told you your friend worked at Patterson's Furniture?" Wade frowned and set the dried containers on the counter.

"Well, she didn't say the store's name, but I went on-line and found out where she worked."

He sighed and shook his head. "I thought we agreed you weren't going to get involved."

"I'm not getting involved. I was simply curious."

"Do you realize that's where Mr. Herman worked?"

"No." That was a surprise.

"I was over there this afternoon, interviewing the owner, who swore he knew nothing about the pills we found."

"Of course." It wasn't like the man would admit to pushing drugs.

Wade nodded and chuckled. "He said he didn't actually hire Herman, that the store manager did, so he called the manager over. And, talk about evasive. This guy insisted he had no idea how Herman could have ended up with oxycodone pills. 'Maybe someone came by after hours and sold them to him,' he said. Which, of course, I don't believe. As for why he didn't report Herman as missing Friday, he said he just figured Herman had found the work more physical than he'd expected and quit."

"So, both Brenda and Jerry worked for Patterson's Furniture." I repeated the information for my own clarity. "And now both are dead." I looked at Wade. "That's got to be more than a coincidence."

"P.J. . . ." He stretched out my name, a warning tone to the syllables. "Forget it."

Looking into his eyes, those beautiful blue eyes that have fascinated me from the day I met him, I wanted to assure him I wouldn't get involved. Not this time. Not when I was only days or weeks from becoming a new mother.

"I'm just pointing out that two people dying the same day, two people who worked for the same store, might be more than a coincidence," I said and started the dishwasher. "Especially when a federal agent comes around asking questions about that store. Does Detective Farrell know your OD victim also worked for Patterson's Furniture?"

Wade smiled and shook his head. "I don't know, Miss Detective, I haven't told him, but I will make sure he's aware of that. Now—" He slipped an arm around my shoulders. "Come into the living room and sit down for a while. Aren't you sore from that accident last night?"

"A little," I admitted, walking with him out of the kitchen. "By the way, Howard said our local pig farmer admitted he had pigs loose last night. So there."

Wade chuckled. "Are you saying pigs don't fly?"

Chapter Sixteen

On Wednesday the weather played its usual turnabout. The temperature rose and snow turned to rain. Jason and Wade left the house at their usual times, and by ten o'clock, I'd called the mechanic in Zenith, the one Howard had recommended. To my relief, the man said if I brought my car in that afternoon, he had a loaner I could use until he replaced the airbags and made the necessary repairs to my car. That meant I not only could make it to my regular Mothers-to-Be meeting, I could also stay in town and enjoy my once-a-month dinner with Grandma Carter.

I hadn't wanted to miss either. I loved getting together with Grandma, and I wanted Connie to listen to my baby's heartbeat. Paige Joy hadn't been moving around much this morning, and I was worried. Being bounced back and forth and thumped by an airbag couldn't be good for her. I would feel better if I knew everything was all right.

With several hours to go before I left for the meeting, I went to work on a federal tax form for the third and last client on my list. Once I had those taxes completed and filed, I would start Wade's—we wouldn't file as a couple until next year—which would take some time since his idea of keeping records involved stuffing receipts, notes, and documents into shoe boxes. I had two boxes to go through.

A sharp pain in my side took my breath away, and I stood, hands on my belly, waiting. Was this the start of labor?

Dozens of thoughts raced through my head. If I were going into labor, how long should I wait before calling Wade or Connie? Did I have everything I needed here at the house, or because of the accident, should I go to the hospital?

Undecided, I paced the living room. Baraka went to the front door, indicating he wanted to go out. A good idea, I decided. His last fart had gagged me.

The rain had subsided to a drizzle, and I stepped onto the porch to watch Baraka start his customary search for the perfect spot to cock his leg. A pair of crows in the tree across the road cawed. Warning others that the dog and human were outside? Or was I giving the birds too much credit? Howard said crows were highly intelligent, but did they really set up sentries to alert others about my activities?

In tandem the crows cawed again, then flew from the tree. I visually followed their flight toward Howard's house, then noticed a car parked on the shoulder of the road, not far from my driveway. A silver SUV, its lights on.

In trouble?

I watched it, trying to see if there was anyone in the vehicle. Its windshield wiper made a swipe, and I thought I saw someone on the driver's side. I debated walking down to check if the driver needed help. The SUV wasn't that far away, and I'd learned that in the country, people helped each other. But something didn't feel right. I couldn't see any damage to the car. If the driver was simply having engine trouble, he could come to me. Even if he didn't want to walk the short distance, he could get out of the car and signal for help. And if he'd already called for help, there was no sense in me getting wet to learn that.

I heard the SUV's engine start, watched it pull back onto the road and head my way. It slowly passed in front of my house, but tinted windows stopped me from seeing inside. And then, once by, the SUV sped up. In seconds it was out of sight.

Strange, I thought. *Very strange.*

* * *

I hadn't felt any more sharp pains since that first one, so once Baraka finished outside, I let him back in, and returned to my computer. At one o'clock, since I still hadn't felt any more pains, I drove my car into Zenith, stopped at the bank to make a deposit into my business account and cashed the personal check the Sporbachs had given me. I then drove to the mechanic's shop just north of town.

The sign for Schipper's Auto Repairs wasn't large, simply a sheet of plywood, barely four-by-four nailed to two short posts. It was set back from the road between a ranch-style house and a large pole barn, but I hadn't noticed it before. Hadn't noticed how many cars were parked in front of the barn, some with their hoods up, others with obvious damage. I guess I hadn't paid attention because up until now I hadn't had a need for a mechanic.

Nate Schipper, I discovered, was a graduate of Zenith High and had worked for six years as a mechanic at the Chevrolet dealership in Kalamazoo before buying this property. "We're expecting, too," he said, pointing at the house. "Zenith is a good place to raise a family."

I hoped so, though having been raised in the city, I was still adjusting to living in a rural area where everyone seemed to know everyone else's business. Earlier, when I'd called to see if he could fix my car, the moment I mentioned my name, Nate knew I'd gone off the road and hit the Hammon's mailbox.

"Yeah, Howard stopped by and said you might call," Nate said as he walked me over to the side of his barn. "He said you'd probably need a loaner. This Chevy's not in the best of shape, but it will get you around until I can install new airbags in yours."

I hoped he was right about the car getting me from place to place. The loaner was a faded red, six-cylinder Chevy Impala with almost two hundred thousand miles. Several scratches and dents marred its exterior, and the moment I opened the car door, I could smell stale cigarette smoke and see a burn spot on the passenger's seat and stains on the floor mats.

I almost decided against taking the car, but if I wanted my car fixed, I didn't really have a choice. The positive side was he said the loaner car got good gas mileage. With a smile, I took the keys and headed for Kalamazoo.

After a while, I didn't notice the cigarette smell, and the car actually didn't handle badly though it did seem to pull to the left. I arrived early for the meeting. That is, early for me. Tamara was already inside the building, standing in the hallway outside of our meeting room. "We have to wait," she said when I headed for the door. "Connie's inside, arguing with the minister."

I could hear voices through the closed door, Connie's and another woman's. "Why are they arguing?"

"Seems someone broke into the church last Saturday," Tamara said. "Down here the wastebasket in the bathroom was turned over, its contents strewn all over the floor, and the paper towel holder was smashed. Upstairs, in the sanctuary, all of the hymnals had been pulled out of the racks in front of the pews and tossed on the floor. I guess the minister's office also was broken into, but I don't know what damage was done there, or what might be missing. From what I've heard through the door, she's blaming us."

"Us?" I didn't understand. "Why would we want to mess up a church that's allowing us to meet twice a week?"

"I don't know. I guess—"

The door opened and Tamara stopped talking as a tall, gray-haired, black woman stepped out into the hallway. "Today, but that's it." The minister shook a finger toward the open doorway. "I don't care if you had nothing to do with what happened. I'm making a rule. From now on, only members of this congregation will be allowed to use this building. No outsiders."

"Phew," I murmured, watching the minister head for the stairs, her back as rigid as her words.

"Phew is right," Tamara said and pushed herself away from the hall wall. "Shall we go in and see if our loyal leader survived the battle?"

* * *

Connie waited until we were all there before she explained the problem. "I think having the church broken into just a day after a woman was killed out front has been too much for Reverend Jones. And the timing isn't all that bad. Some of you are near your due dates, and since a couple of you have indicated you want me as your midwife, chances are I would have had to start rescheduling these sessions."

"I almost called you this morning," I said. "I felt a strong pain right along here." I rubbed my hand over my right side. "I was sure I was starting labor."

"But nothing more?" Connie asked, looking at me.

"Nothing more. I got up and walked around a bit, let my dog out, and went out on the porch. Everything felt fine." I didn't add that seeing the silver SUV made me forget I'd been worried about going into labor.

"Well, don't hesitate to call if you think you might be going into labor, even if it is a false alarm." She looked at the rest of the group. "That goes for all of you. Even if you're going to have your baby in the hospital, I'd like to know when you go into labor." She smiled. "I feel like you're all my daughters."

Maria made a derisive sound. "I hope you better than *mi madre*. She kick me out when I am seventeen."

"I'm sorry to hear that," Connie said.

"Iz okay," Maria said and smiled. "I land on feet, and *Madre* now dead."

I didn't know what to think about Maria's last statement, and from Connie's expression, I could tell she wasn't sure what to say, either. No one seemed to. Finally, Connie cleared her throat and said, "Changing the subject, did any of you know the woman who was hit by a car out front of the church?"

Before I had a chance to speak up, Tamara said, "I did. Years ago, I was in a soc' class at Western with her. She and I used to compare notes before exams. I was surprised when I saw her Friday. Surprised she remembered me."

"You talked to her?" I said. "Did she tell you she was being followed?"

"Being followed?" Tamara shook her head. "No. She stopped me just as I was about to enter the church, asked where I was going. When I told her about this group, she wanted to know if there was somewhere private downstairs where she could make a phone call. I told her I didn't know about any other rooms being open, but there was a bathroom. She walked downstairs with me. Last I saw of her, she went into the bathroom."

"Is that where you saw her, P.J.?" Connie asked. "Talked to her?"

"Yes." I briefly related what I'd overheard. "I told Brenda to call 9-1-1, but I should have done more to help her." I still felt guilty.

"Yes, good friends help," Maria said.

Connie frowned at Maria. "She told her to call 9-1-1. Sometimes we can't help people. They have to help themselves."

"Maybe, but if me, I would have asked for help." Maria looked directly at me. "If you such good friends, why your friend not ask?"

"I don't know why." Except, I did. "I was in such a hurry to get to the toilet, I—"

"Don't try to second guess yourself, P.J.," Connie said. "And what about you, Maria? Did you see her? Talk to her?"

Maria stiffened, her eyes narrowing. "Why you ask me?"

"Because, as I recall, you came in late Friday. Something about a phone call from your husband. Did you see the woman?"

"No." Maria looked at all of us. "No one here to blame. Right? Paper said it was accident."

"I don't think it was."

I didn't mean to say that aloud, and the moment I did, everyone's gaze switched to me. "Do you know something we don't?" Connie asked. "P.J., did your husband tell you something?"

"No." I laughed at the idea. "Just the opposite. He keeps telling me to forget it, not to get involved."

"Yes, forget it," Maria said. "Iz better to do what husband wants. Everyone happy then."

"Maybe." Tamara kept looking at me. "Come on, P.J. Do you know more? Have they figured out who was driving the car that hit her?"

"Not as far as I know, and Wade's right, I shouldn't get involved."

"My boyfriend wouldn't think of telling me what to do," Sarah said.

Anna laughed. "That's because you're young and not married. Now, in my case, by not having a partner, I can do what I want whenever I want."

"Okay, okay," Connie motioned with her hands that it was time to change the conversation. "Let's talk about what we're going to do now that we can't meet here."

Brenda's name wasn't mentioned again, but I couldn't shake the feeling that I'd let her down.

Chapter Seventeen

"Are you sure you're all right?" Anna asked me as we walked to our cars after the meeting. "Monday night I was already worried about you having to make that long drive back to Zenith. And later, when I heard about the pileup on I-94 just outside of Galesburg, I hoped you hadn't gotten caught in that. I didn't think about the road out of Zenith being bad." She chuckled. "Didn't think about pigs being on the road."

I stopped walking. "It wasn't funny."

"I'm sorry, P.J." Anna shook her head, still grinning. "But the way you told it at the meeting, about them having completely disappeared by the time your husband got there, it did sound funny."

"If I hear one more comment about disappearing pigs, I think I'll scream." Even the teller at the bank in Zenith had mentioned my disappearing pigs.

"You have had a rough few days. When you and I met Monday, you didn't even mention having your house broken into on Sunday."

"I shouldn't have mentioned it during today's session. I'm sure Connie thinks I'm crazy. Crazy like my mother." I sighed, wishing I hadn't told the group all the crazy things my mother did when she was pregnant with me. "Probably you all do."

"No," Anna insisted. "You know your house, know where things should or shouldn't be. It's just that . . ." Again, she chuckled. "Well, what you told us sounded strange. Really strange."

"Baby brain strange?" I tried to smile. "I don't know. Maybe I am going crazy."

"Or, maybe," Anna said as we started walking again, "someone did break into your house. After all, besides the missing thumb drive, you said your dog was outside when he shouldn't have been."

"I should have locked that door when I left."

"In the neighborhood where I grew up, a locked door wouldn't have stopped someone from breaking in. If anything, that big dog of yours should have scared your burglar away, which might be why he was thrown outside." Anna stopped beside her car. "Do you think they tranquilized him?"

"Wade doesn't think so. When we arrived home, Baraka acted subdued but not like he was out of it. And you're right, most people look at him, and because of his size, assume he's vicious, but I've never seen him act aggressive when people come over. Mostly he sits and watches them." I laughed. "However, having a Ridgeback stare at you can be intimidating."

"Well, you said nothing valuable was taken, so you lucked out there." Anna waved as Tamara walked past. "See you," she called out to her before turning back to me. "Thanks for sending those pictures of the bank statements. I printed them. They came out pretty good. Good enough to show the differences." Shaking her head, she opened her car door. "I can't believe I left that original statement in the folder. How stupid."

"Have you heard anything from Mrs. Welkum? Did she call or anything?"

"Nothing." Anna shook her head. "That makes me even more nervous. What is she doing? What might she do?"

"The question is, what are *you* going to do?"

"Not a thing until Monday. That's when the board meets. I'll show them those pictures of the doctored bank statements and tell them what I think. After that, it will be up to the board to decide what to do."

"I showed the pictures to Wade."

"What did he say?"

"Basically, what you're planning. He said it's the board's responsibility to investigate. Once they've determined the extent of the theft and gathered all the available records, an outside firm should be hired to do an audit. If there's sufficient evidence, the suspected embezzler should be confronted."

"So, who do you think it is?" Anna asked.

"Has to be Mrs. Welkum, doesn't it?" That seemed self-evident. "Her daughter's not around, so she couldn't have doctored that February statement."

"I guess," Anna said, "but I don't want it to be her. P.J. Homes4Homeless is doing good things. Madeline Welkum started the charity with her own money. Her name alone has made things happen. Twenty homes have been purchased, refurbished, and given to vets and families who had no homes. Looking at the books, as far as I can tell, she hasn't been taking a salary, not a regular one, so maybe the missing checks are payments to her, reimbursements for what she's spent out of her pocket, or something like that."

I knew Anna didn't really believe that. "If so, why write and cash checks that she marks as void? Why doctor bank statements so those checks don't show up? If she deserves the money, why not simply list it as an expense?"

"I don't know." Anna slid into her car. "And I don't know what will happen to the charity if she's arrested. I never thought I'd have to do something like this when I agreed to be on the board. I think they asked me so they could say the board was diversified. "Look at me—" She indicated herself with a wave of her hand. "One Black. One female. One lesbian. Diversified."

I laughed at her description of herself. She definitely fit all of those categories. "Stay out of trouble," I said and stepped back as she started her car.

* * *

I drove from the church to my grandmother's house. The rain wasn't much more than a fine mist, but the temperature was dropping, and as I walked up to her front porch, it felt like icy needles hitting against my cheeks. Entering the warmth of Grandma Carter's house was a pleasure.

"Boy, am I glad to see you," Grandma called from the kitchen.

"Why? What's wrong," I asked, surprised by the anguish I'd heard in her voice.

"It's your mother."

Grandma sat at her kitchen table. That she didn't get up worried me. Usually, I received a hug when I arrived. "What happened to Mom?"

"Sit down." Grandma motioned toward the wooden chair near her. "You're going to want to be sitting."

I sat, my stomach tightening as I waited for her to go on.

"You know how normal your mother's been acting since she got on that new medicine and started dating Ben?"

"Yes," I said, drawing out the word since I knew Grandma's question meant something had changed, and I hated to hear that.

Last summer Mom's doctor had finally found a medicine that Mom willingly took and her hallucinations and paranoia had stopped. She'd found a job with Goodwill and had met Ben Ross. The two of them had been dating off and on ever since. For months I'd had a normal mother, one who helped me on my wedding day, went shopping with me for baby clothes, and lectured me about my weight gain.

"So, what happened?" I repeated.

"Your mother and Ben were arrested last night."

"Arrested? For what?"

"For indecent exposure." Grandma sighed. "They were found swimming in a motel pool at three in the morning."

I knew most motels limited the hours their pools were open but breaking that rule wouldn't get a person arrested for indecent exposure. Which meant one thing. "Mom went skinny dipping."

"Yep," Grandma said. "Both your mom and Ben were buck naked."

I closed my eyes and leaned back against my chair. "What were they thinking?"

Grandma laughed. "Come on, P.J., you know your mother."

She was right. I knew my mother's thinking didn't always make sense, that over the years she'd been arrested for multiple misdemeanors. Whenever she went off her pills, she saw weird things—like UFOs—and did weird things. "I thought Ben was making sure she was taking her pills. Shoot, I thought he was levelheaded."

"She says she's taking her pills, that this has nothing to do with any of that. She says they were celebrating."

"Celebrating what? How to get arrested?"

"Their wedding."

That news shocked me even more than the idea of Mom being arrested. I sat forward again. "Mom and Ben are married?"

"That's what she says. She told me Ben has a friend who can marry people and that they are now married."

"A friend, huh?" I had a feeling Mom's marriage was another of her illusions. "Where is she now? In jail?"

"No, she's at Ben's place. She said they have to appear in court sometime next week." Grandma raised her eyebrows. "She asked me to find her a lawyer."

And my grandmother would. From the time I was ten and we received the report that my dad had been killed by a bomb in the

Mideast up to now, Grandma Carter had been the one to come to Mom's rescue. Mine, too. Over those years, Grandma had helped pay our medical bills, hired lawyers to get Mom out of trouble, and taken us in when Mom forgot to pay the mortgage and we lost our house. Grandpa Carter also helped, but he died when I was fifteen.

"You remember that lawyer you hired last summer for Ida? Think you could contact him and see if he can help?"

I knew who Grandma meant. I met Ida Delaney, a woman in her seventies, when I gave a talk at a local library about avoiding scams. Ida had dementia, and for some reason thought I could help her nephew who was trying to blackmail some unsavory men. When the police became involved, Ida ended up staying with Grandma for a while, and we hired a lawyer. "Arthur Hicks," I said. "Sure, I can call him, but Mom and Ben are the ones who will have to talk to him."

"While you make that call, I'll fix you some tea," Grandma said, sounding more upbeat than she had when I first arrived.

I had to leave a message when I called Hicks, but ten minutes later he called back. After we exchanged pleasantries, I explained, as best I could, what my mother and Ben had done and why they needed his services. I also let him know I didn't expect him to do this pro bono, not as he had for Ida.

I then called Mom.

I should have been more enthusiastic when she told me that Ben and she were married, but I wasn't. She sounded like a teenager, giggling and sighing as she related how someone Ben knew was the minister of a church—one I'd never heard of—and how, for their wedding, this minister dressed liked a hippy. "He wore a tie-dye robe and a garland of flowers around his head," she said. "Well, actually, they were artificial flowers stuck in a sweat band, but it looked neat. Reminded me of those pictures your grandmother has of when she marched in peace rallies."

I'd heard about those days and seen those pictures. On occasion Grandma still marched for different causes, usually ones that involved women's rights.

"The minister's wife banged on a tambourine and threw torn up bits of toilet paper, like flower petals, on the carpet as I walked down the hall to the living room," Mom said. "And after the ceremony we drank blueberry wine the minister had made himself and ate brownies."

"Brownies?" I repeated.

"Yes, they were marvelous." She giggled. "Much better than that cake you had at your wedding."

"Are you still eating brownies?" I asked, wondering if some brownies laced with marijuana might explain a late-night dip in a motel pool sans clothing.

"Finished the last one last night, just before we decided to go swimming."

Bingo. "Make sure you tell Mr. Hicks that, Mom," I said, knowing I would also let Arthur Hicks know she might not have been completely responsible for her actions. Neither she nor Ben.

"Will do," Mom agreed.

Finally, I did tell her congratulations, though I'm not sure why. In all probability she and Ben weren't really married and unless Arthur Hicks could convince a judge they didn't know what they were doing, they might be spending the next few months in jail and paying a fine. Poor Mom. She might have a high IQ, but even ignoring the schizophrenia, she lacked common sense.

"I guess we just wait and see," I told Grandma.

"All we can do," she agreed. "Meanwhile, are you hungry? And how are you doing? When I talked to you yesterday, you said you were sore from that accident."

"I am getting hungry," I admitted, "and feeling better today. Connie, the nurse who runs that Mothers-to-Be group, checked me over and said the baby is fine. That was a big relief." I had been worried. "I'll see her again on Friday, and then I have my two-week appointment with my doctor Monday. That is, if Paige Joy hasn't arrived by then." I sighed. "I am so ready for this baby to come."

Grandma stood and headed for the refrigerator. "Babies come when they're ready. Baked chicken sound good? Potatoes and peas?"

"Sounds wonderful." I also stood. "What can I do to help?"

As Grandma prepared the chicken, I peeled three small potatoes. Working side by side with her was a familiar experience for me. For years Mom and I had lived in this house, prepared food in this kitchen, and ate together at Grandma's table. Good memories and bad had been shared here. I considered myself lucky; most of my memories were good ones.

"How are you doing on those taxes you had to finish?" she asked when we sat back down to wait for everything to cook.

"I've finished the last of the ones I agreed to handle this year," I said, pleased with myself. "Just Wade's and mine left to do."

"Organized and everything in control, as usual."

I laughed. "It's more like I try to be organized, but somehow I always seem to lose control. Things just seem to happen. Think about it. There I am, simply in need of a bathroom, and who do I run into? Brenda Cox. I hadn't seen or talked to her for almost two years, and an hour later, she's dead, killed by a hit-and-run driver who no one can identify. Why? Why did I overhear her saying her boss had threatened her? Was her death an accident as Wade and the police are saying or was it murder?"

"P.J." Grandma's voice held a warning tone. "Don't you go and get involved."

"I know, I know." I avoided looking directly at her. "I won't."

"Uh-huh." She didn't sound convinced. "I mean it, P.J." She stood and went to check on the potatoes. "Believe me," she said from the stove, "I was shocked when I saw it was Brenda who was killed. She was a wonderful person, staying with you that time I was in the hospital, but I'm sure she wouldn't want you getting involved in whatever she was involved in. Not in your condition."

She came back to the table and placed a hand on my shoulder. "Honey, some things just happen. Listen to Wade. Let them figure out what's up."

I looked at Grandma's hand, veins and tendons clearly visible beneath thin wrinkly skin. She'd lived more than seventy years and had experienced a multitude of unexpected events, including my mother's mental illness. I would agree, some things did just happen. On the other hand, sometimes it seemed like there was a reason.

"Grandma, I can't just let it go. Brenda was there for me when I needed her. Maybe it's crazy, but I feel like I was meant to be in that bathroom when Brenda was there, that there was a reason why I overheard that conversation. Also, Brenda worked at Patterson's Furniture and last Friday she died. Last Friday someone else I knew, though not well, died. He also worked at Patterson's Furniture. To me that's more than just a coincidence."

"Two hit-and-run accidents the same day?"

"No, Jerry died of an overdose. But do you see what I mean?"

"Patterson's Furniture," Grandma said. "Never heard of it. Where's it located?"

"Somewhere off Douglas Avenue, north of West Main. I looked it up on-line the other day. They had a cute child's rocking chair."

Grandma looked at me and frowned. "P.J., stay away from there."

Chapter Eighteen

I was hungrier than I'd realized, and dinner was delicious. Grandma drank wine; I drank milk. We talked about her book group, the crocus and jonquils that were starting to peek through the ground, and how much Jason had grown in the last few months. What we didn't talk about was Brenda or Patterson's furniture, and when I left Grandma's house, a dozen cookies for Wade and Jason on the seat beside me, I really should have headed home. It was already starting to get dark, and I had a forty-minute drive ahead of me. Nevertheless, it wasn't far from Grandma's house to Patterson's Furniture, and I was curious. I wanted to see where both Brenda and Jerry had worked.

I took West Michigan Avenue to Douglas Avenue and turned right. At first I passed homes that dated back to the early nineteen-hundreds. Some had been divided into apartments or duplexes, and many, I knew, were rented during the year to Kalamazoo College students. I didn't see any furniture stores in this area. It wasn't until I neared the U.S.-131 Business Loop that I passed Patterson's Furniture.

I made a U-turn at the next intersection, drove back past the store, and turned into the paved lot on its south side. Although it was past six o'clock, a sign in the window by the entry door flashed "Open," and the store's interior lights were on.

I couldn't see anyone inside the building, and there were no cars parked near the entry door, but a black truck with rusted fenders and a delivery van with the words Patterson's Furniture on its side were parked back by a Dumpster. Engine still running, I sat in my car trying to decide exactly what I wanted to do next. According to the information I'd found on the Internet, Brenda worked here as a bookkeeper. That meant this was where she'd been looking at pictures on her computer, where she'd been threatened by her boss. From here she headed downtown, ending up in the church where I overheard her talking on the phone.

Another car pulling into the lot jarred me out of my thoughts. A dark-colored, beat-up sedan parked near the entry door and a wiry-looking, bearded man got out. He started for the entry door, then paused and looked back at his car. The door on the passenger's side opened, and a preteen girl hurried to join him.

The two entered the store, and I made a decision. If a man and his daughter could shop for furniture this late in the day, so could a pregnant woman. I turned off the engine, grabbed my purse, and got out of my car.

A buzzer went off as I stepped inside. The man and his daughter were now near a display of mattresses, and I could see a tall, muscular man dressed in well-worn jeans and a faded gray T-shirt walking toward them. One other man stood near a door at the back of the store. Short and stocky, he was also dressed in jeans and a baggy blue sweatshirt. Both men looked to be Hispanic. Not that their nationalities mattered to me, but the way they were dressed didn't fit my image of a furniture salesman.

"Be with you in minute," the one walking toward the man and girl called to me.

"Okay," I called back, glad to have time to simply glance around.

The store looked about as I remembered from the overview on its webpage. One thing my computer hadn't shown was the no smoking sign by the door, which seemed comical since I could smell a hint of marijuana. But maybe it came from the clothing of the customers, not the store's backroom. Maybe.

In front of me were the usual groupings: living room furniture, dining room, and bedroom. Nearby an array of lamps, vases, and a variety of decorative items sat on desks, bookcases, and stands. A ceramic crow figure caught my attention. Although twice the size of the crows that harassed me every time I stepped out of the house, it looked to be a perfect replica of the bird, from its jet-black color to the beady glass eye staring at me. A perfect gift, I thought, for Howard.

I carefully picked up the crow to check the price. It wasn't that much, but looking at the bird closer, I could understand why. Rather than being fired as one piece, it had been fired as two halves that were later glued together. Although the seamline was barely visible, what I held was not an original but a mass-produced crow.

I smiled, remembering the sign on the website: *Crafts and Furnishings: Made in Mexico by indigenous native craftsmen.*

Crafty craftsmen was more like it. Two halves glued together produced an empty cavity that could be filled with drugs. I wouldn't put it past the Mexican drug cartels to use crow statues to smuggle cocaine and heroin across the border. And here was Ken's buddy Jerry, working at Patterson's Furniture, ready to receive the shipment.

I noticed the employee helping the father and daughter watching me. He made me think of a bouncer. Did he know what I was thinking?

I smiled, carefully placed the crow back on the display table, and stepped away. Whether it was mass produced or not, I might buy the crow for Howard, but first I wanted to look at the nursery furniture. I'd liked what was shown on-line. Getting to that section, however, required working my way past a long, wooden dining table and around a stack of chairs before I made it to a crib crammed between two small dressers.

I was looking at a colorful mobile attached to the crib's railing when, from behind me, I heard, "*Es bonito, sí?*"

I turned to see the short, stocky man who had been standing by the storeroom door was now just inches away. Up close, he looked much younger than the other salesman, maybe early twenties. We were almost the same height, and he was smiling, but even though he was physically less intimidating than the other man, his nearness made me nervous. I edged back, closer to the crib.

"Good for *bebé*." He glanced at my protruding belly and made a rocking sign with his arms. "Sleep safe."

"Oh, no. I already have a crib. What I was looking at is this." I tapped the mobile on the crib, setting it in motion. "But I don't want it."

He frowned. "No like?"

"Yes, it's nice, but I'm just looking. You know, window shopping." He looked confused. "I wanted to see what you had."

From his expression, I wasn't sure how much English he understood, so I placed my right hand above my eyes and turned my head from side-to-side, as if looking for something or someone. I don't know if my gesture conveyed my meaning or not because, when my gaze reached the checkout counter, I forgot about the man beside me. Earlier, I hadn't noticed the glassed-in area behind the counter. A sign next to an opening in the glass said CASHIER.

"Oh, Brenda." I sighed, suddenly overwhelmed by the realization that less than a week before she had used that area to perform her job.

"Brenda?"

"What?" I looked back at the man standing by me. Had I said Brenda's name aloud?

"*Qué?*" he said, frowning. "What 'bout *Señora* Brenda?"

"She was a friend," I said, deciding I had to say something. "*Una amiga.* She worked here, *sí?*"

"*Sí*, maybe." He glanced over at his coworker, then back at me. His smile had disappeared, and his posture was now guarded. "You want buy something?"

Considering his reaction, I decided it was time to leave. I'd discovered what I wanted to know. The store looked like a normal furniture store, Brenda had worked here, and simply mentioning her name made an employee nervous. Time to act like I couldn't find what I wanted. Again, I looked around, as if trying to find something, then gave an exaggerated sigh and let my shoulders sag. "Darn it," I said, hoping I sounded disappointed. "I saw a child's rocking chair on this store's website. I really liked it, but I don't see any like it here."

My salesman's cheerful demeanor returned. Smiling, he raised a hand about knee high. "*Mecedora* for *bebé?*"

I wasn't sure what a *mecedora* was, so I made a rocking motion with my right arm.

He nodded. "Sí, we have."

I still wasn't sure he understood what I was looking for. "For a toddler. For a *niña tres o quatro anos.*"

"*Sí*, we have. *Nueva.*" He turned and started for the storeroom.

"*Que esta pasando*, Miguel?" the other salesman, who was still with the father and daughter, called out.

The one called Miguel said something back in Spanish that I couldn't understand and pointed at me. The other salesman nodded, and Miguel proceeded into the storeroom.

Moments later, he returned with exactly what I'd seen on the website. A rocking chair perfect for a toddler. It had tiny, colorful flowers on the back and seat and a music box attached to the rocker. Packing material surrounded the music box, but my eager salesman assured me it would work.

"Is good, right?" he said, grinning. "*Bueno*."

"Yes, *Bueno*." He'd sold me. "How much?"

The price was what I remembered seeing on the website, and I knew I wouldn't find anything else quite like it. "I'll take it," I said and pulled out my credit card.

"Juan!" Miguel called to the other salesman, who was still with the father and daughter. "*Señora* want buy."

I still couldn't follow what Juan said back to Miguel, but finally Miguel smiled. "He say okay, I take care of you. But no credit card. Cash only."

"Really?" I pointed back toward the entrance to the store where a sign on the window indicated all major credit cards were accepted. "But it says . . .?"

"Credit card machine no work. Boss take wife to doctor. Fix tomorrow."

I prefer to pay for large items, such as furniture, with a credit card, but I couldn't argue against a broken credit card machine, and I did have the gift money from the Sporbachs. "Then, I guess it's cash."

Miguel repeated the price, plus the addition of state tax, and I pulled out the envelope the bank teller had given me. Miguel had just handed me the receipt when the father and daughter left the store and Juan joined us.

"What's up?" he asked, looking at the rocking chair by my side.

"I sell," Miguel said proudly.

"You sold her *that* rocking chair?" Juan's attention turned to me. "I'm sorry, *Señora*, that chair isn't for sale."

"But I just bought it." I looked down at the chair by my side. I couldn't see anything wrong with it.

"You—" He seemed to be trying to find the right words. "It hasn't been completely unpacked."

The only unpacking I could see was the wrapping around one of the rockers, which I assumed protected the music box. "That's okay. I can unpack it myself."

"It hasn't been logged in."

"Then write down whatever information you need and log it in." The more he argued, the more determined I was to have the rocking chair.

He shook his head. "You don't understand. We cannot sell this chair to you."

"Why? Why not?" I'd come to this store because two people who had worked here had recently died. Now a salesman didn't want me to buy one of the items sold in the store. There had to be a reason, but to discover that reason, I needed the rocking chair.

"Look," he said, glaring at me, "you can pick it up tomorrow. We'll—"

I didn't let him finish. Firmly, I placed a hand on the back of the chair. "I'm not driving back into Kalamazoo from Zenith to pick up what I have right here, and my husband is a homicide detective for the Kalamazoo Sheriff's Department, so I never know what his hours will be. He told me to come here and buy the rocking chair you advertised. I have done so. Now, is there a problem?"

Juan and Miguel looked at each other, but neither said a word. Finally, Juan smiled. "Okay, *Señora*, you win, the chair is yours."

His smug look made me wonder if I really had won. I turned to Miguel. "Would you mind carrying the chair out to my car for me?"

Miguel looked at Juan who nodded, and I released my hold on the chair. "Nice doing business with you, Juan."

"And with you, Mrs. . . .?" He waited for my name.

"Kingsley," I said, deciding it would be better to use Wade's name in this case. "Mrs. Wade Kingsley."

I followed Miguel as he carried the rocking chair out of the store to the loaner car. Once both the chair and I were in the car, I locked the doors and started the car. The clock on the dash showed it was getting late. Later than I usually returned home after having dinner with Grandma. I dug through my purse for my cell phone, and when I found it, punched in Wade's number.

"I'm heading home," I said when he answered.

I heard another man's voice in the background, one I recognized. "Is Chambers there with you?" I asked, just as I noticed movement inside the furniture store.

The "Open" sign went off.

Wade said, yes, that he and Deputy Chambers were having a drink. More than one drink, I had a feeling, hearing Chambers' laugh.

Juan stood inside the store, staring out at where I was still parked. My stomach tightened. Sitting here, in the dark, was stupid. "I need to get going," I said and started the car. "But I just had an interesting experience. I'll tell you more when I get home."

"P.J., where are you?" I heard Wade say just before I clicked off the phone.

Chapter Nineteen

Two symptoms of schizophrenia are seeing something that isn't there and the constant feeling of being watched. As I drove home, I experienced both of those symptoms. It was after I'd turned off I-94 onto the sparsely traveled backroads that would take me through Zenith and on to my house that I noticed the headlights. It was too dark for me to tell if it was a car, SUV, or truck behind me, but for miles and miles it stayed the same distance back and made the same turns I made.

As I entered the Village of Zenith, I slowed down and looked into my rearview mirror. I thought the car following me would catch up and I could get a better view, but it was gone. When or where it turned off, I didn't know, but no car followed me, no SUV, or truck. The street was empty.

I felt foolish then for thinking someone was following me. If I still lived in the city, as I had for years before Grandpa Benson died and I inherited the farm, I wouldn't have noticed a car behind me at this hour. In the city, unless it was very late at night, there were always cars and trucks on the streets, coming and going. But it was different in rural areas.

I stopped at Zenith's one and only blinking red light. I'm not sure why. There wasn't a car in sight, not behind me, in front of me, or on either side street. Smart people were at home, which was where I should be.

Once through Zenith, I picked up speed, but still kept the loaner Chevy below fifty-five. Although the drizzle we'd had most of the day had ended, every so often I could see shiny areas on the road ahead where a thin layer of ice covered the pavement. Black ice. I also kept watch long the sides of the road for deer. One thing I didn't need was an animal dashing out in front of me, causing me to slam on my brakes and go into a spin—deer or pigs.

I was on the last two miles of my drive home, not far from where two nights before I had seen the pigs and ended up in a ditch, when I once again noticed headlights. A car was coming up behind me, its headlights on high. The reflection in my rearview and sideview mirrors nearly blinded me, and my first thought was the car was going too fast for road conditions. As the vehicle rapidly closed in on me, I lightly tapped my brakes, hoping the driver would notice and slow down.

If he did, I couldn't tell, and merely tapping my brakes made my car slide a bit to the right. I turned the wheel to correct the slide and wished I were driving my own car, not a loaner. The feel of the car wasn't quite the same. I overcorrected and felt the back end of the Chevy fishtail a little.

Just a little, but it was enough to make my stomach lurch. I loosened my hold on the wheel and hoped the car would correct itself.

"Slow down," I said, as much an order for me as for the car behind me.

The lights in my mirrors became brighter, almost blinding. Close. Too close.

"Get off my—" I yelled, then gasped. The car was beside me, barely inches away. Crowding me.

I gripped my steering wheel afraid the slightest movement of my hands would move my car closer to the one beside me. I ventured a quick glance to my left, could tell the vehicle beside me was a light-colored SUV, but couldn't see much more. I didn't dare really look for any length of time. As it was, the loaner pulled to the left.

I felt my car bump against the other car, and I quickly corrected my steering.

Overcorrected.

Once again my car started sliding to the right. I turned the steering wheel to the left, then back to the right. I needed to get control. Except, I couldn't. The Chevy continued to slide, its backend swinging to the left.

I heard the crunch of gravel and knew my front tires were on the shoulder. I jerked the wheel to the left, then to the right. I had no idea where the other vehicle was or what it was doing, all I cared about was regaining control of the car I was in.

It didn't happen.

The front of the Chevy skated off the icy pavement, across the gravel shoulder, and down into the drainage ditch that ran along side of the road. I heard a loud screech, like fingernails on a chalk board and felt a jarring bump. Pitched forward, I braced my arms so my belly and chest wouldn't hit the steering wheel, all the while pressing down on the brake with my right foot. The seatbelt's shoulder strap tightened, holding me in place, and the Chevy came to a jarring stop, its engine still running.

The air bag hadn't popped out, which surprised me, but the seatbelt had kept me from serious injury. I pushed myself back, sucked in a breath, and looked out the side window to see where the other vehicle was.

It had stopped on the road ahead, its brake lights illuminating its backside. I still couldn't tell if the SUV was silver or white, and it was too far away for me to make out the license plate. I kept staring at it, afraid it would start to back up. What could I do to protect myself? I popped open the console and looked for anything I could use as a weapon. The console was empty.

Heart racing, I dug into my purse for my cell phone. I had it in my hand when the brighter red of the brake lights went off and the SUV moved forward, not back. "What!" I yelled, relief mingling with anger.

The vehicle continued on, picking up speed. "Damn you!" I shouted at the retreating vehicle. "You could have killed me."

I watched those two red taillights grow smaller and smaller until I couldn't see them at all. Only then did I refocus on the Chevy I was in. I tried to back the car up, but nothing happened. The engine revved, the wheels spun, but the car did not move.

Finally, I stopped trying and turned off the engine. With a sigh, I clicked on my cell phone.

This time I had plenty of battery left.

At first Wade thought I was kidding when I told him I was stuck in a ditch only a short distance from the house, but as soon as I told him what had happened, his reaction turned to concern. "Are you all right?"

Once I'd assured him that I was okay—no physical damage to my body and, as far as I could tell, and the baby seemed to be fine—he lectured me. "You shouldn't be out, driving on icy roads in the dark. What if you had been injured, had gone into labor?"

"I didn't, but we need to get this car out of the ditch and off the road," I said. "Soon, before another car comes along and hits the backend."

Minutes later I saw Wade's Jeep coming down the road toward me. He pulled up, parking at an angle so the Jeep's flashing red and blue lights would warn on-coming vehicles. I watched Wade get out, look my way, and shake his head. I was about to roll down my window and tell him not to make any smart remarks when someone opened the Jeep's passenger's side door and stepped out.

I groaned as I recognized the tall, skinny man in civilian clothes. Deputy Chambers, my least favorite officer in the Sheriff's department. He immediately turned on his flashlight and aimed it into my car, blinding me.

I lowered my window. "Get that out of my eyes."

He harrumphed and aimed his flashlight toward my backseat. "What's that?"

"A rocking chair," I said, "for a child."

Again, he grunted, then stepped back, allowing Wade to come close. "You okay?"

"I'm fine." I turned my head to watch Chambers work his way around the Chevy, his flashlight illuminating different sections of the car. "Why did you bring him?"

"We were still talking when you called. It seemed like a good idea." Wade reached through the open car window and touched my shoulder. "You've got to stop scaring me like this."

I undid my seatbelt and opened the car door. He stepped back so I could get out. Carefully I stood and stretched. Everything seemed in working order.

"What exactly happened?" Wade asked.

I repeated what I'd said when I called. "He was right beside me. I felt him hit my left front fender, and that made me lose control."

Wade looked at the front fender. So did I.

"Can't tell," Chambers said, joining us. "Car's got dents and scratches everywhere." He looked at me and smiled. "Sure you didn't run into more pigs?"

I glared at Wade. "You told him?"

He shrugged.

Chambers chuckled. "He told everyone at the station. Marge really got a kick out of that. Oh, and I hear you still think people are breaking into your house."

Wade looked up at the cloud-covered sky, and I knew he wished Chambers would keep his mouth shut. Just the mention of Marge's name upset me. I certainly didn't need her knowing I ran my car off the road. As for Chambers, he hadn't believed my house was broken into a year ago, thought I was crazy like my mother. No reason he would believe me now, especially since I wasn't sure Wade believed me.

"In the morning, I'll write up an accident report," Chambers told Wade. "For your insurance company. Meanwhile, I think I know why she's stuck." He took Wade around to the other side of the car. "It's that rock."

The two of them tried to move the rock, but it was wedged under the frame. Finally, Wade said, "Well, we can't leave the car here. Let's hope pulling it out doesn't damage the undercarriage."

A half hour later we were in the house. The loaner didn't steer quite right after it was pulled out of the ditch and the muffler clanked against the pavement all the way home, but the car was now parked in the yard. Chambers had left, Jason and Wade were eating some of the cookies Grandma Carter had sent home with me, and I was exhausted. Who ran me off the road was a question that would have to wait until morning.

Chapter Twenty

Thursday morning I woke with a stiff neck and aching shoulders. Even my hands hurt, I supposed from gripping the steering wheel so tightly the night before. Daylight filtered through the bedroom curtains, and from where I lay, I could see Wade standing in front of the full-length mirror, the tails of his partially buttoned dress shirt hanging over the waist of his trousers. For a moment I wondered why he was putting on his business suit, then remembered, just before we went to bed, he'd said he'd have to be in court again today.

I couldn't suppress a groan when I pushed myself out of bed and onto my feet. It wasn't just my neck and shoulders that hurt; my entire body ached.

"You okay?" Wade asked, leaving the mirror to come over to me.

"I feel like I was run over by a Mack truck." I rubbed my neck to loosen the muscles.

"You've got to stop putting cars in the ditch." He wrapped his arms around my shoulders and hugged me as close as my bulging belly allowed. "I don't want to lose you, P.J."

"And I don't want to lose you, either." I snuggled my nose against the bare skin of his exposed chest and inhaled the scent of Dove soap. Damp chest hairs tickled my cheek. "How long have you been up?" I hadn't heard him get out of bed or take a shower.

"About an hour."

I turned my head so I could see the clock on the nightstand. It was nearly eight o'clock. "You should have woken me. What about Jason?"

"Up, dressed, and fed. I figured you needed the sleep." He released his hold and stepped back to resume buttoning his shirt. "I told him I'd drop him off at school. What you need to do today is relax. Watch some TV. Read a book. You're going to be plenty busy when our daughter arrives."

I loved how Wade said, "our daughter." I'd been so afraid when I first discovered I was pregnant that he'd turn his back on both me and the baby. Instead, once he recovered from the shock, he'd welcomed the idea. And even though I told him he didn't have to marry me, he insisted he would have proposed even if I hadn't been pregnant.

I hoped that was true.

Since moving into the farmhouse, he'd helped me rearrange our bedroom to make room for a crib and bassinet and had hired an architect to draw up plans for an addition off this end of the house. With luck, good weather, and some of the money I'd inherited from my grandparents, by the end of summer, we should have a walk-in closet off this bedroom, a master bath, and a second downstairs bedroom, which for a few years would be a nursery.

That reminded me of my purchase at Patterson's Furniture. "Honey, I'm going to call and have that loaner car towed back to the repair shop today, so, before you leave for work, could you bring the rocking chair on the backseat of the car into the house."

His shirt buttoned, Wade tucked it in and zipped up his trousers. "Rocking chair?"

"The one on the backseat. You saw it last night, didn't you? It's a child's rocker, so it's not very big, but—" I pointed at my belly. "Miguel put it in the car for me. I think I might have trouble getting it out."

"Miguel?"

"He works at Patterson's Furniture. He's the one who talked me into buying the rocking chair. Well, he didn't actually talk me into it, but he showed me the chair and I—" I stopped. No need to explain everything. "It's on the backseat of the Chevy."

"Why were you at Patterson's Furniture?"

The tone of Wade's question made me realize I probably shouldn't have brought up my visit to Patterson's Furniture. How could I explain that I wanted to see if it was a real furniture store and see where both Jerry and Brenda had worked.

"P.J.?" Wade's eyebrows rose, his tone censoring. "I thought we agreed that you wouldn't get involved in this."

"I just wanted to see the store," I said, hoping I looked and sounded innocent. "See if they might have anything, that is any furniture, that would be appropriate for a little girl, and I found something. The rocking chair."

"And on your way home you get run off the road."

"I—" I wasn't sure what to say. "Okay, maybe my being at the store had something to do with that. Or, maybe it doesn't. There's been a light-colored SUV hanging around here recently. I saw it yesterday, and Howard said he's seen it drive by several times."

"And you didn't think to mention that?"

"I didn't think of it last night. And maybe it's all just a coincidence, my seeing that SUV and my being at that store yesterday. Maybe . . ."

Wade shook his head. "Do not go there again."

His order jarred me. I haven't had to answer to anyone about personal decisions for a long time. Even as a child and teenager, more often than not, I played the role of decision maker for my mother. As for my father, whenever he was around, he treated me like a princess. I don't remember him ever ordering me not to do something.

I love Wade, but I wasn't about to kowtow to him. "What did you say?"

He opened his mouth, I'm sure to repeat his command, then closed it. Either the way I was glaring at him or common sense made him decide to change his tactic. "Please," he said. "Please don't go back to that store. We don't know what's going on there, but we're sure Mr. Herman's death is connected to his employment there. And, you said yourself that your friend had been threatened and thought she'd been followed when she left the store. Less than an hour later, she was hit by a car."

"So, you do believe she was murdered?"

"I'm not dismissing the possibility."

Hearing his concern, I decided overreacting to his order wasn't fair. He was worried about my safety, mine and the baby's. I should be pleased, and I was. "Don't worry. I won't go back. I don't know about the store's owner, he wasn't there, but the two guys I dealt with acted really weird. Oh, and I'm sure I smelled marijuana."

Wade nodded. "I noticed it, too."

"That's right. You said you were there."

"Tuesday and again yesterday. Investigating. That's part of my job description."

I got his meaning. I also understood why Juan let me take the rocking chair after I mentioned Wade's name." Do you think they're dealing drugs, and Brenda was going to report it, and that's why she was killed? Maybe she—"

"Enough." Wade turned me toward the bathroom. "Go take your shower, Mrs. Nosy Detective."

I decided that was one order I would follow

Chapter Twenty-One

After Wade and Jason left, I called Schipper's Repair Shop. Nate hadn't heard about my accident the night before, and, when I said the muffler was about to fall off and the car didn't steer right, he thought I was talking about my Chevy, not the loaner. He assured me my muffler was fine and he didn't notice anything wrong with the steering. When he finally understood what I was saying, he didn't sound pleased, not even after I told him I'd filed a report with the sheriff's department and would contact my insurance company.

I was out in front of my house, inside the fenced area, tossing a ball to Baraka when Nate drove into the yard with his tow truck. Baraka gave a woof and ran up to the gate, tail wagging. Once out of his truck, Nate stood back, obviously eyeing Baraka's ridge and size.

"He's friendly," I said and quickly explained that the ridge on my dog's back didn't indicate viciousness.

Baraka jumped up against the gate, and Nate came closer to scratch Baraka behind his ears. "He might be friendly, but I don't think I'd chance coming into your yard without you here. Those are big teeth."

He then turned back to the Chevy he'd loaned me the day before. After walking around the car and looking under it, at the muffler that now touched the ground, he came back. "I don't see any damage other than the muffler. Are you sure another car hit you?"

"It was so close, I'm not sure if it hit me or if I hit it."

"Either way, I would expect more damage to the fender."

"It was just a tap. The road was slippery." I wasn't sure why I had to explain. "I'd think you'd be glad there wasn't more damage."

"Oh, there's enough damage," he said and started for his tow truck. "I won't know exactly how much until I get this back to the shop. Meanwhile, I'm afraid I don't have any more cars for you to run off the road."

"I didn't run it off the road, I—" I stopped myself. Why repeat what I'd already told him? "That's all right," I said and sighed. "I've been given orders to stay home and relax."

"Probably safer if you do. Safer for all of us." He grinned. "As for your car, I should have it ready early next week. I lucked out and found replacement airbags in Detroit." He waved a hand at the Chevy in my yard. "I gotta charge you for this, you know."

I understood.

After Nate hauled the loaner car out of the yard, I tried to relax as Wade had instructed, but I couldn't. The events of the day before kept playing through my mind. Were Mom and Ben really married? Would Arthur Hicks be able to keep them out of jail? Why didn't Juan want to sell me the rocking chair? And who was driving the SUV that ran me off the road? Who and why?

Finally, I gave up. I had no answers, and since the temperature had reached the mid-fifties, and the clouds were breaking up, letting the sun through, I decided a walk in the woods might relax me. "Come on, Baraka," I said, heading for the kitchen door where my hip-length, padded winter jacket hung on a hook above my snow boots. "Wanna take a walk?"

My dog reached the door the same time I did, tail wagging and body alert. As I slipped on my boots, then my jacket, all I could think was how nice it would be after the baby was born, when I could again see my feet and easily bend over.

I checked Baraka's injured paw. The cut had already sealed and for more than a day he hadn't been limping. As far as I could tell there was no reason to bandage the paw.

He didn't move when I opened the door, didn't dash out of the house, simply stood looking out. I didn't say anything or move. I'd trained him to wait for my command, but having found him outside Sunday, I wanted to see what he would do. Finally, he looked up at me, his velvety brown eyes questioning.

"Okay," I said, and he trotted out of the house and down the steps.

What his behavior told me was even if I had left the door ajar Sunday, for Baraka to paw it open and go outside, there would have had to be something out there that he would want to get at. But what?

I had no answer.

Once outside, I thought about locking the door, then decided not to bother. I wasn't going to take a long walk. Not the way I felt.

Baraka danced back and forth at the bottom of the steps, his focus on me. I made a sweeping motion with my hand toward the path that would take us by the old chicken coop and into the woods. He dashed in that direction.

His paw definitely wasn't bothering him.

I followed him past the chicken coop. Once started construction on the addition to the house, the coop would be torn down. None too soon, in my opinion, considering the building still smelled of decay and mold even after the hours I'd spent cleaning out the laying boxes along with tossing the old magazines, newspapers and bottles my grandfather had piled on the floor, year after year.

I will be forever grateful to Harlan Benson for my inheritance of the house and forty acres, but not for the mess he left me. Although I was told my grandparents did raise chickens for several years, once those hens and roosters were gone, Grandpa Benson turned the chicken coop into a dumping area and the woods behind the house into a junk yard. Cleaning up the area seemed an unending task. Before the snow fell, Wade and I filled a twenty-yard Dumpster; yet, discarded car parts, tires, and chicken wire still created a hazard zone between the coop and the woods. Next month we would order a larger size Dumpster, and maybe hire someone to help with the cleanup.

As I walked along the path that went through the woods, I remembered back to when I was nine, just a year before my father disappeared from my life. I'd asked him then why there was so much junk around Grandpa's place. " 'Cause he's too lazy to haul it to the dump," Dad had said, then laughed and motioned toward a rusted bedspring half-covering a broken ceramic toilet. "And someday, Honey, all this junk will be yours."

He was right.

Junk, trees, tillable acres, a two-story house and outbuildings, I inherited them all. It was the woods I loved the most. I could feel my body relax as Baraka and I walked by pines and hemlock, their green needles a contrast to the barren branches of the maples and oaks. A rabbit dashed across the path and Baraka took off after it. I stopped where I was and watched my dog zigzag through the trees, his golden red coat and sleek body reminding me of a female lion on the chase. And then the rabbit went to ground and the race ended. I started walking again as Baraka pawed at the hole that had swallowed the rabbit. Finally, I called his name, and he came bounding to my side, a smile—or what looked like a smile—on his face.

I walked to the far end of my woods and thought about the changes that had occurred in the last twelve months. Julia and John Westman no longer owned the farm northwest of mine and I hadn't seen Nora Wright, whose farm was almost directly north of mine, since last summer. So far no one had shot at me, which I greatly appreciated, and no one had threatened me or my grandmother with a shovel.

Some changes had been good.

Feeling more relaxed and a little tired from the walk, I turned and headed back to the house. Even Baraka had expended his initial burst of energy and only occasionally trotted off to the side to investigate a pile of snow that hadn't yet melted. We were halfway back to the house when the crows started cawing. That's when I remembered I'd forgotten to buy the ceramic crow I saw at Patterson's Furniture store. It would have been a nice gift for Howard.

I shrugged off the thought. I certainly wasn't going back there.

The trees blocked my view of the sky, but the incessant cawing seemed to be coming from an area near my house. Warning that someone had arrived?

I picked up my pace; Baraka also seemed more alert. We were beside the chicken coop when he started to growl. A low, throaty, threatening growl. That's when I saw someone coming out of my house through my kitchen door. Short and stocky, from the side he looked like the salesman from the furniture store, but I wasn't completely sure.

"Hey!" I yelled.

He looked my way, and I knew exactly who it was. "Miguel!"

Baraka bolted forward, barking as he headed for the door. Miguel yelled something in Spanish and jumped off the side of the stairs. Without looking back, he ran to the truck parked in the driveway.

"Miguel, wait!" I yelled, also running in that direction. A clumsy imitation of running. I didn't get far.

Melted snow and ice had turned a low spot on the path into slime, and my right leg slid out from under me. I automatically twisted to the side, falling on my hip rather than on my back and using the side of my arm as a buffer. Still the thud radiated through my body. All I could think about was my baby. My poor baby, who was getting banged and thumped and possibly injured.

For a moment I didn't move. Past the edge of my house I heard Miguel swear, then Baraka yelped. The truck door banged shut, followed by the revving of an engine. There was the crunch of gravel under tires, then no noise, and finally a squeal as those tires took hold on the paved road in front of my house. By the time I pushed myself up to my feet, I knew he was far away.

"Baraka!" I yelled, praying my dog was all right, that the yelp I'd heard hadn't been due to anything serious happening to him.

"Baraka, come!"

I sighed in relief when he slowly came into view, his tail between his legs, and his entire body taking on a shameful appearance.

I walked toward him, telling him over and over that he was a good dog, that he'd tried, and that I hoped he was all right. He rubbed his head against my side, the spark he'd had during our walk gone. I ran my hands over his back and sides, felt him flinch when I touched his left front shoulder. With him by my side I walked to where the truck had been parked and looked for anything Miguel might have dropped.

What I found was a small rock with blood on it.

Chapter Twenty-Two

"Yes," I once again repeated to Wade. "The baby and I are fine. She's acting as she always does, poking her fists and feet into my sides" I was being bruised internally as well as externally. "And no, I don't think the blood on the rock came from when Baraka cut his pad. It was fresh when I first saw it."

I'd called Wade as soon as I'd taken off my muddied boots, jeans and jacket and checked to see if anything downstairs had been taken. TV, computer, Xbox—all the valuable items a burglar might steal were untouched. As far as I could tell, my purse hadn't been touched. My wallet, credit cards, even the envelope with what was left of the money the Sporbachs had given me was still there, and the loose change that Wade dropped into a cup on the dresser was at the same level as I remembered.

I leaned my cell phone against that cup of change and kept talking as I slipped on a clean pair of maternity jeans. "I think he swore because Baraka bit him."

The jeans, with their maternity insert, had seemed ridiculously oversized when I first purchased them. Now I could barely get the pants around my middle. "Yes," I continued as I cinched the tie-strings. "I was careful. I put gloves on before I picked it up, and I put it in a paper bag." Exactly as he'd explained wet evidence such as blood should be handled and packaged.

"I'm sure it was one of the men from the furniture store. The short one. They didn't want me to buy the rocking chair. Kept giving me reasons why I couldn't have it. I think Miguel came here to get it back. But he wasn't carrying it when I saw him. You did take it out of the car, didn't you?"

When he assured me he had, I asked the next logical question. "Did you put it upstairs?"

His answer surprised me. "The woodshed?"

Clothes changed, I slipped on my shoes. "Okay, I'm going to go look."

I didn't bother with a jacket, simply went down the back steps and over to the shed where wood was stored to fuel our wood-burning fireplace during the winter. Most of the wood was now gone, and it only took me a moment to spot the rocking chair on a shelf along the back wall.

"It's there," I told Wade and shivered, the cold air making me wish I had grabbed a jacket. "Why did you put it in here? And up on a shelf?"

Wade's explanation that since our daughter wouldn't be using the rocking chair for a while and it would be safer up off the dirt floor made sense, so I decided I would leave it where it was. "If I'm right and he was after the rocking chair, I don't think he thought about looking in there," I said and headed back into the house. "And, if he wasn't after it, I have no idea what he was looking for. Nothing inside the house seems to be missing."

I hesitated when Wade told me to report the break-in. "And tell them nothing was taken?" Or, that I'd foolishly once again left the back door unlocked. "What do you want to bet Deputy Chambers will be the one to come take the report? You know he thinks I'm crazy like Mom."

Wade assured me home invasion was a crime in itself.

I continued talking to him as I walked back through the living room area to my office. I knew I had a pen and paper there. I wanted to write down what happened so I wouldn't forget anything. "Now

I'm glad I have the rock with Miguel's blood on it. At least you guys can't tell me I imagined seeing a man come out of the house. Once his DNA is—"

I don't know why I looked at my computer, or why I noticed the thumb drive.

Or, rather, didn't notice it.

"Wade, he did take something. The new thumb drive is gone."

* * *

Sure enough, it was Deputy Chambers who arrived at the door and took my report of a break-in. I tried to ignore his not too subtle hints that I might have imagined the whole thing, just as I must have imagined some car running me off the road the night before. He finally agreed to take the blood-stained rock as evidence and said he'd have it tested. I made a note to myself to have Wade make sure that happened.

After Deputy Chambers left, I stretched out on the couch. I was exhausted and sore. Because of the baby, I didn't want to take anything stronger than Tylenol, but my neck and shoulders ached from my two car accidents, and my hip now hurt from slipping and falling in my backyard.

Baraka came over and rested his chin on my chest, the look in his eyes sympathetic. I stroked the top of his head and his ears, the hair silky soft. I felt the baby's fist punch against my abdominal wall, and Baraka jerked his head back. I laughed at his expression. Head cocked, he looked at my stomach suspiciously. "She's trying to pet you," I told him.

He snorted and lay down next to the couch.

Knowing he was there, ready to protect me, was reassuring. I don't know how long I slept. It was my cell phone ringing and Baraka jumping to his feet that woke me. For a moment I couldn't remember where I'd left my cell phone, and it had stopped ringing by the time I made it to the dining room table. Still feeling groggy, I started to check my recent calls list, but stopped when the land line started ringing. I knew that phone was in my office, and I reached it before it stopped ringing.

It was the school.

"He's been in court," I explained when the principal said she'd tried calling Wade, but he wasn't answering. "He probably has his phone turned off. Why, what's wrong?"

I smiled when she explained what had happened. "He got in a fight with another boy? You think the boy's finger is broken?" That wasn't good. "But Jason's okay?" That was good. "Yes, I understand," I told her. "Either Wade or I will be there right away."

Not as easily done as said I discovered when I also couldn't get hold of Wade and realized I didn't have a car.

Howard came to my rescue. "No problem," he said. "I'll pick you up in fifteen."

A ride in Howard's old blue Ford was always an experience. The exterior was scratched and battered; the interior was his personal Dumpster. "You cleaned your car up for me," I said when I opened the passenger door. The front looked almost pristine. The back seat, however, was still littered with an array of tools, old newspapers, a heavy tan jacket, empty Styrofoam coffee cups, and a box of shotgun shells.

"Thought I should clean up for a pregnant lady. I even cleaned this." He reached down for something stuffed under his seat. To my surprise, he pulled out a revolver with a four-inch barrel.

A year ago seeing the gun would have petrified me. Now, knowing Howard, I simply said, "Do you always carry that under your seat?"

"Yup. Never know when it might come in handy. Which is why I'm showing you where it is, in case you ever need it."

I shook my head. "Howard, I can't imagine my needing to use your gun, and what if Jason finds it?" Wade, I knew, had talked to

Jason about gun safety, but seven-year-olds were curious. Wade was very careful about his firearms.

"Your husband and I have talked about that. We both feel it's time for the boy to learn how to handle a gun and care for it. If he's trained in gun safety, he's not apt to play with one and accidentally shoot someone."

I wasn't sure I agreed, but I would leave that up to Wade.

"So, are you ready?" Howard asked.

I was, though I was dreading the upcoming confrontation.

It took less than ten minutes for Howard to drive to the school. I hadn't gone with Wade the day he enrolled Jason at Zenith Elementary. Since then, I'd dropped Jason off and picked him up a few times, but I'd never been to the principal's office. Howard knew the way and knew the secretary. April Toft greeted him warmly when we arrived, then she led us to a small conference room and asked if we wanted coffee. I said no; Howard said yes. The school principal brought Howard's coffee when she entered the room.

Sandy Singer was an attractive woman: blond, blue-eyed, and slender. She wore a blue pantsuit with a blue-and-white checked blouse and two-inch pumps. I guessed her age around early forties. Her handshake, when I introduced myself and explained who I was and why Wade wasn't present, was firm but not overly aggressive.

She already knew Howard.

I was beginning to believe everyone in the village of Zenith knew Howard.

"What happened, Sandy?" he asked. "I know Jason. He's not an aggressive boy. I can't see him starting a fight."

"According to Danny Hart, 'Jason—' I quote '—went bonkers.' " Sandy Singer smiled. "Danny says he was minding his own business and Jason started hitting him, and when he tried to stop Jason, Jason bent his finger back until it broke."

I remembered the lesson Wade had given Jason on how to stop someone from pushing him. "Did anyone see this happen?" I asked.

Mrs. Singer named three boys.

"From what Jason has told us," I said, "Those three and the boy named Danny have been bullying Jason ever since he started school here. Danny seems to be the instigator. So did any other children, besides those four, see what happened?"

"No, it occurred behind the building, in a corner near the kitchen. They said no one else was around when Jason attacked Danny."

How convenient, I thought. "What does Jason say happened?"

She smiled. "That he's tired of being pushed around. He seemed rather proud of what he did."

I didn't know what to say. I could understand Jason feeling proud of fighting back. I'd been teased in school because of my name and because kids knew my mother had called the police claiming aliens had landed in our backyard. I never fought back, but as soon as I was old enough, I legally changed Priscilla Jayne to P.J.

Howard spoke up. "May we talk to Jason?"

"Of course." Sandy Singer stood. "He's in my office. I wanted to talk to you first. I'll bring him in now."

She left the conference room, closing the door behind her, and I looked at Howard. "Wade taught him that move with the finger."

"Sounds like he learned it good."

"Jason was supposed to yell for help if the boys cornered him. So maybe—"

I didn't finish. The door opened and Jason came into the room, followed by Mrs. Singer. He smiled when he saw us, then lowered his head. "I guess I'm in trouble, huh?"

"Tell me what happened," I said, hoping I sounded un-censoring.

Jason shrugged. "Danny kept saying things about you and Dad. Said you were crazy, that everyone knew you were crazy and that you went into that ditch the other night because you were drunk, not because of any pigs in the road." He looked at me. "But I knew you weren't drunk."

"And I know there were pigs in the road," Howard added.

"When they said those things, what did you do?" Mrs. Singer asked.

"Got mad." Jason looked down again. "Tried to hit Danny."

"Tried?" I asked.

"I missed." His expression was shameful.

"And then?" I wanted the full story.

"He started pushing me. Pushed me into that corner." His gaze went to the principal's face. "I knew I had to do something to get away. I didn't mean to break his finger. Really, I didn't."

"I believe you," she said, "but you must understand, I can't condone fighting. Whether you hit him or not, you started the fight."

She looked at me. "Today's Thursday. Jason is suspended from school for the rest of today and all of tomorrow. On Monday I want you or your husband or both of you, along with Jason, to meet in my office with Danny and his parents. This bullying has to stop." She touched Jason's shoulder. "Do you understand?"

He nodded and the meeting was over. Sandy Singer asked to speak to me for a minute in private, so Howard took Jason to get his things and pick up any homework he should do. I told them I'd meet them at the car. Once they were out of sight, Singer again closed the conference door. "I want to give you a head's up. Danny's father, before he left with Danny for the emergency room, said he was going to sue your husband. Knowing the family, he probably will."

"I'll let Wade know."

"If it comes to that, I think there are a couple teachers who will testify on Jason's behalf." She winked. "And maybe a principal."

I thanked her and left.

Chapter Twenty-Three

Friday morning Connie called cancelling the Mothers-to-Be gathering at her house. "Sarah's in labor. Or, at least she thinks she is." Connie chuckled. "I think it's a false labor, but she wants me there. And it is her first baby."

It's a first baby for all of us, I thought but said nothing.

"Must be something in the air," Connie added. "Maria had her husband take her to the hospital Wednesday because she thought she was in labor. Turned out to be indigestion."

"You said, 'Better to be safe than wait too long,' " I reminded Connie.

"Which is why I'm on my way over to Sarah's right now. But I wanted to check on you. Are you all right? No problems from that accident you were in Monday night?"

I laughed. "My problem is I can't seem to keep a car on the road or my feet under me." Without going into details, I told Connie about the SUV crowding me off the road Wednesday night and my fall Thursday when I tried to stop someone who had broken into my house. "Everything seems to be all right with the baby," I said. "She moves around, kicks and punches me, just like usual. No spotting, and I haven't had any cramping." What did hurt were my neck, hip, and shoulders.

"Feel an urge to clean things? Put your nest in order?"

Again, I laughed. "If you could see this house, you wouldn't ask that question. It looks like we were ransacked."

"Which you said happened."

"Yes, but what I'm looking at is here all the time." My normal messiness added to by a grown man and a seven-year-old boy.

"I'm sure it's not that bad," Connie said. "Any idea who broke into your house? Anything missing?"

"Nothing major." I didn't mention the missing thumb drive or that the burglar was an employee of Patterson's Furniture. Until I figured out why Miguel had taken that thumb drive, I didn't want others to know.

"Well, I'm at Sarah's." The background engine noise disappeared from Connie's side of the conversation. "You take care of yourself, and I'll let you know when the group will meet again and where."

I said goodbye and set the portable phone back in its carriage. The mess I'd mentioned was everywhere: Wade's bath towel draped over the back of one of the dining room chairs, shoes—two pairs of mine and one of Jason's—scattered by the front door, Jason's cereal bowl, spoon, and empty juice glass on the table. I'd told him to put them in the kitchen, but once again he'd escaped upstairs without doing so. I thought about having him come back down and doing as told, but the idea of confronting him sounded tiring. Easier to take care of the bowl, spoon, and glass myself, which I did. I added them to the ones in the dishwasher but didn't bother to add soap or start the cycle. The dishes could wait to be washed, just as the bed could wait to be made and the dusting could wait and . . .

I returned to the living room, shooed Baraka off the couch, and lay down. I hadn't slept well the night before. Besides the discomfort of aching muscles and being nine months pregnant, too many thoughts had raced through my head. Why did Miguel break into my house? Why take a thumb drive? I would understand if he'd taken the rocking chair. Juan hadn't wanted me buying that chair. I could see him sending Miguel to get it back.

But how did Miguel know where I lived? Had someone followed me when I left the furniture store?

Some of those questions were ones Wade had asked me last night. After he finished testifying in court, he'd gone to the station and read the report Chambers filed. Wade didn't say, but I'm sure Chambers questioned my sanity. With nothing except a thumb drive missing—and I was pretty sure Chambers thought I'd merely misplaced it—I wouldn't blame Wade if he also questioned my sanity. But he promised they would test the blood on that rock for DNA.

How to handle Jason's fighting had also kept me from a good night's sleep. Wade had lectured his son on the virtue of working out differences without resorting to fighting, but then he congratulated Jason on using the bent finger method to stop the Hart kid. In my opinion, he was sending a mixed message.

This morning, however, Wade did issue Jason's punishment. If my stepson thought his suspension from school meant a holiday, he was wrong. There would be no playing with the Xbox for one week, all of the homework his teachers had sent home with him was to be finished and ready to turn in on Monday, and he was to write an essay on why fighting didn't solve anything.

I must have dozed off on the couch because it took me a while to realize the chimes I kept hearing were coming from my cell phone. Back when I had my old phone, the ringtone always made Baraka howl. Considering that at the moment my dog's head was right below my ear, I was glad I'd changed the ringtone on this new phone and that Baraka didn't howl at chimes. Now I simply had to find where I'd left my phone.

The chimes stopped before I found it, but the screen indicated a missed call from Ken Paget. I rang him back. "What's up?"

"Hey, I heard you were in an accident. You all right?"

"Sore from being bounced around, but otherwise okay. Which accident did you hear about?"

"Which? You've been in more than one?"

I told him about the pigs on Monday and the SUV on Wednesday. It was the pigs he'd heard about, but he wanted to know about the SUV, especially after I mentioned seeing one parked near the house Wednesday morning. "That doesn't sound good," he said. "Not good at all. Do you think that night it was waiting for you to come home?"

"I don't know. It seemed to come out of nowhere."

"And it rammed into you?"

"Actually, I think I bumped into it. The road was slippery, and I wasn't used to the car I was driving. That I ended up in a ditch may have been an accident. That it was a light-colored SUV may have been coincidental."

"Do you really believe that?"

"I don't know. Ken, some days I think I am going crazy. That night I even thought someone was following me from the furniture store."

"Furniture store? What furniture store?"

"Patterson's." The moment I said the name, I knew I was about to get a lecture, and I was right.

"You were at Patterson's Furniture store before being run off the road? *The* Patterson's Furniture store where Jerry worked?"

"Yes."

"My god, P.J., why? Why did you go there?"

Ken was beginning to sound like Wade, and I didn't like it. "I went there because my friend Brenda also worked there, and because the same day your friend Jerry died, she was killed. I wanted to see if I could figure out what was going on there, why the Customs and Border Protection agency, was involved."

"And did you?"

"No, of course not." I hated to admit it had been a foolish idea.

"You need to stay away from there, let the police investigate her death. More than drugs are involved."

The tension in his voice held my attention. "More like what?"

"Diamonds," he said. "They're smuggling diamonds."

"Patterson's? How?" The moment I said it, I knew how. "In the crows, right?"

"Yes." He sounded surprised. "How did you know?"

"I saw one when I was in the store Wednesday. It was on a table near the entrance. I picked it up because I thought I might buy it for Howard. Looking at it, I realized the way it was made it could be used to smuggle drugs."

"Jerry evidently thought the same, but he didn't buy this crow. He has, or rather had, a tendency to walk off with merchandise without paying. I know he was caught once when we were in our teens. He's never mentioned any other times, but I've seen him with things in his possession that I'm sure he didn't actually purchase. His job at Patterson's, from what he told me, was perfect for a man with sticky fingers. He unloaded and unpacked merchandise when it arrived, worked second shift, and was there after the store closed. The perfect opportunity to take one of the crows."

"But it wasn't filled with drugs?"

"Nope. Diamonds." He laughed. "I've had it since Tuesday, and, if I'd known what was inside, I would have been a nervous wreck."

"How many diamonds?"

"A couple dozen. Uncut and some quite large. They were in one of those bubble-wrap bags inside the body cavity."

"How did you discover they were there?"

"Today I broke it, accidentally. Tuesday, I came out to see what sort of a mess the trailer was in and do some cleanup. I was surprised to see the crow was still here. It was back in the bedroom and I guess the crime scene people thought it was part of my stuff. Anyway, when I left that day, I put the crow in the trunk of my car. Like you, I thought I might give it to Howard. He does like to talk about crows, and he brought that bag of Epsom salt over, even if I never did get it.

"I then proceeded to forget about the crow until today. Last night my neighbor here at the trailer park called and said he saw two guys come out of my trailer. They took off when he yelled at them, so he came over and looked inside. He said they were definitely searching for something. Closets, cupboards, and drawers were all opened, contents pulled out. As soon as I finished up work today, I came over. Besides cleaning up the mess, I started gathering Jerry's things to donate to the Goodwill. I was looking for something to put his clothes and shoes in when I remembered I had a bunch of those plastic bags from the grocery store in my trunk. The moment I saw the crow, I had a feeling I knew what those guys were looking for and what the phone calls were about."

"What phone calls?" Ken hadn't mentioned phone calls.

"Twice this week I've gotten a call from someone disguising his or her voice. The person sounded really angry, said the diamonds weren't mine, and if I knew what was good for me, I would return them. The first time I got a call, I thought it was a wrong number, but last night the caller said my name. I think he, or she, has an accent, but I really can't tell."

"What kind of accent?" I asked, though I had a feeling I knew what he would say.

"Spanish, maybe. Mexican. It's not pronounced, but it's there."

"A couple Mexicans work at Patterson's."

"More than a couple, I think," Ken said. "As I told your husband, Jerry was sure the store is run by a Mexican cartel."

"So, the crow was in the trunk of your car. How did you find the diamonds?"

"I dropped it. When I went to get the grocery bags out, I accidentally pulled the crow out, too. It fell on the pavement and broke. And when I picked up the pieces, I saw the bubble-wrap bag. Inside it were the diamonds."

"Wow." I didn't know what else to say.

"Wow is right. I brought everything into the trailer, shattered crow statue and the bag of diamonds. I'll call your husband in a while and turn the diamonds over, but you should see them. One is huge. Can you get away from doing taxes and come over here?"

"Darn it, Ken, I can't. I have no car and Jason is home."

"Jason's home? Is he sick?"

"No, he's suspended. He got into a fight yesterday."

"Jason?" Ken chuckled. "Xbox Jason?"

The two of them had met at my wedding and had bonded over video games. I quickly explained the situation, and Ken said, "Good for him. I was picked on as a kid. Being a nerd isn't easy. 'Course now, half those kids are paying me big bucks to fix their computers." He paused, then went on. "Well, I'd love to drive over and show you these pretty stones, but now that I know why I was getting those calls and what those men were looking for when they broke in here, I think I'd better give your husband a call and see what he—"

Whatever Ken hoped to see was drowned out by Baraka's loud barking as he dashed by me, heading for the kitchen. These were warning barks, not welcoming ones. "Just a minute," I told Ken. Phone in hand, I hurried after my dog.

Baraka was at the window that looked out on the driveway, his body rigid and the hairs from the top of his head to the base of his tail actually standing on end. I could see why. Or, rather, I saw a black truck with rusted fenders that looked like the one I'd seen both at Patterson's Furniture Wednesday and in my driveway yesterday. The driver's side window was rolled up, but I was pretty sure the driver was Miguel. He was looking my way, and for a moment neither of us moved. And then the truck jerked backwards, scattering gravel as its tires spun in reverse.

I watched the truck back onto the road, give a slight shudder, then speed forward. Still barking, Baraka ran for the front door, and I followed, but by the time I could see the road, the truck was too far away for me to read a license plate.

Heart racing, I sagged onto the nearest dining room chair. It took me a moment to remember I was still holding my phone. I brought it back up to my ear. "Ken? Are you still there?"

There was no response.

What I did hear were footsteps thumping down the stairs. "What's going on?" Jason shouted the moment he came into view. "Why's Baraka barking? Is someone here?"

"No, he's left," I said and set my phone on the table. I needed to quiet my dog, and I needed to find a way to explain to Jason why I couldn't stop my legs from shaking.

Chapter Twenty-Four

As soon as my heart stopped racing and my legs stopped shaking, I called Wade and told him about the truck. "I was talking to Ken when it happened," I explained. "All at once Baraka started barking and there it was."

"This truck simply pulled into the yard and then backed out?"

"Not like he'd made a mistake and pulled into the wrong yard." That occasionally happened. "More like he didn't think anyone was home, but then he saw me and got away as quickly as he could."

"With your car gone, could be." For a second, Wade said nothing, then asked, "Why did Ken call you?"

He sounded suspicious. I think Wade worries about my relationship with Ken the same way I worry about his relationship with Marge. Since in my mind there is nothing to worry about, I hurried to explain Ken's call. Wade still sounded suspicious when I finished. "You say he found diamonds in a crow?"

"A ceramic crow, He'd just said he was going to call you and turn them in when that truck pulled into the yard and Baraka started barking."

"Well, he didn't call."

That surprised me.

"And he's at the trailer?"

"He was when I talked to him."

I heard the rustle of papers and guessed Wade was at his desk. His next statement confirmed that. "I'm almost through here. I'll swing by the trailer on my way home, see what's up. I thought we got everything connected to Mr. Herman's death or we wouldn't have released the trailer."

After talking with Wade, I called Ken. I was going to tell him Wade would be stopping by. What I got was Ken's voicemail. "Call me," I said.

The adrenaline rush of the truck incident countered my need for sleep, so I went back to my office to work on our taxes. I'm not sure how much time passed, but I was finishing Wade's 1040 when Jason came back downstairs. "Can I go outside for a while?" he begged. "Kinda like recess?"

"Sure." I hated to admit it, but I'd forgotten he was even upstairs. When I am working, I forget time and everything else. That's going to have to change once Paige Joy arrives.

I was sitting at the table paying bills when Jason came back inside. The way he scooted by, heading for the stairs seemed odd. Usually he's talkative, eager to describe something he saw or found outside. Today he didn't even look my way.

"Everything all right?" I asked before he made it to the stairway.

He stopped, looked at me, then away. "Yeah, sure," he said and dashed up the stairs.

Something was wrong.

For a moment I thought about following him, then I gave up the idea. In the few months Jason has lived here, I've learned that sometimes it's best to give him a little time before asking for an explanation. Plus, going up those stairs in my condition was becoming more and more difficult.

The reason for his behavior would have to wait until he came back downstairs.

* * *

When Wade arrived home, Ken became my concern rather than Jason. "I didn't get away from the station as quickly as I'd hoped,"

Wade said as he changed out of his work clothes into jeans and a sweatshirt. "I stopped by the trailer, but your buddy wasn't there, and it was locked up. If he found diamonds, he needs to turn them in."

"Which he said he was going to do."

"I hope he didn't also find more of those pills his buddy had. Those small blue tablets stamped 'M30' contained fentanyl as well as oxycodone. The combination totally shut down Herman's brain function."

"Ken didn't say anything about pills. Just diamonds." With Wade standing in front of me, I tried calling Ken again, and again my call went into voicemail. Since Wade had brought up the subject of pills, I relayed the message to Ken. "Stay away from blue pills stamped 'M30.'"

That was all I could do

Chapter Twenty-Five

By Saturday morning, whatever had bothered Jason seemed to have passed, and he was back to his normal self—arguing that he'd finished all of his homework Friday and had written an essay on why fighting was bad, so why couldn't he play video games? I could tell Wade was getting irritated with his son's whining, but I hoped he wouldn't give in. In my opinion, Jason spent too much time watching TV and playing video games.

Wade's sister Ginny came to the rescue.

"Skiing?" I heard Wade say over the phone. "Skiing is fun. He's being punished for fighting."

I'm not sure what Ginny said to Wade, but by the time he ended the call, she'd convinced him that having Jason spend the weekend with her up north skiing would be better than having him stay here. One hour later she was at our front door.

Ginny is tall, blond, and has one of those willowy figures that looks great in everything from sweats to cocktail dresses. Whereas her brother tends to be reserved, she is warm and congenial, which—along with her low, seductive voice—I'm sure has helped make her interior design business a huge success. She and I hit it off from the first time we met.

After hugs and assurances that I was doing fine, Ginny sent Jason upstairs to get his clothes, while she and I did a little catching up on what we'd been doing since we'd last talked. Wade latched his son's skis onto Ginny's car, and by ten o'clock, aunt and nephew were in her BMW heading north for Cadillac, Michigan. Ginny promised they'd be back before Jason's bedtime Sunday evening.

Wade and I watched her car disappear from view, then Wade turn me toward him. "Okay, it's Saturday morning. I don't have to go to work, Jason is away for two days, what would you like to do?"

"Hmm." I cuddled against his side. "I don't know. What would you like to do?"

"I know what I'd *like* to do," he said and nibbled my earlobe. "But, considering your present condition, I think we'd better put that idea on hold."

I pulled back from his side and looked down at my huge belly. "I'm sorry. I just don't feel it's a good idea."

"And I agree," he said, once again easing me close. "I can wait. But do you realize how beautiful you look right now? How much I love you?"

I didn't have a chance to find out. My cell phone rang at that moment with the ringtone I'd assigned for calls from Grandma Carter. "Hold that thought," I said and stepped away from Wade. "That's Grandma. I've been waiting to hear what's up with Mom."

"They're getting married," Grandma said the moment I answered. "This afternoon, and they want you there. You, Wade, and Jason."

"Married?" I looked at Wade, and he raised his eyebrows. "I thought they were already married."

"This time it will be legal. That lawyer, Hicks, put it all together. Your mother and Ben will be married by a judge. So, can you come?"

"My mother and Ben are getting married," I told Wade, "and they want us to come."

"You sure she wants me there?"

I knew why he asked. Wade and my mother have never had a real good relationship. She thinks I'm crazy for marrying someone in law enforcement, after all, her interaction with the police has primarily been when they've arrested her; he thinks she's crazy.

I posed the question to Grandma. She assured me Mom had included Wade in the invitation. When I relayed the message, he shrugged and grinned. "Sure, why not?"

I told Grandma that Jason wouldn't be able to make it and why but that we would, and she gave me the time and place. "And afterwards," she said, "we'll all go out to dinner. My treat."

* * *

We spent the morning making sure our bedroom was ready for Paige Joy's arrival—and for Connie's assistance in our daughter's arrival. Although I was eager to shed this object that had inhabited my body for the last nine months, I was also nervous about her birth. Would she be all right? Healthy and normal? Would giving birth be painful or exhilarating? Would everything go as planned?

Wade tried to convince me I was worrying too much, but I could tell he had his own concerns. "Relax," he told me, and to help me achieve that state of mind, after we showered, he gave me a backrub, and we stretched out on the bed until it was time to dress for my mother's wedding.

I talked Wade into wearing a suit, and I wore the nicest maternity outfit I had that still fit. We were supposed to be at the courthouse by four-thirty, but for some reason Wade decided to make a phone call just before we were to leave, and I was afraid we might be late. Finally, he joined me in the Jeep, no explanation given, and we headed for Kalamazoo.

Grandma was standing outside the courthouse when we arrived. A heavy wool coat covered her wool dress, but she still looked cold. I didn't waste any time getting out of the Jeep and hurrying the two of us into the building. Wade followed, once again talking on his cell phone. *Cut the conversation*, I signaled as we neared the security area. He, of the three of us, should know the protocol for getting into a courthouse. Since he always carried a weapon, it would take a while for him to show his badge and ID and satisfy the guards that he was no threat.

"Your mother and Ben are already inside, along with Arthur Hicks, talking to the judge," Grandma said. "I was afraid you wouldn't get here in time."

I glanced at Wade. He was now talking with one of the security officers, chatting away. My husband clearly wasn't eager to participate in my mother's wedding. "Wade," I called to him, then motioned for him to join us.

He lifted a finger, indicating he wanted me to wait, then nodded at something the officer said. Finally, he broke away and joined us. Grandma by then had looked up the courtroom where the ceremony was to take place, and she led the way down the hall.

I'd never been to a wedding ceremony held in a courtroom. It certainly wasn't like stepping into a church. There were only eight of us in an area that was normally filled with a judge, jury, and everyone connected with a case. Even the décor, if you could call it that, was bland. Shades of brown made up the unadorned walls, stark furnishings, and plain flooring. The only touch of color was the American flag.

In contrast, my mother wore a yellow dress and carried a bouquet of red roses, and Ben had a red rosebud in the lapel of his brown suit jacket. They were talking to a man in a gray suit who was standing behind a wooden pedestal. The moment Arthur Hicks saw us enter the room, he took us up and introduced us to the judge. After a few words, the judge had us stand back, and the whole ceremony went by quickly. The judge spoke, then Mom, then Ben, and finally the judge proclaimed them man and wife. After that it was simply a case of the appropriate signatures being placed on the wedding license, including Wade's and mine as witnesses. Arthur thanked the judge and promised to buy him a drink next time they played golf, and Grandma announced she'd made reservations at a restaurant only two blocks away, and that everyone was welcome, including the judge.

He turned down her invitation, but Arthur said he'd be glad to come. Mom, Ben, and Arthur chose to walk to the restaurant, but Grandma climbed into Wade's Jeep with us, and by five-thirty we were all seated at a large round table near the back of the restaurant, everyone but me enjoying a glass of champagne.

In my opinion, club soda, even with a twist of lime, isn't the same as champagne.

"I liked the other ceremony better," Mom said, and looked over at me. "The one last Tuesday. It was so cool. The minister, or whatever he's called, wore that tie-dye robe and wreath of flowers on his head. And his wife played a tambourine and sang. I mean, it was great. We laughed and drank wine."

"And ate brownies," Grandma said and harrumphed.

"And ate brownies," Mom repeated, grinning as she looked at Arthur. "I suppose there won't be any brownies tonight."

"Or swimming," Hicks added, sipping his champagne and obviously enjoying himself. "Just wedded bliss."

Ben laughed and slid an arm around Mom's shoulders. "Wedded bliss every day," he said and kissed her cheek.

Watching my mother and my, now, stepfather I wondered what their marriage would be like. Ben wasn't what I would call handsome—his eyes were a little close-set and his nose rather long and narrow—but he had a nice smile and a deep, hearty laugh. Mom called him a sweetie. In the nine months they'd been together, they had a few fights and separations, but for some time now they'd been getting along quite well. Although Mom hadn't actually moved in with him, Grandma said Mom spent most nights at his place. "As long as he makes sure she takes her pills, that's fine with me," Grandma told me.

As much as it was a surprise, I know Grandma was glad Mom and Ben were now married. Grandma was not getting any younger, and she has always worried about who would watch over Mom if she could no longer do so. I've told her I would, but I'm also glad Ben has taken on the role. I love my mother, but when she's off her medicine, she can be a strain.

I heard Wade's phone ding. He pulled it out of his pocket, gave it a glance, and pushed his chair back and stood. "Excuse me for a minute, I need to take this call.

"He came back?" I heard Wade say as he walked away from our table. I immediately wondered if he was talking about Ken.

Mom laughed, and I turned my attention back to her. In spite of her complaint that this wedding had not been as much fun as the one on Tuesday, she and Ben seemed to be having a good time laughing and telling jokes. Arthur was also laughing. The man was a gem. An expensive gem, from what Grandma told me he charged. She and I would probably be paying his bill, but, in my opinion, he was worth the money. He'd gotten the indecent exposure charges dropped. Mom and Ben wouldn't be spending their honeymoon in jail or paying a big fine.

"I'll be able to hold my granddaughter when she arrives," Mom said, grinning. "I just hope she doesn't cry as much as you did."

Her gaze went beyond me. "Ah, there's another pregnant lady here tonight."

I turned and looked behind me. Maria Gonzales, from the Mothers-to-Be group, was heading toward our table. Or, more accurately, she was heading for the bathrooms just beyond our table. I don't think she even saw me as she passed. Her focus was zeroed in on the sign for Ladies.

The waiter brought a tray of appetizers and another bottle of champagne to the table. Grandma had gone all out for this wedding supper. One more thing I should help her pay for. I would talk to her later.

Wade tried to rejoin us without being noticed, but Mom spoke up before he slid into his chair. "Now, Son, what was so important that you had to leave this wonderful party? What could be more important than listening to your mother-in-law talk about all the trouble your wife gave her as a baby?"

I cringed. Wade doesn't like to be called "Son," not even from his own parents, and from what I've heard, Mom hallucinated a lot right after I was born. There was no telling what she would say now after two glasses of champagne. Or had she had three?

"Someone tried to break into our house again," Wade calmly said and grabbed one of the last barbequed chicken wings from the appetizer tray.

"Again?" I stared at him, wanting more information.

"Howard stopped him," Wade said and winked at me. "Before we left the house, I called and asked him to keep an eye on the place. He got the license number."

"Did the guy get into the house?" I was thinking about Baraka. I didn't want my dog hurt.

"Nope, Howard said the guy had just gotten out of his truck when he saw him coming. Short guy? Kinda stocky?" Wade waited for my response. I nodded, and he went on. "The guy didn't waste any time getting back into his truck. Backing up, he almost ran into Howard's car, and, according to Howard, he practically flew down the road."

"So, he's still out there."

Wade patted my hand. "We now have the license plate number. We'll get him."

"Here's to the cavalry," Mom said, holding up her glass of champagne in salute.

"It's got to be the rocking chair he's after," I said. "That's why he keeps coming back."

"Maybe, but why take those two thumb drives? The first time the house was broken into and you said your thumb drive was missing occurred days before you bought that rocking chair."

I didn't have an answer, and Arthur, Ben, Mom, and Grandma all wanted to know exactly what was going on. Wade and I told what we knew, starting from the Sunday we came back from seeing the butterflies up to what had happened today. The questions and answers were interrupted when the waiter took our order and by the time our food arrived, our conversation had switched from break-ins to why I'd decided to have the baby at home.

Talking about giving birth, and that my time was coming close, I remembered seeing Maria pass our table to go into the bathroom. I hadn't seen her come out. Not that I couldn't have missed her. I turned in my seat and looked around. "Is something wrong?" Wade asked.

"No, at least, I don't think so." Although I couldn't locate Maria anywhere in the restaurant, chances were I'd simply missed her. On the other hand, . . . "Excuse me. I need to go to the bathroom."

Connie's comment Friday that she'd thought Maria might have gone into labor had me worried. What if Maria was in labor? Right here, in the restaurant's bathroom? During one of our Mothers-to-Be sessions, Maria had said she was worried about having her water break in front of others, that it would be embarrassing. Would she stay in a bathroom to avoid being embarrassed?

To my relief, Maria wasn't still there. I wasn't sure what I would have done if she had been in labor. Probably, I would have called Connie.

Maybe it was thinking about going into labor, but I suddenly felt a sharp pain in my groin. For a second it took my breath away, and

I gripped the side of the nearest sink. Slowly, the pain passed, and I could breathe again.

It took me a few minutes to make sure the pain didn't return. Finally, I used the toilet and washed my hands. I was smiling when I returned to the table and I didn't say anything about the pain, but I was glad the wedding dinner didn't last much longer. By the time Grandma took a picture of Mom smashing a piece of wedding cake in Ben's face, I was ready to go home, take off my shoes, and put up my feet.

I wasn't eager when Wade suggested we stop by Ken's store before heading home.

Chapter Twenty-Six

The lights were off in Paget's Computer Repair Shop, a closed sign in the window, which wasn't a surprise considering it was late. I tried calling Ken again. Almost immediately I received a message that his voicemail was full. "I don't even know where he lives," I told Wade.

"He has an apartment nearby. I was there last weekend." Wade drove on for another block, then turned right. He parked the Jeep in front of a two-story brick apartment building. "Wait here. I'll see if he's home."

I noticed Wade checked his gun before walking up to the entrance to the building. He also paused at the doorway and motioned for me to lock the Jeep's doors. Which I did. Though not a bad area of town, I didn't feel totally safe sitting alone in a car at night.

At least ten minutes went by, so I figured Ken was in his apartment talking to Wade. Maybe giving Wade the diamonds he'd found. I almost talked myself into getting out of the Jeep and joining them when I saw Wade exit the building. I could tell from his expression that something wasn't quite right. "What?" I asked as he got into the car.

"He's not there," Wade said. "As I was knocking on his door, a woman in the apartment next door came out. When I told her who I was, she said she was glad to see me, that she was worried about Ken. She saw him yesterday afternoon. She was surprised he wasn't at his shop, but he said something had come up that he had to take care of. She said he acted nervous, didn't chat with her, as he usually did, just opened his door and went into his apartment.

"About an hour later, she heard someone pounding on his door, yelling for him to open up. She was about to go out and tell the guy to be quieter when the pounding stopped, and when she looked out, no one was there. Curious, she waited a while, then went over and knocked on Ken's door. She said she was going to see if he'd like to share some soup she'd made. The way she said it, I gathered he often joins her for dinner."

I nodded. "Yeah, he said they do."

"Anyway, Ken didn't answer when she knocked on his door, which surprised her. She hadn't heard him leave. This morning she decided to check and see if he was all right. Again, he didn't answer when she knocked, so she let herself in for a 'Safety check.' " Wade smiled. "She's a good looking, middle-aged woman, and I have a feeling they might share more than soup. Tonight, once I showed her my badge, she let me in."

He paused and pulled his seatbelt on.

"And?" I urged.

"He wasn't there. Not this morning when she looked and not when I looked. I checked the entire apartment for any signs of a struggle. Nothing. However, I did find his bedroom window open, the screen on the ground outside the apartment, and his cell phone on his dresser, which would explain why he hasn't responded to our calls."

"You think he went out his bedroom window when that guy started knocking on his door?"

"Certainly a possibility. Tenants' cars are parked behind the building. His car wasn't in his assigned spot."

"You need to call the police, tell them he's missing."

Wade chuckled and started the Jeep. "And tell them what? A grown man left his apartment through his bedroom window, not his front door?"

"And hasn't come back?"

"It's not against the law to stay away from your home."

"But he left his phone."

"Maybe he thought he had it with him." Wade checked for traffic, then pulled onto the street.

I didn't know what else to say. Maybe it wasn't against the law to stay away from your home, but why would Ken do so? Unless . . . "They were after the diamonds."

"They who?"

"The man pounding on his door Friday night. The one phoning him. Threatening him."

"If he is being threatened he needs to turn those diamonds over to the sheriff's department. Once we have them, they'll leave him alone."

"What if he didn't have them with him Friday night? What if they were still in the trailer? They were there when he called. Did you see anything when you were at the trailer?"

"I didn't go inside yesterday. He wasn't there. To go inside, I'll need a search warrant."

"Then get one."

Wade grunted, and for a few miles didn't say anything more. I knew he didn't appreciate me telling him how to do his job. He didn't want me involved at all. But how could I ignore what was going on? What I wished, most of all, was that I hadn't cut Ken off when he called Friday, or that I'd been able to go to the trailer and see the diamonds. If I had, I would have made sure he got them to Wade. I seemed to be failing my friends lately.

That thought was interrupted when Wade said, "Tell you what. Monday I'll see if I can get a search warrant for the trailer. And, if by then we haven't heard anything from Ken, I'll call Kalamazoo Public Safety and let them know what's up. Okay?"

"Okay." Wade's ideas pleased me, but there was one problem. "Don't forget, we have that meeting at the school on Monday."

Wade nodded. "I haven't forgotten."

* * *

Sunday morning I was looking forward to spending time alone with Wade. I planned on fixing us a big breakfast, then simply relaxing with the paper, or, if it warmed up a bit, the two of us taking a walk in the woods with Baraka.

Before we even got out of bed, Wade's phone rang. I scooted closer to his side as he answered, hoping the call was from Ken. We still hadn't heard from him.

It wasn't Ken; it was a woman's voice I heard. Lying by Wade's side, I could tell she was crying.

My first thought was Ginny, that something had happened to Jason, but then Wade spoke. "Calm down, Marge. Stop crying. I can't understand what you're saying."

Marge.

I closed my eyes and clenched my teeth. I should have known it would be her, the ever-persistent Marge who called at the worse times, her excuses flimsy. She needed his advice or information.

That's what she said. I knew better. She wanted his body.

Or was I being paranoid?

Wade slid out of bed and headed for the bathroom. He closed the door behind him, shutting me off from hearing anything else he said. I tried to calm my breathing, tried to give the woman the benefit of the doubt. Maybe she had a major problem. Maybe there was a reason she'd called this early on a Sunday morning.

When Wade came out of the bathroom, he'd already ended the call. "Sorry, but I've got to go," he said and grabbed a pair of jeans from the closet. "Marge's car won't start, and she's supposed to be in Ann Arbor at her mother's this afternoon with a special cake she is scheduled to pick up right now."

"She can't call Triple A?"

"She said she did, but they can't get anyone to her for at least an hour and this woman who's made the cake will be going somewhere before then." He pulled a sweatshirt over his head. "I won't be long."

There were a dozen things I wanted to say, none of them nice, so I decided to keep my mouth shut. "Go back to sleep," he said and came over to kiss me on my forehead "Take advantage of this break. I'll let Baraka out before I leave."

I did lie in bed, but I didn't go back to sleep. Various scenarios played through my head, all of them involving Marge Bailey seducing Wade. Finally, I threw back the covers and got up. Enough fuming. I was not going to spend my day imagining another woman with my husband.

After showering and getting dressed, I found an upbeat music station on the radio and turned the volume on full blast. I then had some toast and orange juice for breakfast and tackled what I'd put off for over a month while I did taxes—I cleaned my house. Dishes from the dishwasher were put away, stray items of clothing that were laying around on the floor, draped over furniture, and stuffed in corners were dumped in the closet or laundry basket. I dusted, mopped floors, and vacuumed. I wasn't sure if all of this housekeeping was a sign that I was nesting—as Connie called it— and would soon deliver Paige Joy, or if I simply wanted my house to look good when Ginny—whose house always looked clean and neat—brought Jason back.

My burst of energy also helped expend my anger at Wade for leaving to go help Marge, and by the time I put the vacuum away, I was exhausted and didn't care if Marge Bailey seduced my husband. Being single, I told myself, was a lot easier than being married. Single, I didn't care what my house looked like.

By the time Wade returned, I was sitting on the couch in the living room, watching the noon news. I didn't say a word when he sat beside me. I wasn't about to ask him why starting a car had taken so long.

For several minutes we sat that way, neither of us speaking. I could feel Wade's tension, hear his breathing. He kept opening his mouth, as if to say something, then closed it and took in a deep breath. Finally, he spoke. "She tried to seduce me," he said. "There was nothing wrong with her car. The moment I arrived, she wanted me to come inside. She had coffee ready and homemade cinnamon rolls. Her car had started after all, she said. She'd already picked up the cake she needed, but as long as I was there, why not have breakfast with her?"

Wade paused, and I could tell he was looking at me, waiting for my response. Without looking at him, I said, "And, so you did?"

He sighed. "I did."

I kept staring at the TV, the weatherman promising warmer temperatures. Wade's answer had my internal temperature rising, but I said nothing.

"I needed coffee," he said, as if that explained everything. "And it's been a long time since I've had homemade cinnamon rolls."

I looked at him, my eyebrows raised in disbelief.

"Honest," he said, "I thought she just felt guilty for bringing me over to fix her car when it didn't need fixing. I didn't realize what was up, not at first. Not until she started talking about how upset I'd seemed lately and how she admired me for marrying you to make the baby's birth legitimate."

How dumb can you be? I thought.

He expelled a deep breath. "She started going on about how kindhearted I am, and that I needed a woman who really understood me." He chuckled. "Kindhearted. That's not something I would list as one of my stronger points."

I disagreed but said nothing.

"She said you'd entrapped me, and it wasn't fair, that I shouldn't have to spend the rest of my life tied down to someone I didn't love." Wade shifted his weight on the couch so he was turned toward me. "That's when I realized she was the one who didn't understand. I told her she had it all wrong, that you didn't trap me into marrying you, that I was attracted to you from the moment I saw you. I said it more than once, but she just wouldn't listen."

She didn't want to listen, I thought. Wade might be smart about a lot of things, but he was sure dense when it came to understanding women.

"She told me no one would think poorly of me if I divorced you after the baby was born." He gently placed a hand on my abdomen. "As if this were the only reason I married you."

"So, you told her she was wrong. Then what?" He certainly hadn't come right home.

"She got all emotional. Started crying, hanging onto me, and telling me she was the one I should have married, she knew how to make a man happy."

"Did she kiss you?"

He averted his gaze. "I couldn't get away from her."

"So you stayed?"

"No." He said it firmly, then backtracked. "That is, I stayed for a little while. She was so upset I was worried about her."

I rolled my eyes. "Oh, come on, Wade. Really? You stayed a little while? Like three hours?" I started to get up. I wasn't going to sit and listen to his excuses.

"No. P.J., stop it!" He caught my arm and kept me from standing. "I did not spend three hours with her. Maybe ten minutes at the most. And then I left."

"Oh yeah?" Ten minutes did not equal the time he'd been gone. "You left here before nine o'clock. It's now past noon."

"Because after I left her house I drove to the station. I wanted to see what they'd found out about our burglar."

If he was trying to get off the subject of Marge, he'd succeeded. "What did you learn?"

"That the license plate is registered to a company truck. One owned by—"

I finished for him. "Patterson's Furniture."

"Yes." He looked surprised by my answer. "You already knew?"

"I told you the guy I saw was Miguel, the one from the Patterson's Furniture store. That truck was parked outside of the store the night I stopped there. They didn't want me to buy that rocking chair. I don't know why, but I think Miguel's been trying to get it back." I looked at Wade. "Is it still in the woodshed?"

"I'll go check."

Chapter Twenty-Seven

Wade brought the rocking chair into the kitchen and set it on the linoleum. Thursday, when I had looked for it in the woodshed, I'd merely checked to make sure it hadn't been taken. Now, with it sitting on the kitchen floor in front of me, I could see something had been taken. "Did you remove the packing material covering the music box?" I pointed at the small, hard-plastic box attached to the left rocker. "That was wrapped in brown paper when I saw it in the store."

"No, I didn't take anything off. It must have come off when you pulled it down from the shelf."

"I didn't take it down from the shelf."

"If you didn't . . .?" He frowned.

"Miguel?" I thought back to Thursday. "No, it couldn't have been him. I looked after he left. The rocking chair was still on the shelf."

I gave it a gentle push and a tinny rendition of "Rock-a-bye Baby" played. For a moment Wade watched the chair rock, then he put a hand on the back of the seat and stopped it. "Well, I didn't take it off. When I took the chair out of the loaner car, I decided, since our little girl wouldn't be using it for a while, I would leave it on to keep the mechanism from getting dirty. That's also why I put it up on that shelf. To keep it from getting dirty or scratched when next winter's load of wood was delivered."

"So, who pulled it down? Who took the wrapper off?"

Wade shrugged. "Someone must have come here between Thursday and today. Maybe while you were taking a nap."

I glared at Wade. "I don't take that many naps, and *he* would have let me know if someone was in the shed."

We both looked down at Baraka, who was sniffing the seat of the rocking chair.

"Then I don't know, but someone got whatever was under that wrapper." Wade lifted the chair and held it upside down so he could get a better view of the music box. "My guess is under the brown paper they had a plastic bag filled with heroin or cocaine wrapped around the music box. It wouldn't be the most efficient way of transporting drugs, but—"

I had another thought. "Maybe it wasn't drugs. What about diamonds? If they were being packed inside of a ceramic crow, why not around a rocking chair's music box?"

"I suppose." Wade tapped on the back of the rocking chair. "Seems to be solid. You'd be amazed by the ingenious ways these guys hide drugs. False walls in furniture. Cocaine mixed with molten plastic." He ran a fingertip over the plastic cover of the music box. "Which means we should test this."

"Really?" I didn't like the sound of that. "If that plastic has cocaine mixed with it, wouldn't the person who pulled it down from the shelf have taken the whole rocking chair?"

"Maybe he didn't realize he was supposed to get the music box, too. Maybe that's why Miguel returned two additional times." Wade set the rocking chair back on the linoleum. "I have to take it in, P.J., you know that."

I knew. "It's just such a pretty rocking chair. The bright colors. The flowers."

Wade leaned over and kissed me. "It is pretty, and I promise we'll find something for our little girl that will be just as pretty. Okay?"

I shrugged, and he picked up the rocking chair. "I'm going to take this out to the Jeep. I copied some of the pictures taken inside Ken Paget's trailer to have with me tomorrow. If he found diamonds in a crow statue that we didn't take, I'm wondering what else we might have missed. Maybe you can see something."

"I've never been in Ken's trailer," I said as Wade headed for the door. "How would I know what you missed?"

"You pick up on things," he said. "Little things I sometimes overlook."

His words pleased me, and I realized I was no longer angry with him. Not as angry as I'd been earlier. He might not think he was kindhearted, but he was. I couldn't blame him for going off to rescue Marge. I couldn't even blame her for wanting him for herself. As I watched him through the kitchen window, I smiled. She wanted; I had.

My cell phone chimed that I had a text. I turned away from the window and went into the living room to get my phone. The text was from an unknown number. All the message said was: TELL WADE TO CHECK THE FREEZER.

WHAT? I quickly typed back. WHO IS THIS?

Wade came into the house carrying his briefcase and started for the dining room. "I'll put these printouts on the table and you—"

"Wait. I just got a strange message." I showed him my phone just as another message came through: KEN

"Ken?" Wade frowned.

"I guess." I typed: ARE YOU ALL RIGHT?

A few seconds later, I read: WITH A FRIEND. YOU NEED TO BE CAREFUL. STAY AWAY FROM PATTERSON'S

Ken didn't need to tell me that. I regretted my one visit.

TELL WADE TO CHECK FREEZER.

HE'S HERE, I typed back and handed my phone to Wade. He read the messages, then tapped a button. Next thing I knew, he was talking to Ken.

"What's up, Paget?"

I couldn't hear Ken's response, but I saw Wade frown. "You could have called me from the bar." He shook his head at whatever Ken said in response. "No, there was no one there when I stopped by." Wade nodded and listened before speaking again. "Good idea. By the way, I stopped by your apartment Saturday. Your neighbor told me what happened Friday night. You should have come to the station, reported all of this . . . No. No excuses."

Wade grumbled, held the phone away from his ear, and frowned at it. Then he clicked off and handed the phone back to me. "He hung up."

"So, what did he say?"

"That he did try calling me Friday, but my line was busy, so he decided to go to the bar and get a beer. When he got back to the trailer, two guys were hanging around outside, so he headed back to Kalamazoo. He didn't think they knew where he lived, but then they—or at least one of them—showed up Friday night and he decided to take off."

"What did he say about the diamonds?"

"He hid them in the freezer before he went to the bar." Wade looked outside, then shook his head. "You know what? I'm not going up to his trailer today. We'll have an official warrant tomorrow, and I'll have another deputy with me. If those diamonds haven't been found by now, they should still be there tomorrow."

In the dining room, Wade set his briefcase on the table. "Now that I know we're talking about stolen diamonds, I understand why an agent from CBP is involved. Smuggling diamonds is a violation of the Clean Diamond Trade Act. But why would Patterson's get involved with smuggling diamonds? Drugs, I understand. The

Mexican cartels are always looking for ways to get their product across the border. And from Kalamazoo, transporting cocaine and heroin to Chicago or Detroit is easy. The items we took from the trailer that day were ones we thought might have held drugs. We didn't think of diamonds. Now that we know there were some in a crow statue, take a look and see if you think there's anything else we missed."

Wade pulled several black-and-white scanned pictures out of his briefcase and placed them on the table. Each showed a portion of a trailer's interior. Ken's trailer. "These were taken after the body was removed."

The first picture included the kitchen and living room area. "What, no outline of where the body lay?"

Wade chuckled. "That's only on TV and in the movies."

There was no chalk outline, but there were several small, plastic tents with numbers on them. Those, I knew, had been placed beside anything the crime scene investigators felt might be related to Jerry's death. In the pictures, I saw tents next to pieces of clothing scattered across the floor, evidently where Jerry pulled them off and dropped them. One tent had been placed next to an ash tray with a marijuana joint, and in the kitchen area, there was a yellow tent next to a plastic bag of pills, which I assumed, were the oxycodone plus fentanyl pills. There were tents next to a spoon, cigarette lighter, and syringe on the counter near the sink, and two on a wooden end table—one beside a worn leather wallet and the other next to a small brown paper bag that appeared to be full of something.

I looked up. "What was in the paper bag?"

"The Epsom salt Howard says he left for Ken's plants."

I went back to the pictures. Besides the section of the trailer where Jerry's body was found, a couple pictures included the narrow hallway that allowed passage to a half-bath and a small bedroom. Two others focused on a larger bedroom and bathroom that took up the trailer's back section. The ceramic crow was on a table next to the bed. "That's it," I said showing Wade. "Ken said the diamonds were in bubble-wrap inside the crow's body."

"See anything else we might have missed?"

A colorful vase sat on a dresser. "I saw these in the store, too. Did you take it as evidence?"

Wade shook his head. "I don't remember seeing it on the list. I'll look for it tomorrow."

"It might just be a vase," I said and stepped back from the pictures, "and I don't see anything else that wouldn't normally be in a trailer. It's almost one o'clock. You hungry?"

He smiled and put the pictures back in his briefcase. "I thought you'd never ask."

* * *

I fixed sandwiches and after we ate, I stretched out on the couch with my head on Wade's lap while he watched a basketball game on the television. I was exhausted, physically from my housework and mentally from worrying about what Marge was up to. Wade casually ran his fingers through my hair, massaging my scalp. I was nearly asleep when he said, "You knew, didn't you?"

"Knew what?" I mumbled.

"That Marge wanted to be more than a friend. That her call this morning was just a ploy to get me over there."

I sighed and looked up at his face "I guessed as much. The way she looked at you that first time I met her I could tell she wanted to be more than friends. And then, all those late-night calls."

"I just didn't see it," he said. "I should have realized what was going on, shouldn't have left you this morning. We should have had the day to ourselves." He leaned down and kissed me, then whispered, "I love you."

"And I love you," I said, feeling more content than I had all day.

I dozed for an hour or so while Wade watched the game. The ring of his cell phone woke me. I sat up, and he went over to where he'd left his phone on the table. His "Hello" was followed by a noncommittal "Yes, that's me" and another "Yes."

His responses sounded formal, and I tensed. A quick glance at the wall clock showed it was now nearly four o'clock. If Ginny hoped to have Jason back by his usual bedtime, they should be on the road headed home. Was this a call to inform Wade of an accident?

Wade nodded at something the caller said, his expression neutral, then added, "Yes, I initiated it."

That didn't sound like anything he would say if Ginny and Jason had been in an accident. I released the breath I'd been holding, let my shoulders relax, and realized I needed to use the bathroom. As I walked by Wade, I mouthed, "What's up?"

He raised a finger, indicating he'd tell me later.

He was off the phone, reheating a mug of coffee, when I returned. Once again I asked, "What's up?"

"Van Buren Sheriff's Department found a black truck submerged in one of the lakes north of Paw Paw." Wade paused, took a sip of his coffee, then went on. "Just the truck. They're starting a search for a body."

"They're sure it's the truck that's been here?"

"License plate matches."

"Accident?" The way people connected to Patterson's Furniture had been dying lately, I had a feeling this wasn't.

Wade smiled. "Not likely. That truck was completely submerged. To get that far into the water, the truck had to be going over a hundred miles an hour when it left the road. The accident was that the truck was found. The fisherman who spotted it and called 9-1-1 said it's been months since he's gone out on that lake, that it's rarely fished by anyone. Under normal circumstances, it might have been weeks before the truck was spotted."

"So, do you think Miguel drove it into the lake to hide it, then swam back to shore?" I didn't want him dead.

"Maybe." Wade didn't look convinced. "Or maybe the divers will find his body in that lake." He set his coffee mug on the counter. "I think it's time I contact that CBP agent you talked to."

Chapter Twenty-Eight

Ginny had Jason call us when they were driving by Grand Rapids. She estimated their time of arrival at one hour and pulled into the yard almost on the minute . . . just in time for dinner. Both she and Jason were exhausted and hungry. Thank goodness I'd anticipated them joining us and had enough food. They filled the dinner conversation with stories of runs they'd made, falls they'd taken, and people they'd met. Ginny had started taking Jason skiing when he was four, and he was a pro compared to me. Usually, she took him to Timber Ridge or Bittersweet, near Kalamazoo. They'd been twice this year. As far as I knew, this was the first time she'd taken Jason up north. According to him, the slopes at Caberfae Peaks in Cadillac were a piece of cake.

Ginny lifted her eyebrows when he said that, making me think he wasn't quite the pro he thought he was.

I expected Ginny to take off right after dinner, but she came into the kitchen when Wade took Jason upstairs to get ready for bed. "I want to talk to you two when he's not around," she said.

She sounded concerned and I wanted to ask her what was wrong, but I forced myself to wait until Wade could join us. Plates, glassware, and mugs were loaded into the dishwasher, pots and pans hand-washed, and the counter scrubbed. Between my burst of housekeeping in the morning and what Ginny and I accomplished while we waited for Wade, I swear the kitchen and dining room were the cleanest they have ever been. Even Wade said so when he joined us.

Of course, I was ready to kick him for the comment.

"Ginny wants to talk to us," I said, not sure if what she had to say was good or bad.

"About Jason," she supplied and motioned toward the living room area. "Let's sit in there."

Wade sat beside me on the couch and Ginny pulled up a chair so she was in front of us. Her voice always reminds me of Marilyn Monroe's—low and sexy—but she kept it even lower than usual when she began. "He's afraid. Afraid of some kid in school, and afraid for you, P.J." Her gaze zeroed in on me. "Not 'of you' but 'for you'. What has been going on?"

I started my part of the tale with what I'd overheard when I stepped into the bathroom and heard Brenda talking. Wade told her the events he'd been involved in, and we ended with the phone call he'd received a few hours earlier about the submerged truck. "So far we haven't heard anything about the divers finding a body," Wade said, slipping an arm around my shoulders, "but it's sounding to me like that furniture store is involved with both drug smuggling and diamond smuggling and maybe a lot more. As for P.J.'s involvement, my guess is they think that woman from the bathroom gave P.J. something. Something they want back."

Ginny looked at me. "Jason said something about you being run off the road by pigs. Twice. He said they're trying to kill you."

I chuckled. "The pigs aren't trying to kill me, at least I don't think so. They were simply on the road, and that happened only once," I paused, thinking about Wednesday's incident. "I'm not sure what actually happened the second time I went into the ditch. Maybe I was intentionally run off the road, or maybe it was simply an accident."

"I'm looking into that."

Wade's comment surprised me. He hadn't said anything to me about investigating that accident. I gave him a quizzical look.

"I have to follow through on something, but once I know for sure, that problem will be taken care of."

"Follow through on what? What do you know?"

He shook his head. "Once I know for sure, I'll tell you."

Ginny gave us a curious look, then interrupted. "Okay, what about this kid at school? Jason is really afraid of him. He seemed proud of breaking the boy's finger, but now, he says, the kid's going to come after him. How old is this kid?"

"Seven?" I said and looked at Wade. I wasn't really sure.

"Almost eight," Wade supplied. "I've had a couple run-ins with his father. I talked to Jason when we were upstairs. We'll see how tomorrow goes."

"Well, I don't like having my nephew bullied. Just remember, Michigan has school of choice. If necessary, you could move him over to Galesburg schools. If you took him to school, I could pick him up after school."

Wade nodded. "I don't think it's going to come to that, but thanks."

Ginny left soon afterward. Once she was gone, I asked Wade what he knew about the car that more or less ran me off the road Wednesday night. He hugged me, kissed my cheek, and said, "I told you. I'll take care of that."

End of conversation—at least in his mind. I kept wondering what he knew that I didn't.

* * *

Monday morning Jason acted squirrely, running up and down the stairs several times, supposedly for forgotten items he needed to take to school—his finished homework, a library book, and a pencil he'd borrowed from a schoolmate. He gulped down his breakfast, all the while talking a mile a minute about someone he met while skiing with Ginny. However, his burst of energy ended when it came time for us to leave for the meeting at school; then he moved like a snail. "Come on," Wade urged. "Put on your jacket and go out to the Jeep."

Jason was nervous, and so was I. Wade, on the other hand, acted as if this were simply another trip to the school to drop off his son.

"Any idea what's going to happen during this meeting?" I asked.

"Nope."

"What if the Harts sue us?"

"I don't think it will come to that."

Maybe not, but I did notice Wade was wearing his badge clipped to his belt and his gray sports coat that showed the outline of his holster. To intimidate the Harts? Maybe. When I asked, he said, "Nope. It's for later. After we finish at the school, I'll have you drop me off at Paget's trailer. I'm meeting Detective Gespardo there. Dario has the search warrant. He'll take me to the station after we process the trailer."

"How will you get home?" I wasn't comfortable driving the Jeep, but with my car still in Schipper's Auto Repair shop, I didn't have much choice. I needed a way back home after our meeting with the principal.

"Dario will drive me home. This way, in case I don't get home by three, you'll have a way to get to your doctor's appointment."

"You think you'll be later than three?" I wasn't eager to bring Jason to the doctor's office with me.

"I'll try, but I never know how things are going to go."

I did know Wade couldn't predict how his day would go, so I didn't say anything more, simply got my coat, made sure Baraka had food and water, and went out to the Jeep. Wade locked up and followed.

None of us said anything during the short drive to the school. I sensed Jason's tension, his body stiff as he walked between us into the building, his gaze straight ahead. April Toft, the office secretary, took us to a larger conference room this time, one with a long wooden table and several chairs on either side. Children's artwork decorated the otherwise plain pale green walls. She asked if we wanted coffee. Wade said yes, I said no.

And then we waited.

Fifteen minutes after the time we were supposed to meet with the principal, she and the Harts entered the conference room. We stood, the table between us and the four of them. I've heard the term "a chip on his shoulder" many times, but seeing Mr. Hart—eyes narrowed, mouth scrunched into a straight line, and chin lifted—I actually glanced at his shoulders to see if there was a chip on one or both.

There wasn't, but his rigid posture relayed he was ready for a physical fight. Principal Singer indicated the chairs on their side of the table, but none of them made a move to sit down. I felt sorry for the principal. She looked as if she'd been in a battle. Her cheeks were flushed and her voice strained when she made the introductions: "Mr. and Mrs. Hart, these are Jason's parents, Mr. and Mrs. Kingsley."

"Yeah, I know the infamous Detective Kingsley," Hart growled.

"How are you, Daniel," Wade said, nodding. I noticed neither man moved to shake hands.

"You are going to pay for this," Daniel Hart said. "Look at what your kid did to my son."

Danny Hart had been between his mother and father and not clearly in sight. His dad grabbed him by the collar of his jacket and pulled him forward. I could see Danny's right hand now. One of those elastic-type bandages had been wrapped around the boy's entire hand and wrist.

There was a clumsiness in the way the hand was wrapped that didn't look professional, but I guessed they might have had to loosen the bandage at some point and then rewrap it. Nevertheless, it didn't seem reasonable that a broken finger would require that much bandaging. "What exactly did the doctor say?" I asked.

Daniel Hart looked at me for the first time since he'd entered the room. "He said the finger's broken, that's what he said."

"Which finger?" I persisted.

"This finger." He pointed his middle finger at me in a way that not only identified which of his son's fingers had been broken, but also relayed another message.

"Interesting," I said, refusing to indicate the gesture bothered me. "When I broke my finger, they simply put a splint on it."

"This was a bad break," Danny snarled, sounding a lot like his father. "A really bad break."

"So, what are you going to do about this?" Daniel Hart demanded, again looking at Wade. "We got hospital bills, and this has traumatized my boy. I talked to a lawyer. He thinks I should just sue you, but I'm willing to let this go for fifty grand. Forget the courts and what it would do to your reputation."

I took in a breath, not quite sure what to think. If this went to court, there would be lawyer fees and court fees. But to pay these people fifty thousand dollars for something their son started?

I didn't realize I was shaking my head until Wade spoke up. "As you can see, my wife says no. And, Daniel, I think you might want to reconsider going to court. We have some witnesses who will testify that your son has been harassing my son. Also, look at the size of your son and my son. Do you really think a judge or jury will believe your boy is the victim? And even though that bandage job looks pretty serious, I can get a court order for the actual X-rays and doctor's report. That evidence, along with the school's accident report, might be very interesting."

Daniel Hart's next words were more explicit than a hand gesture. Principal Singer tried to intervene. "Gentlemen, I'm sure this can be discussed in a civilized manner. Mr. Hart, as I told you earlier, accidents happen. The boys should not have been fighting, and—"

She didn't have a chance to finish. Hart swore again, pushed her aside, and, with a hand against his wife's back, shoved her toward the doorway. Danny followed his parents out of the room, but at the doorway turned, looked at Jason, and with his good hand gave the finger.

Mouth open, Sandy Singer watched the three leave, and then she sank into the nearest chair. "I tried to talk some sense into him," she said. "He came into my office with all sorts of demands. I . . . He . . ." She shook her head and sighed.

"He does have some anger management issues," Wade said and sat back down. Both Jason and I did, too. "He's been picked up for a couple bar fights and for threatening a store clerk. I think one judge ordered him to attend anger management classes. Either he didn't or they didn't do much good."

"His son," Principal Singer said, "seems to be following his father's example." She looked at Jason. "I wish you'd come and told me he was bothering you. Told me or your teacher."

Jason hung his head but didn't say anything.

She looked at me. "As I said last week, a couple teachers have observed a problem between the two, but nothing overt. Sometimes, with boys, it's difficult to tell if they're playing or if it's bullying, but the teachers should have said something to me. It's something we're going to work on." She nodded, as if agreeing with herself, then looked at Wade. "Do you think he'll sue you?"

"Maybe. His type seems to go that route. I certainly wasn't going to pay him fifty thousand dollars."

"He threatened to sue the school, too. I'll talk to the district lawyer."

"Have those teachers who told you they noticed some kind of interaction between the two boys write down their observations.

And talk to a—" He looked at Jason. "Who did you say saw Danny push you around and trip you?"

His head still lowered, Jason mumbled two names, both girls. I reached over and rubbed his shoulders. He shrugged my hand away.

"I'll talk to them," Principal Singer said and stood. "And I'll keep you informed as to what I learn."

I sensed she considered the meeting over. I had one more question. "What do we do about Jason and school?"

She looked at him. He still had his head lowered. "Jason, what do you think we should do?"

For a moment I didn't think he would answer, but finally he looked up at her. "I didn't do nuttun' wrong."

"You started a fight."

"He started it. He told me I was too chicken to fight."

She shook her head. "So, you let him goad you into hitting him."

"I tried, but his arms are longer, and he kept pushing me back into that corner."

"You broke his finger."

" 'Cause he was pushing me."

"So anytime someone pushes you, you're going to break their finger?"

"No." He looked down again. "I didn't really mean to break his finger. I just wanted him to stop."

"What should you have done when he started pushing you?" Principal Singer asked.

Jason looked at his dad. Wade said nothing, but I could tell he was hoping Jason would remember the training session they'd had that one morning. "I should have—" Jason started, then looked back at the principal. "I should have yelled for help. Shouldn't have let myself get alone with Danny and his buddies. Should have yelled 'Help, get the teacher.' "

"Right," she said. "Any time someone starts bullying you, you need to report it."

"But then they'll call me a tattle-tale."

Wade spoke up then. "Sometimes you need to speak up, Jason, even if the kids call you a tattle-tale. You've seen the pictures of the shootings at schools, how kids get hurt because no one said anything. You need to let others know when there's a problem."

"Yeah, I guess." Jason gave a small nod.

Sandy Singer took over then. "I think Jason should stay home for the rest of the day. I don't know if Danny is here now or if his parents took him home. I'll check and call them. I think both boys need one more day to think this over. Then, tomorrow—" She directed her instructions to Jason. "I want you to come to my office when you arrive at school. I'll take you to class. I'll take both you and Danny, if he shows up. I want all of your classmates to understand there is to be no fighting and no bullying."

And that was the end of the meeting.

Chapter Twenty-Nine

While I waited in the office for Jason to turn in the homework he'd completed and pick up a new assignment from his teacher, Wade went out of the building to make a phone call. He had the Jeep pulled up to the curb by the time Jason and I came out. "Everything set?" he asked Jason. "You have homework to do? I don't want you considering this a vacation. No Xbox and no TV until three o'clock when you'd normally be home."

"Yes, Sir."

I saw his pout but said nothing. Chances were Jason would sneak in some TV watching while I napped. Although it was barely mid-morning, I was exhausted. Between worrying about what was going to transpire during the meeting this morning and not being able to find a comfortable spot to lie, I hadn't slept well. I struggled to haul myself into the Jeep and groaned when the baby moved. My due date was still a week away, but both Paige Joy and I were ready to part company.

I struggled to fasten my seatbelt, and Wade finally had to help. With a sigh, I leaned back. "You still going over to Ken's trailer?"

"Dario's already there. You okay?"

"Just tired of being pregnant." I motioned for him to get the Jeep moving. "I'm okay."

Jason's school was less than a mile away from Zenith's mobile home park. A couple of my clients lived in the park, and Jason said one of his classmates lived there. The grounds were well-kept and it had paved streets, sidewalks, and a clubhouse. I'd heard there were over seventy sites and as we drove down one of the streets, I saw only one vacant lot. Wade pulled up in front of an older looking trailer. A rusted maroon Buick was parked in the carport attached to the trailer. Jerry's car, I assumed. A marked sheriff's patrol car was parked behind it. Dario Gespardo got out of that vehicle as soon as Wade stopped.

I first met Dario last summer when Abby Warfield's house exploded, killing her. I'd taken her dog, which was not injured but looked sick, to my vet. Gespardo considered that a no-no, and since I'd been the last known person to see Abby alive, he also considered me a suspect in her murder. Dario had been with the sheriff's department for over thirty years, and Wade considered him a mentor and friend. Since our marriage, Wade and I had spent a couple evenings with Dario and his wife, but I still felt the man suspected me of being up to something illegal. I'm sure my having a mother with a criminal record—albeit based on her mental problems— didn't help Dario's perception of me.

"Hi, Gesp," Jason called from the back seat.

Dario waved to him, and then to me. Wade got out and pushed the seat back to make room for my expanded middle. He had it in position by the time I waddled around to the driver's side. "Missus said to say hi," Dario said as Wade helped me into the vehicle. "She remembers how miserable those last few weeks were. I imagine you're ready to pop."

"Pop" wasn't a term I liked when thinking of giving birth, but I smiled and nodded.

"You going to be all right?" Wade asked. "Maybe I should just take the afternoon off and drive you to the doctor's myself."

The idea was appealing, but I shook my head. "I'll be fine."

He didn't look convinced. "If you think you might be going into labor, call me. And if you can't get a hold of me, call the station. They'll find me."

"I will." I turned my attention to the trailer they were about to investigate. "No signs of Ken?"

"Neighbor came out when he saw me pull in. Said he hasn't seen Mr. Paget since Friday." Gespardo turned his attention to Wade. "I decided to wait until you arrived before going inside."

I wished I could look inside the trailer. Wade must have guessed what I was thinking. "You might as well take off now," he said. "Have some lunch and get some rest."

I read the message in his eyes. *Leave the investigation to law enforcement.*

"Yes, sir," I said and gave a mock salute before looking at Dario. "Say 'Hi' to your wife."

"Can we have mac and cheese for lunch?" Jason asked as I steered the Jeep away from Ken's trailer. "The real kind?"

I understood what he meant. Soon after Wade and Jason moved in with me, I thought I would impress them by making macaroni and cheese the way Grandma Carter made it—from scratch. I added lots of shredded cheddar cheese to a white sauce, cooked the macaroni until it was tender, drained the macaroni, added butter, and mixed everything together. Jason took one taste and told me it wasn't "Real" macaroni and cheese. That was when Wade mentioned his ex-wife always made it out of a box.

"I'm not sure I have any 'real' mac and cheese," I told him.

"You can buy some. The store's right there."

Although I couldn't see him, I'm sure Jason was pointing at the grocery store next to the mobile trailer park. He was right, I could stop and pick up some boxed macaroni and cheese, as well as a few other items I knew we needed. But did I have the energy?

"Please," he said sweetly.

I gave in. "Okay. But you need to stay in the car while I shop." Although Jason wasn't bad to shop with, he did pester for sweetened cereals and ice cream.

The locally owned grocery store didn't have as wide a selection of items as the big box stores in Battle Creek and Kalamazoo and the prices were slightly higher, but it was nice to be greeted by name when I came through the door and whenever I couldn't find something I wanted, one of the clerks would find it for me or the owner would order it. Pushing a cart, I started by heading for the bread aisle. One thing I'd discovered over the last few months was two men—even though one was only seven—went through a lot more bread than two or even three women. Peanut butter and jelly was a staple for the Kingsley males, and I liked it, too.

Coffee followed bread. Although I still wasn't drinking as much coffee as I had before getting pregnant, we went through those canisters fast. And, as long as I was in that aisle, I picked up another box of chamomile tea. I was heading for the produce section when I sensed someone had come up right beside me. Almost shoulder to shoulder right beside me. The moment she said, "Well, if it isn't the manipulator," I knew who it was.

Marge Bailey.

I'd only met her once and that had been months ago, but I remembered her clearly. She might be a forensic photographer, but she looked like a model: tall, slender, her long brown hair flowing past her shoulders. Her facial features weren't perfect, but she knew how to accentuate the positive with makeup, a talent I'd never learned nor had the desire to learn.

Even as I looked at her, she sized me up. Her smile was wicked. "He feels sorry for you, you know. Feels guilty for the condition you're in." Her gaze slid to the bulge at my middle. "But we know it's not his fault, don't we?"

I didn't know how to answer that, so I said nothing.

"Wade and I had a nice talk about you yesterday," she said. "He said you're seeing things now. Can't keep your car on the road." She chuckled. "Pigs? Really?"

Her goading attitude irked me. As much as I wanted to ignore her, I couldn't. "Speaking of delusional," I said, "Wade and I had a nice talk about you, too."

Her smile disappeared, her eyes narrowing. Just slightly, and only for a moment. Then the smug look returned. "You know I'm joining him in a few minutes. In the trailer park."

She casually ran a fingernail over the back of my hand. A shiver ran down my spine and I jerked my hand away from the grocery cart. Away from her touch.

Marge grinned. "We decided to keep things as they are until after you have this baby. But don't worry. He'll make sure you and the baby are all right before he starts the divorce."

I knew she was bluffing. At least, I hoped she was, but I still found it incredible that Wade found me beautiful, and that he would pick me to marry over Marge. Me with my chance of mental illness. Me with a crazy mother and a curiosity that seemed to constantly get me in trouble. I looked Marge directly in the eyes. "He's free to go whenever he likes."

"Oh, how noble you sound." She sneered at me. "And how noble of you, when you heard his ex-wife was going to move his son across the country to California, to stopping taking birth control so you could give him another son."

"I did not stop taking birth control."

That came out louder than I'd expected, and a woman standing beside a bin of potatoes looked my way. I cringed. I was letting Marge get to me. I knew I shouldn't. I should walk away, but she had me crowded next to the display of cauliflower. I grabbed one and lifted it toward her in a threatening way. "Excuse me," I said. "I want to weigh this."

She did step back, and I pushed my cart toward the scale hanging at the end of the row. Marge followed. "You put him in a position where he had to marry you."

I glared at her. "He's free to go any time he wants."

"If that's so, tell him. Don't make him go through life miserable."

I plopped the cauliflower onto the scale, but I didn't even look at what it weighed. Eyes closed, I tried to think of what to say . . . or not say. I took in a deep breath. Blood pounded in my ears, and I felt like throwing up. Slowly I let my breath out, and, still unsure what to say, opened my eyes.

Marge was gone.

I looked around. The woman who'd been standing by the potatoes was staring at me. "Are you all right?" she asked.

No, I wanted to shout, but I managed to nod and say, "I'm okay."

"It's a shock when you meet the 'other woman'," she said, emphasizing the words. "I know. I had it happen to me. I told my husband if he left me for her, he'd be sorry."

Now I was curious. "Did he leave you?"

"Oh yes. Not right away, but a couple years later." She laughed. "And he's been sorry ever since." She glanced down at my belly. "But maybe that won't happen in your case. When are you due?"

"Soon." The way I was feeling any time would be fine. And, if this woman thought she was encouraging me, she was wrong. I didn't want to spend my life wondering when Wade would leave. I started to push my cart away, but she called after me, reminding me I had a cauliflower on the scale. I grabbed it, dropped it in the cart, and headed for the checkout stand. It wasn't until I was in the Jeep and driving back to the house that I remembered I hadn't bought any packages of macaroni and cheese.

Chapter Thirty

I wasn't sure if I wanted to laugh or bop Jason over the head when his response to my forgetting to buy the mac-and-cheese was, "That's okay. Aunt Ginny said you might have baby brain sometime."

Angry brain better described my thought process. *Tired brain.* The Harts had made me angry; Marge Bailey had made me angry. And not knowing what was going on with Ken was making me angry. More than that, I was tired. Tired of feeling like a blimp, of waiting for this baby to arrive, and seemingly having no control over my life.

I fixed soup and toasted cheese sandwiches for lunch. Jason gobbled his down. I barely touched either. Once he went upstairs to work on his homework, I stretched out on the couch. I had a couple hours until I needed to leave for my doctor's appointment. Time to unwind.

I wasn't aware of falling asleep, but the ring of my phone woke me. It took me a minute to remember what day it was and where I'd left the phone. The answering machine clicked on before I reached it, and I recognized Nate Schipper's voice. "Your car's ready. You can pick it up any time."

I quickly turned off the answering machine and engaged the phone. "That's great. Any chance you could drive the car out to me around three o'clock? I could drop you off on my way to my four o'clock doctor's appointment."

His answer wasn't what I wanted to hear. He wouldn't be able to get away from the shop until after five.

"Okay, I'll see what I can do," I said. I really didn't want to drive Wade's Jeep into Kalamazoo. Even though it was an unmarked vehicle, and most people wouldn't recognize it as part of the sheriff's department's fleet, I wanted my car, the one I was familiar with.

I hated to bother Howard, but he had offered help if I ever needed it. The moment I ended my call with Nate Schipper, I dialed Howard's number. By the sixth ring, I decided he probably wasn't home, but just before I hung up, he answered. "You okay?" He sounded breathless. "How close are the contractions?"

"I'm fine. Not in labor. No contractions."

"Oh, good . . . I guess." He still sounded breathless.

"It's my car." I explained the situation, and, as usual, Howard came to my rescue. Twenty minutes later his blue Ford pulled into the yard. Once again Howard had cleaned the passenger's seat off for me, however, I hadn't explained that Jason would need to go with us. It took a few minutes for Howard and Jason to push tools, papers, and ammo to the side so Jason had room.

On the drive into town, Jason told Howard about our confrontation that morning with the Harts. I simply listened. It was interesting to hear Jason's take on the meeting and the pride in his voice when he talked about his dad. "He told him to go ahead and sue us, and Danny's dad ran like a scaredy cat."

That wasn't exactly how I remembered it, but I didn't say anything.

"Speaking of cats," Howard said, looking my way, "Would you mind loaning me Jason for a while this afternoon? The reason it took me so long after you called is I've got a barn cat that just had kittens, and I need to move them from where she had them to a safer spot. I tried doing it myself, but every time I moved one and went back for another one, she picked up the first one and took it back to the nest. I need an extra set of hands. Someone nimble, like Jason."

Before I had a chance to say anything, Jason spoke up. "Could I, P.J.? Could I? I could help Howard, and you wouldn't have to worry about what to do with me when you go to the doctor."

"You're sure?" I asked Howard. "I have no idea when either Wade or I will be back."

"No problem. I'm thinking, besides helping me move the kittens, he can show me how to play a game on my computer. It's a new one I just got. Futuristic battles to save Earth."

I didn't have to look behind me to know Jason was eagerly agreeing to the idea. By the time we reached Schippers Auto Repair the two of them had everything decided. Jason would finish his homework and then I would walk him over to Howard's place where he would stay until either Wade or I picked him up.

To my surprise, when I pulled out my checkbook to pay the bill for the airbags, their installation, and the repair to the Chevy's fender, Howard stopped me. "Mike's paying for this."

I'd forgotten Howard had said Mike Mullen would pay for the damage since it was his pigs that caused me to end up in the ditch. Nate agreed to send the bill to Mullen's Pig Farm, and that was that. Well, almost. Nate said he still wasn't sure what the bill would be to fix the loaner I'd wrecked. Those repairs would be my responsibility.

Repairs needed because of bad road conditions or did that SUV intentionally run me off the road? I wondered if I would ever know.

I told Nate to call when he had a cost.

It seemed good to be driving my own car again. Back at the house, Jason headed upstairs, eager to get his homework done so he could go to Howard's, and I once again stretched out on the couch, hoping I could get an hour's rest before leaving for Kalamazoo.

Although I didn't fall asleep, I wasn't fully awake when Baraka started barking. Within moments, Jason came tromping down the stairs. "Who's here?" he asked, heading for the front door.

"I don't know." I pushed myself to my feet, and slowly made my way to where Jason and Baraka stood by the door.

I recognized the tall, willowy woman the moment she stepped out of the black sedan. Once again she wore a black pantsuit and carried a black briefcase. Agent Andrea Tailor had returned.

"Baraka, it's okay. Quiet," I ordered, laying a hand on my dog's back to reassure him.

"Did you do something wrong? She's not smiling," Jason said as Agent Tailor came through the gate and started toward the porch.

"No, I didn't do anything wrong, but we will want some privacy." I pointed toward the stairs. "Have you finished your homework?"

"Almost." He didn't move. "Is she going to zap you so you don't remember anything?"

"Zap me?" I looked down at him, confused.

"She's dressed in black."

I remembered then that we'd recently watched a rerun of "Men in Black," and I laughed. Andrea Tailor was dressed like Tommy Lee Jones and Will Smith, including the dark glasses. "No, she's not going to zap me. Now, scoot. And take Baraka with you."

He didn't move, his focus on Agent Tailor. With the woman now standing on the other side of the door, looking in, I decided it would be easier to introduce her than make her wait until I convinced Jason to go upstairs. So, I did. And Agent Tailor was wonderful. The moment Jason asked if she had a weapon that could make people forget they'd met her, she understood. Jason, however, was disappointed when she said, "That's not my job. My job is to help people remember things."

"Okay, satisfied?" I asked him and again pointed toward the stairway. "Now, we want to talk, privately. Finish your homework and, once I'm free, I'll take you over to Howard's."

Jason hesitated, then nodded. "Come on, Baraka."

I watched Baraka trot behind Jason and up the stairs. The sound of a door slamming closed told me Jason was in his room and would keep Baraka there with him. Or maybe that was what he wanted me to think. I remembered my dad telling me how there was a vent above the dining room area where he used to be able to overhear his parents' conversations. I glanced at the ceiling. Was he up there?

"Coffee, tea, or water?" I asked, deciding it didn't matter if Jason did eavesdrop.

"Water sounds good," Agent Tailor said and sat at the table, opening her briefcase, and pulling out a notebook and a pen.

I brought her a bottle of water and sat on the opposite side of the table. "I have a doctor's appointment at four. I'll have to leave around three."

She checked her watch and nodded. "No problem. This shouldn't take long. Your husband left a message yesterday that you purchased a piece of furniture at Patterson's Furniture store, a rocking chair, and that someone from the store came here and took something from that rocking chair. Do you know what was taken?"

"No, not for sure, but a friend of mine found diamonds stuffed in a ceramic crow that came from the same store."

Agent Tailor immediately responded. "Does he still have those diamonds?"

"He contacted us yesterday and told Wade he'd hidden them in the freezer. Wade and another officer went to the trailer this morning, but I haven't heard if they found anything."

"What trailer?"

"The one Ken owns." I quickly explained about Ken, the trailer park in Zenith, and Jerry. "Jerry also worked at Patterson's. He stole the crow that had the diamonds in it. You haven't heard about him?"

"I heard another employee of Patterson's died the same day Brenda did. Died of an overdose, according to my information. Nothing about a stolen crow or diamonds."

"The Sheriff's Department didn't know about the crow and the diamonds until this weekend."

"Interesting." Agent Tailor jotted something in her notebook. "When you talked to Brenda, she didn't say anything about the diamonds?"

"No. Nothing. When you came here last week, I thought you were investigating drug smuggling. It was Wade who told me something more than drugs had to be involved."

"Why did he think that?"

"Because you're not with DEA. He said DEA handles drugs, not CPB." I chuckled. "You people and your alphabet lingo."

She smiled. "Easier than writing it all out."

"So, did Brenda know about the diamonds?"

"She's the one who told us. She contacted us several months ago, wanted to know what we would pay for pictures showing how they were transporting them across the border. She said she could get pictures without them ever knowing what she was doing, and pictures of bills-of-lading. She was bringing me that evidence the day she was killed. Mrs. Kingsley, are you *sure* she didn't give you anything?"

"Positive."

Agent Tailor sat back in her chair, sighed, and took a sip of water before going on. "She called me twice from the church. The first time was the conversation you overheard. The second time was a short while later, after she'd gone upstairs into the sanctuary. That was when she said she'd placed the evidence in a safe place and would be able to retrieve it in a few days. At the time, I thought she'd left the thumb drive in the church."

"So, are you the one who emptied the waste basket in the bathroom and pulled all those hymnals out?"

"No." She shook her head. "Someone did that the day before I searched. Someone who knew Brenda was in the bathroom and upstairs." Tailor looked at me. "Who else was in the church that day who would have known Brenda was there?"

I understood what she was getting at but didn't think I could help her. "I don't know about upstairs, but downstairs, it was just the Mothers-to-Be group I belong to. Of that group, besides me, Tamara said she ran into Brenda outside of the church and that they went downstairs together. Maria came into the meeting after me, so I don't know if she saw Brenda go upstairs or not."

Pen poised above her notebook, Tailor asked, "What are their full names?"

We never used last names, so it took me a moment to remember. "Maria Gonzales and Tamara Trulain."

She wrote the two names down, then looked up. "Gonzales is a popular name, but Trulain isn't, yet it sounds familiar."

"She designs jewelry," I said. "She brought some to one of our meetings. It's beautiful. I know a couple local stores carry her pieces."

"Okay." Agent Tailor smiled. "I'm always looking at jewelry, so that's probably where I've seen the name." She put her pen down and took another sip of water. "So, back to Brenda. Evidently Morales thinks she gave you the thumb drive."

"Who's Morales?"

"Juan Morales. His official title, according to Brenda, is warehouse manager, though occasionally they have him out on the floor selling furniture."

"Okay, I know who you mean. I met him last week."

"I heard you were at the store." Tailor shook her head. "Be careful, Mrs. Kingsley. We know Morales works for the cartel that's behind the drug smuggling. He's not a nice man. Yesterday, when your husband called me, he said someone has broken into this house and taken two of your thumb drives. If it's Morales—"

I stopped her. "Wade told you I've had two thumb drives taken?"

She frowned. "Haven't you?"

"Oh, yes. Yes, I definitely have." Agent Tailor would never know what a relief it was to know Wade didn't think I was removing those thumb drives myself and forgetting I'd done so. "It's just. . ." I hesitated, not sure how to explain. "It's nice to know I was believed."

"Your husband believes you. And I believe you. Here's why. The day Brenda was hit by that car, the crime scene investigators looked for but did not find her purse. The next day, they did, and it was where they'd looked before."

"That's what Detective Ferrell of Kalamazoo Public Safety told me. Wade thought maybe the homeless man who was in front of the church grabbed it and took the cash, but when he realized his image was on TV, he brought the purse back."

"Actually, there were two men in front of the church that day. By the time I pulled my car over, called 9-1-1, and went back to Brenda, one of the two had disappeared. When the police said they couldn't find a purse, I figured the thumb drive and the evidence I was hoping to get was gone. But then the minister of the church reported vandalism the next day. That was too much of a coincidence, especially considering the bathroom where you talked to Brenda and the sanctuary upstairs were the only areas hit, not the classrooms. It wasn't vandalism. Someone was looking for something."

"The thumb drive." It made sense.

She nodded. "When I was here last time, you didn't mention someone breaking into your place and taking yours."

"I was still trying to convince myself that someone actually had been in here and had taken my thumb drive."

"And the second time someone broke in?"

"That was last Thursday. I'd returned from a walk in the woods, and I saw Miguel come out of the house."

"Miguel from the furniture store?"

"Yes, he helped me the night I purchased the rocking chair."

"And the thumb drive Miguel took wasn't the one Brenda gave you?"

I sat back in my chair, suddenly irritated. "Agent Tailor, what don't you understand? Brenda did not give me anything. Nada. Nothing."

Tailor shook her head. "She must have. Have you checked your purse?"

"Yes. The day I realized my thumb drive was missing—the first thumb drive—I looked in my purse just in case I'd forgotten putting it there. All I found were the usual things a woman keeps in her purse." I rose from the table and went to my bedroom. Moments later I came out with my purse and dumped its contents on the table.

Tailor leaned closer, so I shuffled things around, moving my credit card holder and coin purse to one side, my business card case, checkbook, and car keys to the other. That left my lipstick, a pen, safety pins, a packet of tissues and a snack-size bag of peanuts in the center.

"That's it? You haven't removed anything?"

"The only things I've removed are a lipstick I'd forgotten I had and a couple extra pens."

Tailor looked hopeful. "May I see the lipstick?"

I went back in the bedroom and dug through the drawer where I'd dropped the lipstick. I rarely wore any makeup, lipstick being my one exception, and most of the time I bought shades of pink. The one I'd found in my purse, while looking for my missing thumb drive, was a red. Why I was carrying it around, I didn't know. I couldn't remember the last time I'd used that color.

I brought the lipstick to Agent Tailor, who immediately pulled off the top and rolled up the tube. I knew she was hoping it was a thumb drive made to look like a lipstick, but what she found was simply lipstick. With a sigh, she rolled it back down and replaced the cap.

"And that's it?"

"And that's it," I repeated and put the contents of my purse back into my purse, with the exception of the red lipstick.

I knew that wasn't what she wanted to hear. Slowly she pushed her chair back and stood. "Well, Mrs. Kingsley, thank you for your cooperation. I have no idea now where that thumb drive ended up. Hopefully, no one will be breaking into your house again, but I do suggest you not return to Patterson's Furniture. I think they're getting nervous, and this cartel is known for its brutality."

She shook my hand, but before she stepped out the door, she paused. "Be careful, and if you do find a—"

I knew what she was going to say. "I'll call you."

Chapter Thirty-One

By three o'clock, Jason was at Howard's place, Baraka had been let out for a while, and I'd taken a shower and put on a clean pair of maternity jeans, a baggy blue sweater, and sneakers. My car started the moment I turned the key, and I headed for Kalamazoo feeling life was good. Even the weather cheered me up, the temperature above freezing and large patches of blue sky appearing between clouds. Now all I wanted was good news from my doctor. Words like, "Oh yes, the baby will arrive tonight and by tomorrow your body will be back to its normal size."

I knew she wasn't going to say that, but it would be nice. Over and over, Connie had told us not to be afraid of giving birth, but I'd heard too many stories from other women about their experiences and seen too many movies and TV shows where the woman was screaming while giving birth. I just wanted it over.

* * *

"You are starting to dilate," Doctor Gladwin said and smiled, "but your daughter isn't positioned quite right so I don't think she's going to show up for a while."

Not what I wanted to hear.

The best news, however, was Paige Joy's heartbeat was good and strong and as far as Doctor Gladwin could tell, my car accidents and my fall had caused no harm to the baby. Other positives were my blood pressure was normal, and I hadn't gained any more weight.

"My guess is one more week," Doctor Gladwin said, then chuckled. "But I'd keep Connie's number handy."

Dr. Gladwin knew Connie from when Connie worked at her clinic. In fact, she was the one who had recommended I join Connie's Mothers-to-Be group, and from what Connie has told me, the two kept in close contact. "I have Connie's number on speed dial," I assured her.

My doctor's appointment didn't take long, so I decided to stop by Grandma's place to see how she was doing and if she'd heard anything from Mom since Saturday. I hadn't, but I hadn't phoned Mom, either.

Grandma Carter was in the living room, watching a talk show, and smoking a cigarette. She put the cigarette out the moment I stepped into the house, which I appreciated, but the smell of smoke lingered in the air. It's amazing Grandma doesn't have COPD or lung cancer—or Mom or me. I don't remember a time when I lived with Grandma and Mom that the house didn't smell of cigarette smoke.

"What did the doctor say?" Grandma asked the moment I sat down beside her.

"That I'm starting to dilate, but it's going to be a while."

"But everything's all right with the baby?"

"Fine as far as she could tell."

Grandma nodded. "When's that next mama meeting?"

"The Mothers-to-Be meeting? I don't know. Normally it would be Wednesday, but Connie said our sessions will depend on whether or not she's busy helping one of us give birth. Anna's due soon, Sarah may have already had her baby, and last week Maria thought she was in labor. And—" I drew out the word. "I'm not sure where we would meet now that we can't use the church."

"You could meet here. You said there's just the six of you."

"No." As convenient as Grandma's house might be for a meeting, and as nice as it was for her to offer—which was typical of Grandma—I knew Connie wouldn't want to meet here. "It has to be a no-smoking location."

Grandma shrugged. "Okay, have them go to your place. You guys don't smoke."

"I'll mention it to Connie, but I don't think they'll want to drive forty miles. What do you hear from Mom?"

"Nothing." Grandma chuckled. "Which I guess is good. You know, 'No news is good news'."

"Think this marriage will last?" Mom has had boyfriends before, but up until Ben she hadn't married anyone but my dad.

"I hope so." Grandma looked around the living room. "It's lonely at night with her gone, but for the last few months she's been spending more time at Ben's place than here, so I've gotten used to the solitude. What I like is now I don't need to worry about what would happen if I should become incapacitated or die. I—"

I stopped her there. "You know I would have taken care of Mom."

"I know." Grandma patted my knee. "But you now have your own family. It's better this way. So, do I think this marriage will last? I hope so."

"I hope mine does, too."

"What?" Grandma turned toward me.

I hadn't meant to say it aloud. The words had simply come out. I looked down, away from her penetrating gaze. "I—" I started, unsure what to tell her. "This morning—" Was it just this morning that Marge had waylaid me in the grocery store? No, it had started before then. Way before. I took in a bracing breath and looked at Grandma. "Marge, who is one of the photographers who works for the sheriff's department, is determined to end my marriage to Wade. For months she's been finding excuses to call him late at night, and

Sunday she lured him to her place and tried to seduce him. This morning she stopped me while I was shopping and told me the only reason Wade married me was because he felt honor bound to do so."

For a moment, Grandma said nothing, then she asked, "You said she tried to seduce Wade. How do you know that?"

"He told me."

"And did she succeed?"

"He says no. He said—"

She didn't let me finish. "And do you believe him?"

"Yes." The moment I said the word, I realized how foolish I was being. "Yes, I do believe him," I repeated and smiled. "She's the one who has the problem, not me."

Grandma nodded and patted my knee. "You've got a good-looking guy there, P.J. A nice guy. Over the years there are bound to be women who try to seduce him, who think they would make him happier than you do. You either have to trust him or your marriage will fail. And . . ." She paused and gave me a stern look. "The next time this low-life female tries to make you doubt how much that man loves you, you kick her in the butt."

The way she said it made me laugh. "I will, but it's going to have to be after this baby is born. I can barely lift my leg, much less kick someone in the butt. And thank you." She had made me feel better. "Also, thank you for setting up that dinner after Mom's wedding. I'd like to help pay for that meal."

"Save your money. Use it on the baby." Grandma paused and frowned. "You know, speaking of having babies, the way you went dashing for the bathroom at the end of the meal Saturday really had me worried. I thought maybe your water broke. Did you think it had or something?"

"No, it wasn't that." I tried to remember the exact sequence of events. "Did you see the pregnant lady who went into the bathroom while we were eating?" At Grandma's nod, I went on. "She's in the Mothers-to-Be group. I saw her go in, but I didn't see her come out, and I thought she might be having trouble."

"Oh, you should have said something. I could have told you she came out when Wade was telling us about the truck in your yard. In fact, she stopped right behind your chair. I thought she was going to say something to you, but then she went on."

I wasn't surprised. "That sounds like Maria. She's not the friendliest person in the group. Last week she practically accused me of being a terrible person for not helping Brenda when I saw her in the bathroom."

"You offered. What more could you do?" Grandma clicked off the TV. "Want to stay for dinner?"

"No, I need to get home. I left Jason at Howard's place. I'm not sure when Wade will be home, and I hate to impose on Howard."

"I don't think Howard minds." Grandma walked with me to her front door. "I think he sees you as the daughter he never had."

"Who keeps getting into trouble. He calls me Jessica Fletcher and says I'm turning Zenith Township into Cabot Cove."

Grandma laughed. "You do have a way of stirring up trouble."
way of stirring up trouble."

Chapter Thirty-Two

I'd just gotten into my car when my phone rang. It was Connie. "Hi, hope I didn't catch you at a bad time," she said. "And this is going to sound a bit forward, but would you be willing to hold the next Mothers-to-Be meeting at your place?"

"Now that is weird," I said. "My grandmother suggested that just a while ago. Did she call you or something?"

"No, it was Maria who brought it up. She called me earlier today and said it would be fun to meet at your place and see how you have things set up for a birth at home. If you're agreeable, I think it would be a great idea. We could meet earlier than usual so we'd be gone by the time your stepson got home from school. And there will only be four of us. Sarah did have her baby. Not Friday when I talked to you, but yesterday. A little boy, six pounds five ounces."

"So, she beat us all." I'd been wondering about Sarah since Connie's call Friday. "Is she all right? The baby?"

"The baby has a mild case of jaundice, so they're keeping him in the hospital until tomorrow, but otherwise he seems to be fine. I stopped by to see Sarah just a while ago, and she said the doctor told her not to worry; however, she indicated she wouldn't be coming Wednesday."

"Okay, but you said there would only be four of us. Who else isn't coming?"

"Tamara. She went into labor early."

"Oh, no. Were they able to save the baby?"

"Not from what I've heard, but I don't know for sure. I've tried calling her, but so far all I get is her voicemail."

"Poor Tamara." I knew, since she'd made it to her eighth month, she'd had high hopes of making it to term with this pregnancy. "When you do talk to her, tell her how sorry I am for her."

"I will. So, Wednesday at your place okay?"

"You know how far I live from Kalamazoo." Connie had come out to the house back when I told her I was thinking of having my baby at home and would like to use her as a midwife. "If it's all right with the others, it's all right with me."

"Good. I'll call Anna and tell her and confirm with Maria. I just wanted to check with you first. Because, if you don't feel up to it "

"Sounds like fun," I assured her. "My house is actually the cleanest it's been in weeks and having the meeting at my place means I don't have to drive into town. I might even make some cookies."

"Sounds like a party. Tell me what time would be best for you, and I'll call the others tonight and let them know."

"One o'clock?" I looked at my watch. It was almost five-thirty. "You may not be able to get a hold of Anna until tomorrow. This evening she's meeting with the charity board she's on. I'm not sure what time exactly."

"Okay, I'll let you know some time tomorrow. Meanwhile, how did your appointment with Doctor Gladwin go?"

"Fine. She thinks I have one more week before Paige Joy will make her entrance, and she said to say 'Hi' to you."

Once my call to Connie ended, I started my car, but I didn't head straight home. I knew driving by Ken's shop was probably a waste of time; nevertheless, that's what I did. The "Closed" sign was on the door, the inside lights off. From there, I drove the few blocks over to his apartment building and pulled into the parking area on the backside. I hadn't asked Wade which apartment Ken was in, so

I wasn't sure if one of the two empty spots was his, but I didn't see his car.

I thought about calling the number that had appeared with the text messages he'd sent Sunday, then changed my mind. Instead, I typed, ARE YOU ALL RIGHT?

I waited a few minutes to see if he responded, but nothing came back, so I headed home.

* * *

Wade was home when I arrived and so was Jason. He was eager to report the events of his time with Howard, primarily how they moved mother cat and kittens to a safe spot in Howard's barn and how cute the kittens were. "They don't even have their eyes open. It takes almost two weeks before they open," Jason said, then looked at me. "Will it take that long for Paige to open her eyes?"

"No, hers should be open when she's born," I told him, "but she won't be able to see very well. It will take time for that."

"Howard said I can't have one until it's eight weeks old, that it will need its mommy until then."

I looked at Wade, who cleared his throat. "We didn't exactly say you could have a cat."

Jason's chin rose. "You said I could have one if I didn't let Danny bully me, and I didn't."

I chuckled. "You did say something like that."

Wade grunted. "We'll talk about it later." He waved his hand toward the bathroom. "Go wash up. I brought fried chicken home for dinner."

I was glad to hear that. I was too tired to cook. As soon as Jason closed the bathroom door, I asked Wade, "Did you find the diamonds at Ken's trailer?"

He nodded yes and smiled. "The ice was in the ice. Probably the best place he could have put them. Unless you really knew what you were looking for, you wouldn't notice."

Jason came out of the bathroom, hands dripping wet, and Wade asked him to get the paper plates from the kitchen. "I'll tell you more later," he said and followed his son into the other room. "I'm starved."

During dinner, Wade quizzed me on my day. I summarized my visit to the doctor and with my grandma, told him I drove by Ken's place but didn't see any signs of him and hadn't heard from him, then skimmed over Agent Tailor's information. What I didn't mention was my run-in with Marge. Jason again brought up the subject of a kitten. Again, Wade told him we'd think about it. It wasn't until later, after Jason had gone to bed, that I asked Wade what else he and Gespardo had found in Ken's trailer.

"It was a mess. Cupboards, drawers, and closets had been emptied. Everything was on the floor, including pieces of the ceramic crow. We found two empty beer cans on the floor. We took them and will check for DNA. If it's not Ken's, and we can find a match, we'll charge them for breaking and entry." Wade grinned. "Thank goodness they were drinking beer and didn't want ice."

"So how many diamonds did you find?"

"A half dozen. All uncut. A couple of them were quite large, so we had a jeweler come to the station and look at them. He estimated their combined value close to a half million."

I gave a low whistle.

"We called CBP, and I met your Agent Tailor. She said you'd told her we were looking for the diamonds. She was very happy that we'd found them. She just wishes she had the evidence your friend Brenda was bringing her so she could tie the diamonds to the person smuggling them across the border." He looked at me. "She's still sure Brenda must have given you something."

"Damn. How many times do I have to tell her Brenda didn't give me anything?"

Chapter Thirty-Three

Tuesday morning Wade said he would take Jason to school, that he didn't think there was any need for me to come along, the principal was the one who needed to deal with the two boys. "I'll drop him off, then head into work," Wade said as he finished his coffee. "I still have reports to finish regarding Ken's trailer and those diamonds."

Jason seemed worried. "What if Danny tries to beat me up?"

Wade's response was predictable. "Don't let yourself get into a position where he can, and if you think he might, yell for a teacher to help."

I could tell Jason didn't want to yell for help. As I hugged him goodbye, I whispered, "Just stay close to your friends."

Once the two of them were gone, I did the usual morning chores: washed the morning's dishes, made our bed—and hoped Jason had made his—let Baraka out for a bit, and then checked my email. That's when I noticed one from Anna. The date and time showed it had been sent Monday afternoon.

Mrs. Welkum wants to see me before the board meeting. I think she knows what I'm going to report. Wish me luck. I'll call you tomorrow and let you know how it goes. Anna.

I thought about calling Anna right then. I was dying to hear what went on during that board meeting, how Madeline Welkum reacted, and what the board decided, but I decided to wait. If Anna was having as much trouble sleeping at night as I was, she wouldn't appreciate being woken early. I simply replied to her email with: *Dying of curiosity. Call me. P.J.*

I went through the rest of my emails. Two included questions regarding ways to save on next year's taxes—one of my clients had sold stock at a huge profit without considering how it would affect his taxes and didn't want to repeat that mistake—and one email was a thank you and a request to be informed when Paige Joy arrived.

It was a little after nine o'clock when I finished responding to those emails and I was wondering what I should do with the rest of my day when my land line rang. The call was from Sondra, my neighbor. "P.J., what have you heard?" were her breathless first words.

"Heard about what?"

"The shooting. At the elementary school. It was just on the TV. Zenith Elementary is on lockdown."

"I haven't heard anything." Heart pounding, I headed for my TV and turned it on. "What are they saying?"

"Not much, just that there have been shots. You haven't heard anything from your husband?"

"No." A talk show was on the local channel, but a crawler at the bottom had the information about the shooting, what little there was. *9-1-1 call reports shots fired at local school. Some casualties. Sheriff's department on scene.*

Some casualties. I sank down on the closest chair. "Have you heard anything about the shooter?" I asked Sondra. "Or who was shot?"

"No. Nothing so far."

Even without verification, I knew who the shooter was. *Danny.* And the casualty? "I've got to go up there," I told Sondra. "Thanks for calling."

I grabbed my purse and a jacket and headed for my car. I didn't even look at my speedometer as I drove to the school. A thousand thoughts flashed through my mind, images of Jason looking at me this morning, silently pleading with me for help. Me hugging him and telling him to stick with his friends. Had his friends been shot, too? Had my suggestion killed others? I remembered newscasts of other school shootings, images of children running from school buildings, parents waiting for news, and children crying.

Tears slid down my cheeks. I didn't want Jason dead. I didn't want him hurt in any way. He wasn't my biological son, but I'd grown to love him as if he were mine. I wanted him around when Paige Joy arrived. I wanted her to have a big brother, something I never had.

"Be safe," I whispered as I neared the entrance to the school.

A deputy stood in the middle of the school's driveway. Focused on him, I barely noticed the line of cars and trucks parked along the side of the road. As I neared, the deputy raised his hands in a gesture for me to stop. I wanted to ignore his order and swerve around him, but I forced myself to step on the brake and roll down my window as he approached. "You'll have to park out here and wait until we get the all clear. It's still an active scene," he said.

"But my stepson—" I stared at the one-story rectangular building set back from the road. "I think he's the one who's been shot."

"As soon as we know anything, we'll let you know," the deputy said and stepped back, again blocking my way.

For a moment I did nothing, simply stared at the school building, then I saw the deputy motioning me to move on. Slowly, I backed up and drove on down the road to a spot where I, too, could pull off and park. Purse and cell phone in hand, I locked the car and walked back to join dozens of other parents huddled in groups as close to the school's boundaries as they could get. "What have you heard?" I asked as I joined one group.

"Nothing recently," one woman said and nodded toward the woman standing next to her. "Diane lives across the street. She heard the shots. Three of them."

Diane looked my way. "At first I thought it was fireworks, then I realized no one would be shooting off fireworks at this time of the year or this early in the morning." She looked at my belly. "Do you have a child here?"

"Stepson," I said and left that group to continue on until I reached the deputy guarding the driveway.

"You can't go in," he repeated as I neared. "Please stay back with the others."

"Do you know if Deputy Sergeant Wade Kingsley is here?" I asked.

"No, Ma'am, I do not know." The deputy waved another car away from the driveway. "Please step back," he repeated to me.

Reluctantly, I did as ordered, but I kept looking toward the school building. Somewhere in there Jason was either injured, dead, or, hopefully, hiding. "Please be all right," I silently prayed.

I wanted everyone to be all right; however, in the distance I could hear a siren, the sound growing louder and louder. Soon I saw the outline of an ambulance, lights flashing as it screamed its way toward the school's entrance. At the last moment, the deputy stepped aside, allowing it to pass, but before he could regain his position, a double-cab truck with extra-large tires followed the ambulance up the drive. I caught just a glimpse of the driver, but I knew who it was. Daniel Hart, Danny's father.

Suddenly, I felt lightheaded, and my stomach churned, bile pushing its way into my throat. My legs were shaking, and I knew I needed to sit down or at least lean against something. "You all right, P.J.?" a familiar voice asked, the gentle touch of a hand on my arm. "Do you want to sit down?"

"Yes," I said, and allowed Wade's sister to help me ease down to a sitting position on the curb.

"Have you heard anything?" she asked, crouching beside me.

I shook my head, tears making it difficult for me to talk. "This morning, Jason . . . Jason was afraid something would happen. He was afraid Danny would beat him up. But this is worse, so much worse."

"Think positive thoughts," she said. "Is Wade in there?"

"The deputy didn't know. Oh, Ginny, we should have done what you suggested, pulled him out of here and sent him to Galesburg."

"He wanted to be here," she said and handed me a linen hanky. "He told me that."

I wiped away tears and blew my nose, then looked at the fancy embroidery on the cloth, and had to laugh. "I didn't think anyone used these anymore."

"Just part of the image."

She meant her interior decorator image, of course. An image which, at this very moment, was getting soiled. The stiletto heels of her black boots were sinking into the wet grass, and the hem of her tailored, grey wool coat was dragging in the same mud that was soiling my jacket. She held her hand out for the hanky she'd given me, but I shook my head. "I'll wash it then give it back." I stuffed it in my jacket pocket. "I'm guessing you were either on your way to see a client or with one. How did you know to come here?"

"I was on my way. I heard about the shooting on the radio, so I called them and told them I'd be late." She pointed down the street a short way. "I actually got here before you. I'm parked over there. You want to sit in my car, or do you prefer this cold curb?"

"Car sounds better," I said, my bottom already feeling the chill.

Ginny helped me back onto my feet and we crossed over to her car. More and more cars were arriving, parents stepping out to join others, sharing what they knew and waiting to hear anything new.

Once inside Ginny's car, I tried calling Wade but was immediately instructed to leave a message.

"That probably means he's here," Ginny said.

I left a message. "I'm with your sister, parked across the street from the school. Call when you can."

My phone rang less than a minute later, and I immediately punched the accept button. I didn't look at the caller ID, so when a woman asked, "Is this P.J. Benson?" I was surprised and confused.

"Yes. Who is this?"

"Laura. Laura Parks. I'm the receptionist at Homes4Homeless. I met you last week when you came by with Anna." Laura paused for a moment, then continued, almost whispering. "It's Anna I'm calling about. Do you know where she is?"

I remembered Laura, but I wasn't sure why she was calling me or even how she got my cell phone number. "No, I don't. Why?"

"Yesterday, before I left, she said she'd leave me a note and let me know how the board meeting went," Laura said, her voice still hushed. "I haven't found any note, and one of the board members just told me Anna didn't show up at the meeting last night. I tried calling her but didn't get an answer. I don't know, maybe it's nothing, but something doesn't feel right. I guess I'm wondering if she started labor and went to the hospital. I thought you might know if that was why she wasn't at the meeting."

I had been watching the school as Laura talked, my focus on what was going on there rather than what had happened to Anna. "I haven't heard anything," I said as another ambulance went screaming by.

"Are you all right?" Laura asked. "Are you at the hospital?"

"No, I'm at my son's school. There's a shooting going on." Cars slowly drove by Ginny's car, people looking toward the school. "I can't really talk now, Laura, but I'll see what I can find out. Should I call this number?"

"Yes, please. Maybe I'm being paranoid, but I'm worried about her."

Chapter Thirty-Four

Ginny started her car, turned the fan on full blast, and in moments warm air filled the interior. We didn't talk during this time, simply sat staring toward the school entrance. After several minutes, to avoid the possibility of carbon monoxide, she turned off the engine. I heard, then saw, one of the two ambulances that had gone onto the school grounds come back to the main road, lights flashing and siren blaring. Again, the deputy stepped aside, and the ambulance sped by Ginny's car, heading toward Zenith's main intersection. It went through the flashing red light without stopping, past the library and post office, and on toward Kalamazoo. A part of me wanted to tell Ginny to follow the ambulance, wanted to arrive at the hospital when it did, so I could see who was inside. Reason told me to stay where I was, wait until I heard from Wade or at least knew who had been shot.

I expected to see the second ambulance leave soon after the first, but seconds went by, then minutes, and no other vehicles came from the school. The car was getting cold, so Ginny started the engine again. "Waiting's the hardest part," she said.

I decided to call Anna. I might as well do something while waiting.

She didn't answer her cell phone, so I left a message. Then I called Connie. If Anna was in labor, Connie should be with her, helping her give birth. That was the plan.

Connie didn't answer, so I left a message. "Are you with Anna? If so, call when you can. Oh, and let her know Laura Parks at the charity is worried about her."

"I might win a bet," I told Ginny after I ended the message. "I bet Anna she'd have her baby before I had mine. Looks like I win."

"You look like a sneeze might put you in labor," Ginny said and turned on the radio. She switched from station to station, from music, to sports, to talk. "How is it I can get Chicago news but no local news," she grumbled, and after several tries, she turned off both the radio and the car's engine.

"Look!" I pointed toward the school's driveway. A group of children were walking toward the main road, two adults with them, keeping them together. Small children. "Looks like they've let out the young fives or kindergarteners," I said and opened the car door.

Parents rushed to where the deputy still stood by the entrance. He tried to stop them from going up the drive toward the children, but he couldn't hold some of the parents back. I watched mothers and fathers race forward, then drop to their knees and hug their children. Ginny and I walked over to where the rest of the parents waited.

One mother headed for the two women who had come out with the children and for several minutes talked with them. Slowly she came back to where Ginny and I and dozens of other parents stood. "She said the kindergarteners were never in any danger. They heard shots, but don't know who was shot or how many. They think the police have the situation under control."

I noticed the deputy at the gate nodding as he talked on his shoulder radio. Moments later, he came closer to where I and the others were standing. "They're letting them out in classroom groups," he said. "Please wait until your child reaches the end of the driveway before you go to him or her."

He should have saved his breath. As soon as the next group came into view, parents rushed past him to meet their children halfway. Ginny and I waited . . . and waited . . . and waited. Soon the cars parked along the side of the road had diminished to just a handful and only a few of us stood near the entrance. Finally, one father had had it. "I'm going up there," he said and headed for the school building, ignoring the deputy's demands to stop.

A woman followed him. Then another and another. I looked at Ginny, and we both started for the school. As we neared the building, I saw the second ambulance parked near the school's side entrance door. Right next to it was the black pickup that I believed belonged to Daniel Hart. Several sheriff's patrol cars surrounded the truck. The ambulance attendants were wheeling a gurney out of the school, the small body on it obviously a child's. Boy or girl, I couldn't tell. Bandages covered most of the face.

Two other children sat on a bench near the doorway. One had a white bandage wrapped around his upper arm, the other had a bandage covering his forehead. I didn't see Wade, didn't hear him come up behind me. "Jason's okay," he said, placing a hand on my shoulder and on Ginny's. "Shaken up and crying, but okay. They'll bring him out in a few minutes. They're taking his statement."

I leaned back against Wade's firm body, the tension I'd been holding ever since hearing of the shooting easing out of me. Jason was all right. He wasn't dead, wasn't wounded. But there had been casualties. I looked up at Wade. "What happened? Was it Danny?"

Wade grunted his answer, then stepped back. The sheriff had just brought Danny's father out of the building in handcuffs. "Gotta go," Wade said. "Jason will tell you everything. When he comes out, he can go home."

Wade joined the sheriff, and Ginny and I stepped to the side so the ambulance attendant could close the ambulance doors. Danny's mother came out of the school next, crying. One of the ambulance drivers said something to her, and she nodded, then went to the truck her husband had been driving earlier. The ambulance pulled away, siren blaring and lights flashing, and the black truck followed.

It was then that I saw Howard talking to the principal's secretary. I wasn't surprised to see him at the school. I think he has one of those police scanners and probably knew about the shooting as soon as the police did.

I remembered the school secretary's first name was April, but I couldn't remember her last name. She was nodding at something Howard said, her cheeks shiny with tears. She turned when a short, stocky man with gray hair and a beard limped out of the school building. "Burt!" April cried out and rushed toward the man. "Oh my god, Burt. Are you all right?"

Burt shook his head, his shoulders slumped, and April wrapped her arms around him. I couldn't hear what he said to her, but I could tell he was crying, and I heard April say, "It's all right. You had no choice."

Howard saw us then and slowly walked over to join Ginny and me. "What a morning," he said as he neared.

"Do you know what happened?" Ginny asked before I had a chance to say anything.

"Bits and pieces." He nodded back at Burt and April. "She said Burt stopped him. All I can say is thank goodness. If he hadn't, who knows how bad this could have been."

The way Burt was dressed, in baggy jeans and a plaid flannel shirt, I didn't think he was one of the teachers. Howard guessed my unspoken question. "Burt's the custodian," he said. "April said Danny was going down the hallway, shooting into walls, shooting at anything and everything when Burt stepped out from the cafeteria and hit Danny with a shovel. Hit him right in the head with the edge. Split his face wide open."

I grimaced, the image of Danny Hart's face cut open turning my stomach.

"Then, what does that idiot of a father do when he gets here?" Howard said. "Instead of being glad his son didn't shoot more people than he did and is still alive, the guy goes after Burt. Starts throwing punches. Cussing. And, when one of the deputies tried to stop him, he starts fighting him." Howard shook his head. "I hope they throw the book at the guy."

I agreed, but it was something else Howard had said that bothered me. "You said it was good that Danny didn't shoot more people than he did. We saw one ambulance leave. Do you know who was in that?"

Howard nodded. "Sandy." He paused, and I could tell he was struggling with his emotions. "I don't know if she'll make it. From what April told me, Sandy planned on talking to the two boys, then she was going to take them to class and talk to their classmates. Jason was in her office when Danny walked into the building, pulled the gun, and started shooting."

"Oh, my gosh," was all I could say.

"She probably saved Jason's life. April saw Sandy push Jason behind her. She was shutting the door when Danny shot her. Somehow Sandy must have managed to lock the door because April said Danny couldn't get in. While he was shouting how he was going to kill everyone, April ran down the hall yelling 'shooter in the school.' "

Howard looked over at the two students near the entrance. Each now had a parent close by, along with a teacher or sheriff's deputy. "Her warning," he continued, "alerted the teachers and they went into lockdown. I think those two were hit by fragments of wall sent into the rooms. If April hadn't yelled the warning and Burt hadn't stopped Danny it could have been worse. A lot worse."

"The one I feel sorry for," I said, "is Danny's mother." Her facial expression, when she climbed into the truck to follow the ambulance, had relayed her emotions. "Her son wasn't nice to Jason, but still, he was her baby."

"I'm more worried about Jason," Ginny said. "I sure hope the principal survives."

"They took her to Bronson," Howard said. "As soon as I know Jason's all right, I'm going there." He looked at her, then me. "I'll call and let you two know how she's doing."

"Yes, keep us posted." I was going to say more, but my cell phone rang. I considered ignoring it, then decided to at least see who was calling. It was Connie. All the while watching for Jason to come out, I answered. "Did she have a boy or a girl?"

Connie's response was not what I expected. "I have no idea," she said. "If we're talking about Anna, the last time I talked to her she said she was feeling fine, just nervous about a report she had to give last night. Why, what have you heard?"

"She didn't show up for the meeting. Didn't give that report. And she's not answering her phone."

"Hmm, that is strange." Connie made a clicking sound with her tongue, then went on. "Tell you what, P.J., I'll call the two hospitals in Kalamazoo and see if, for some reason, she ended up in one or the other. I'll let you know what I find out. And, if you hear from her, let me know. Okay?"

"Sounds good."

"By the way," Connie added, "I just heard on the radio there was a shooting at the school in Zenith. That's where your stepson goes, isn't it?"

"That's where I am at right now," I told her. "And I think I see Jason coming out. I'll talk to you later."

I ended the call before she had a chance to say anything. Both Ginny and I waved our arms and yelled, "Jason!"

He ran to me and buried his head against my side. His body shook with sobs, and I reached down and hugged him close. Ginny kneeled beside him. "It's okay, honey," both she and I repeated, over and over. "You're okay."

We were concentrating on Jason, so I'm not sure when Howard left, but by the time Jason cried himself out, Howard was gone. Hand-in-hand, Ginny, Jason, and I walked back to the road and our parked cars. The act of walking, of moving away from the school building seemed to help Jason, and by the time we reached the main road, he was asking questions. Did we know if Mrs. Singer was all right? Was his dad still at the school? Was Danny dead?

The only one I could answer was about his dad. "He left with Mr. Hart."

At Ginny's car, I gave her a hug. "I can't tell you how much I appreciate you being here. Do you still have time to meet with your client?"

"Are you kidding? They can wait. I'm hoping you'll invite me back to the house." She ruffled Jason's hair. "If I come home with you, kiddo, will you tell us what happened?"

He nodded, and she looked at me.

"Of course you're invited."

"In that case, I'll be there in five."

Chapter Thirty-Five

It was mid-morning, but Ginny grabbed a beer from the fridge while I made tea for me and poured a glass of orange juice for Jason. We all went into the living room, and, as if sensing Jason's emotional needs, Baraka sat next to him. At first Jason said nothing, simply drank his juice and petted Baraka's head. Ginny was the one who spoke first. "That had to be scary," she said.

Jason nodded but still said nothing, his expression way too serious for a seven-year-old. In less than a year, he'd experienced an explosion that killed his mother and now a shooting that might have killed his principal, or him. The one thing I remembered the counselor we'd taken Jason to see last fall saying was get him to talk about it. So, I tried. "Tell us what happened."

Jason looked at me. "Danny shot Mrs. Singer."

"I know. Where were you when he shot her?"

"In her office. Next to her. She said, as soon as Danny came, she would take us to class. We were waiting for him."

"And when he showed up . . ." Ginny prompted.

"She pushed me back," he said, his attention switching to Ginny. "Pushed me real hard, and I fell down. And then I heard lots of banging, like when Dad shoots his gun." Jason's voice began to quaver. "And . . . and she fell down."

"What did you do then?" I asked as calmly as I could.

"I got up," he said. "Mrs. Singer told me to lock the door and to do it quick, so I did. Then she told me to get behind her desk."

"Thank goodness you did," Ginny said.

"I asked her what I should do next," Jason said, "but she didn't say anything, so I called 9-1-1, like they do on TV, and asked the lady who answered what I should do."

"That was very smart of you," I said.

He smiled. "That's what Dad said, too."

I'd forgotten that Wade had already seen and talked to Jason.

"What did the lady who answered tell you to do?" Ginny asked.

"She told me I needed to stop the bleeding. But I couldn't. I tried. Really, I tried." His eyes teared up again. "I did everything the lady on the phone said to do. I grabbed the sweater from the back of Mrs. Singer's chair and pressed it against the place where blood was coming out, but the blood kept coming."

I scooted over next to him and slid an arm around his small shoulders. "You did everything exactly right."

"But it didn't stop the bleeding."

The way he looked at me, tears swimming in his eyes, broke my heart. I prayed Sandy Singer lived, for Jason's sake as well as hers.

My cell phone rang, startling me. I ignored it. Jason needed my attention. It rang again. "Aren't you going to answer it?" he asked. "Maybe it's the hospital."

I got up and found my purse and phone, and, in a way, Jason was right. "It's Howard," I said.

Howard started speaking the moment I answered. "She's out of surgery and in recovery. They won't let me see her. Just family. But the doctor said she'll be fine."

I put the phone on speaker mode and had Howard repeat the message so Jason and Ginny could hear, and then I asked, "What about Danny? Is he there or at the other hospital?"

"He's here," Howard said. "I talked to his mother. She blames her husband for all of this. She said last night he started drinking and had his gun out. He kept ranting about teaching Wade a lesson, that no one respected him or Danny. She's sure her husband didn't lock the gun up before going to bed, and she's not surprised Danny took the gun to school and started shooting. He's talked about it. She said she's told her husband they needed to get Danny help, that they should take him to a psychologist, but that he just poo-pooed the idea."

Both Ginny and I shook our heads in dismay.

"What I don't understand," I said, "Is how Danny could shoot with a broken finger. Last time I saw him, his hand was all wrapped up."

"April mentioned that," Howard said. "When I was talking to her earlier today. She said yesterday his hand and wrist were swaddled with an elastic wrap, but when she saw Danny this morning, all he had was a splint on his middle finger. No wrapping. And he was holding the gun with both hands."

Jason nodded and said, "He wasn't shooting very straight."

"You breaking his finger probably saved a lot of lives," Ginny said.

"Yeah, but he wouldn't have been mad at me if I hadn't broken it."

"Danny was mad at everyone, according to his mother," Howard said through the phone. "In her opinion, it was just a matter of time before this happened. She said, once Danny gets out of the hospital, she is taking him to therapy. And, she is leaving her husband."

Jason's demeanor changed after Howard's call. Suddenly he was hungry. While I fixed him something to eat, Ginny called the client she'd been scheduled to meet that morning. "They still want to meet," she said when she came into the kitchen. "Can you handle this alone?"

I assured her I could, and she took off. After he'd eaten, Jason turned on the TV, and I tried calling Anna again.

Again, no answer. I was getting worried.

Jason and I watched the noon news. One of the parents had sent in a video of all the cars parked on the side of the road in front of the school. I saw me standing talking to the deputy. I looked like a blimp. Jason was disappointed the pictures taken in front of and inside the school didn't show him, although his name was mentioned.

And then, that was it. The weather was next, followed by a report about a new store opening. By the end of the news program, Jason was curled up on the couch, asleep, Baraka stretched out on the floor in front, guarding him. I seriously considered lying down for a nap, but not knowing what had happened to Anna had me calling Connie again.

"Nothing," she said. "I have no idea what's happened to her. She isn't in either hospital. I even stopped by her place. She's not there. Do you think she might be with a client?"

"If so, why doesn't she answer her phone? Why didn't she go to that meeting last night?" There were too many unanswered questions.

"I'm on my way over to see Sarah," Connie said. "She called me just a bit ago. She's home with the baby, and I think the reality of being a mother and being responsible for another life just hit her. I'll be at her place for a while, so if you hear anything about Anna, call me, okay?"

"Will do," I promised and hung up.

I was about to call the Homes4Homeless number to see if Laura had heard anything about Anna when Baraka started barking, and I realized a blue Ford had pulled into the yard. "Who's here?" Jason asked from the couch.

"Howard."

I had the backdoor open by the time Howard reached the top step. "How's Jason doing?" he asked as he came into the kitchen.

I didn't have to answer. Jason came through the doorway asking questions. "Is she gonna live? Did they have to give her more blood? I tried to stop the blood, really I did."

"She's going to be fine," Howard assured him. "And she thanks you for saving her life."

"Really?" Jason beamed and came closer.

"I was able to see her for just a few minutes," Howard said. "She did lose a lot of blood, but the doctors said it could have been worse if you hadn't used that sweater and pushed against the wound. I'm proud of you."

"Maybe I'll be a doctor when I grow up," Jason said, sounding sure of himself.

"You'd be a good one," Howard said, then looked at me. "I saw your husband. He stopped by the hospital to check on Sandy and also to talk to the boy's mother. Daniel Hart won't be going home for a while. Besides hitting that deputy, seems he has a felony conviction and wasn't even allowed to own a gun."

"Is Danny gonna be all right?" Jason asked.

Howard sighed and patted Jason's shoulder. "He'll live, but I don't know what his face will look like. He's going to have a scar—" Howard traced a line across his face. "And he's lost an eye. What a shame."

"I hope his mother can get him help," I said. If she didn't, I had a feeling the boy would grow up as mean as his father.

"Well, I need to be heading home. I've got a friend visiting, and we're working on a project, but I wanted to let you know what was up." Howard stepped toward the door, then paused. "Wade said to let you know he'd be heading home soon. Seems he has one more matter to take care of." Howard grinned.

"Good thing you grabbed him when you did." His last statement had me puzzled, but he didn't elaborate. One hour later, I had my answer.

Chapter Thirty-Six

The first thing Wade did when he came into the house was pick up his son and give him a hug. A long hug. Too long, according to Jason who began to wiggle in his dad's arms. "I'm okay, Dad," he said. "I'm okay."

Wade finally set him back on his feet. "Yes, you are." He tousled Jason's hair. "Now, go upstairs. I want to talk to P.J., in private."

"Oh oh." Jason looked at me. "You musta done something bad. That's what Daddy always said to Mommy when she did something bad."

I looked at Wade, but he said nothing, simply motioned for his son to scoot. Once Jason was upstairs, Wade took my hand and led me into the living room. "Sit," he ordered and motioned at a spot on the couch.

I sat, and he sat beside me. I still had no idea what was up, but I knew from the big sigh he gave that he was upset. Finally, he took my right hand in his and said, "When were you going to tell me?"

"Tell you what?"

"That she was harassing you. That she cornered you in the grocery store."

"Oh." Now I understood. "You mean Marge. I didn't say anything because it wasn't that big a deal."

"What about running you off the road. I think that qualifies as a big deal."

That surprised me. "She was the one?"

"I suspected as much Sunday. When I was at her place, I noticed red paint on her right front fender. I hoped it wasn't her, but today when I confronted her, she confessed." Wade shook his head. "She told me she was just trying to scare you, that she didn't mean for you to go into the ditch. As if saying that made everything all right. As if . . ." Wade expelled a long breath. "My god, P.J., you should have told me that she has been watching you. Stalking you."

"I didn't realize she was." But now it seemed reasonable.

"Howard said he's seen a silver Honda car go by here several times over the last few weeks."

"I didn't notice. Really. I've been so busy getting those taxes finished for my clients, I haven't had time to look outside, much less keep track of cars going by."

"So, you had no idea?"

"I remember Howard saying something about a car going by, but last week was the first time I really noticed something strange."

Wade said nothing, but the way he looked at me, I knew he wanted me to explain.

"There was a car parked by the side of the road, up toward Howard's place. I saw it when I let Baraka out. I couldn't figure out why it was there, and when it left, it went by here really slowly then sped up. That bothered me a little."

"But not enough to mention it to me."

"Other things were going on, Wade. I forgot about it. After all, it simply could have been someone having car trouble."

Wade shook his head, and I realized I should have mentioned it, especially since the house had been broken into a couple times.

"What about yesterday?"

"What about it?"

"One of the clerks at the grocery store told me what she'd seen and heard. She said Marge had you cornered over in the vegetable section."

I smiled, remembering. "She made me buy a head of cauliflower instead of a box of mac and cheese."

He frowned. "Cauliflower?"

"It's not important." I took Wade's hand in both of mine and brought his fingertips to my lips. "Honey, she upset me, but only because she sounded so desperate. What does upset me is she was waiting for me last Wednesday night, that she caused me to go off the road. Our baby could have been hurt by what she did." The more I thought about it, the angrier I got. "What are we going to do about her?"

"In a way, that's up to you." He paused to kiss me. "She did confess to running you off the road, and we have witnesses of her harassing you and stalking you. If you want, we can press charges. Otherwise, I want her served with a restraining order. I don't want her anywhere near you or me."

"A restraining order sounds good."

Wade nodded. "After the talk she and I had today, I don't think she has any delusions of romantic feelings on my part, and I've told the sheriff I don't want her assigned to any investigations I'm on."

"Will she lose her job?"

"I don't know, and I don't care."

I snuggled close to him. "I don't think we need to press charges, not unless she breaks the restraining order. Okay?"

He agreed, and I felt it was time to tell him my concerns. As concisely as I could, I explained what was going on with Anna. "She planned on showing the other members of the board the doctored bank statements last night during their regular board meeting, but she didn't show up. I had an email from her earlier yesterday afternoon. She said Madeline Welkum wanted to see her before the meeting. Anna said she'd let me know how the meeting went. She didn't mention anything about having labor pains. Connie hasn't heard from her, and she checked to see if Anna had been admitted to either of the hospitals. She hasn't been. Connie also checked Anna's house. She's not there. Anna's not answering her phone. So, where is she? What happened to her between when she sent that email yesterday to now?"

"Where was she the last time you knew?"

"At the charity house. Laura, the receptionist, saw her there Monday afternoon. Anna told Laura she would leave her a note and let her know how the meeting went."

"And what time was that?"

"I'm not sure." I tried to remember what Laura had said. "Maybe five o'clock. Sometime around then."

"And this Laura hasn't heard anything from her?"

"No." I leaned back against the couch, exhausted from worry. "I know this sounds crazy, Wade, but I feel she needs my help."

I felt him tense. "How can you help her?"

"I don't know." I turned my head so I could look at him. His body language relayed his feelings about me getting involved in other people's problems, yet I couldn't stop myself. "I just feel I need to go to the last place where she was seen, to the Homes4Homeless office."

He started to say something, but I stopped him. "Don't tell me to let law enforcement take care of this. There's no evidence of a crime. There's nothing you or Kalamazoo's Safety Officers could do."

"Or you."

"I want to go."

Chapter Thirty-Seven

An hour later, Jason, Wade, and I were in his Jeep headed for Kalamazoo. Wade had finally agreed that it wouldn't hurt to at least stop by the charity's offices and see if I could learn anything about Anna. After that, the three of us would go out to dinner.

First thing I noticed when we pulled up in front of the charity office was Anna's car wasn't one of the two in the parking lot. "Looks like she isn't here," I said, "but maybe someone has heard from her."

Wade pulled into the lot and parked next to the walkway that led to the building. "Do you want me to come in with you?"

I considered the idea for a moment, then shook my head. "No, let me go in and see what's up. I shouldn't be long."

I slid out of the Jeep, but before I closed the door, he said, "If you're not out in ten minutes, we're coming in. I know how you women start gabbing, and Jason and I are getting hungry. Right, partner?"

"Right," Jason agreed from the backseat.

I wasn't particularly hungry, but I also didn't plan on "gabbing" with anyone. "I'll make it quick," I assured my two males.

Quick, however, was not a word that described a nine-months-pregnant woman. It had only been a little over a week since I'd last gone up the steps to the front porch, but I was panting by the time I reached the decking. I paused for a moment to catch my breath and mentally plan what I would say once inside. Although it was past five o'clock and the office was technically closed, the two cars in the lot gave me hope that someone would come to the door when I knocked.

Turned out I didn't need to worry. The front door wasn't locked. I opened it and walked inside.

Laura wasn't at the receptionist desk, but the door behind her was open and I could hear a shredder running in one of the back offices. "Hello!" I called out. "Anyone here?"

The shredder stopped and a moment later a woman I'd never seen before stepped out of Jewel's office. Her shoulder-length black hair was a tangled mess, and she had dark smudges of mascara under her eyes. Her face had a sallow, unhealthy look, and the magenta wool turtleneck and gray slacks she had on clung to her thin body. From her looks, I assumed she was one of the homeless the charity was helping.

"We're closed," she said.

"I'm looking for Mrs. Welkum," I said. "Is she here?"

The woman frowned. "Who are you?"

"P.J.," I said. "P.J. Benson. That is, P.J. Kingsley. Who are you?"

"Jewel Wiscoff."

"You're Jewel?" Taken aback, I stared at her. "You're Mrs. Welkum's daughter?"

"Yes." She gave a snort. "Her ever loving offspring."

"Is your mother here?" Although there were two cars in the lot, I didn't see or hear any signs of another person.

"She's busy." Jewel started toward me. "Come back tomorrow."

There was something about Madeline Welkum's daughter that made me nervous, and I automatically moved back, toward the front door. "I'm looking for a friend. Anna Carr."

Jewel stopped. "Why do you want to see her?"

I noticed she didn't say Anna wasn't there. I also noticed she glanced toward the door that led to the cellar.

"I need to tell her something. Something about the audit."

The moment I said the word "audit" I knew I shouldn't have. Jewel frowned, her posture stiffening. "You know about the audit. Are you the one who has the pictures?"

"Where's Anna?" I said as I took another step backward. "Where's your mother?"

Again, Jewel glanced toward the cellar door. When she looked back at me, she was smiling. "They're working on the audit downstairs. I think they've been waiting for you."

The way she said it sent a shiver through me. Were Anna and Mrs. Welkum downstairs dead? Were there two bodies lying on cold concrete somewhere below me?

I needed to get out of the house. Needed to let Wade know there was a problem. As far as I could tell, Jewel didn't have a weapon, but in my condition, I didn't want to have to fight my way out. I tried to keep my expression neutral as I said, "Before I help them, I have to get something from my car."

I took another step back.

"No." Jewel quickly closed the distance between us. "You need to see them first."

She grabbed the sleeve of my winter jacket and pulled. She was thin but wiry, and much stronger than I expected; however, I was used to playing tug-of-war with Baraka. I braced my feet and using my shorter stature and lower center of balance to counter her strength, I stopped her from moving me back into the office area and the door to the cellar.

She practically snarled at me, and using both hands, jerked my arm downward.

Off balance, I fell forward.

My knees hit the carpeting, then my belly. Using both hands, she readjusted her hold on my right arm and began to drag me back into the office area. Feet stretched out behind me, I flailed my left arm out and tried to grab onto a leg of Laura's desk. I missed. Jewel kept pulling.

I was halfway through the doorway when I twisted my body to the left and reached for her right hand with my left. My first attempt to bend her middle finger back barely moved it. I knew I wouldn't have much time before she realized what I was doing, so the second time my fingers circled hers, I jerked back as hard as I could.

With a yelp of pain, Jewel let go of my sleeve, took a step back, and kicked out at me. I grabbed her boot with both of my hands and twisted. Off balance, she fell.

I managed to get to my feet the same time she did. As she reached for my jacket, I shuffled backwards, again working my way to the front door. The look on her face was pure determination, but I was just as determined. I batted away her hand when she again tried to grab my arm. I yelled for help, praying Wade or someone would hear.

Wade had said he would come in ten minutes, but I had no idea how long I'd been in the house or if he was just kidding. The moment my back hit the front wall, I started throwing punches without actually aiming.

My right fist connected with the side of her face, but she also managed to grab the front of my jacket. She pulled, once again putting me off balance. I reached back with my left hand, felt the wall, then the edge of the door. I wrapped my fingers around the doorknob, turned it, and pulled as I twisted to the side.

The door opened, cold air entering the room, but Jewel shoved me backwards, pinning my arm between my body and the door. The door clicked shut again, the doorknob now poking into my side. "You are going downstairs," she growled, her face so close I could smell the liquor on her breath and the cigarette smoke that clung to her body.

"No I'm not!" I twisted and pushed against her, using my extended belly as a wedge.

She punched at my belly, and I prayed she wasn't hurting the baby, but I knew I had to get away from her or it wouldn't matter. Once. Twice, I managed to get my hand on the doorknob, but I couldn't get the door open.

And then it did open, the door shoving me forward and into Jewel.

She fell back and I fell on top of her. Quickly, I rolled to the side.

"What the hell!" Wade's voice boomed above me as I grabbed Jewel's leg.

"Stop her!"

I lay on my side, panting, as Wade pulled Jewel to her feet and away from me. She swore and kicked at him, but with little effect. Once he had her arms pinned behind her back, he looked down at me. "P.J., are you all right? Do you want me to call an ambulance?"

My adrenalin rush easing, I pushed myself up to a sitting position. "I think I'm okay," I said, my hands rubbing over my abdomen. "She kept hitting me, hitting my belly."

Jewel gave a yelp of pain, and I was pretty sure Wade had just tightened his hold on her arms. He could pull them out of their sockets as far as I cared.

Slowly I rose to my feet, waited a second to make sure I was okay, then looked at Jewel. The expression in her eyes was pure hatred.

"Go sit down for a while," Wade said, nodding toward the couch. "I'm going to take her out to the car, cuff her, and call this in. Then we can talk."

I looked at the couch by the side of the room. A chance to sit sounded good, but I was worried about Anna and Madeline Welkum. "I'm going to check out the cellar," I told Wade.

He looked around, then back at me. "No. Wait for me."

I should have, but as soon as he went outside with Jewel, I walked back into the office area. Cautiously, I opened the door to the cellar. I was immediate hit with the smells of mold, urine, and something else I couldn't identify. The stairway was dark, too dark to see anything. Staying where I was, I felt around for a light switch, found what felt like one, and snapped it on.

A bare bulb on the wall halfway down the stairway barely illuminated the steps. I heard a noise from below, but I wasn't sure what it was. Mice? Rats? Humans?

"Hello," I called down the stairway. "Anna? Mrs. Welkum? Are you down there?"

Again, I heard a noise, but I still couldn't make it out.

I debated waiting for Wade or going down. Then I heard what definitely sounded like a groan. "I'm coming," I said and took hold of the handrail along the wall. To my relief, it felt sturdy. Slowly I started down the steps.

Concentrating on each step, I didn't notice the spider web until it brushed against my face. I let out a squeal and batted away the slender strands. I don't know if a spider actually ran across my forehead, but I let go of the railing and used both hands to brush my face and hair. Shivering, I continued down the steps.

At the base of the steps, I searched for another light switch. The moment I found one, I flipped it on. As light illuminated the small area in front of me, I took in a breath, and then I yelled, "Wade! Call for an ambulance."

Chapter Thirty-Eight

Anna was tied to a wooden chair, a wide strip of tape covering her mouth. She'd twisted her body so her hips were as far off the seat of the chair as she could get them, but ropes around her chest and legs held her prisoner. Eyes narrowed, she was breathing hard. What worried me most was the pool of liquid I saw on the concrete below her hips. Was the liquid simply urine or had her water broken?

I ignored Madeline Welkum, who was tied to a padded office-chair a short distance away and went to Anna's side. Quickly, I pulled the tape from Anna's mouth.

"My baby's coming," she gasped. "The chair. It's stopping her. She can't get out."

Anna stopped talking and started panting, and I could see the contraction of her belly. I moved around to the back of the chair and tried to untie the knot holding the rope around her legs. Jewel had pulled the knot tight and I couldn't get it loose. Desperately, I looked around for something to use to cut the rope and saw nothing that would work.

Above us, I heard footsteps. "Wade!" I yelled. "Wade, I need you. Come down here. Quick."

His first steps on the stairway were hesitant, but the moment he came into view, he hurried down and to my side. "Use your pocketknife and cut the ropes around her legs," I ordered, "so I can get her pants off. She's in labor."

He did as I asked, cutting the rope and releasing her legs, then, as I pulled Anna's maternity slacks and underwear down to her knees, he cut the ropes that held her arms and hands in place. Her pants were soaked with urine and amniotic fluid, the odor turning my stomach. I tried not to breathe in any more often than necessary as I helped her lie down on a dry area of the floor.

"My daughter," I heard behind me and glanced over to see Wade had pulled the tape from Madeline Welkum's mouth. "You've got to stop her."

"She's upstairs handcuffed to a desk," Wade said. "And my son's watching her until an officer arrives, so she's not going anywhere."

"Did you call for an ambulance?" I asked, taking Anna's shoes off so I could completely remove her pants and underwear.

"I did." He started cutting the ropes that held Mrs. Welkum in place.

"I want Connie," Anna cried. "I need Connie." She stopped talking, her face contorted with pain. And then she cried out, "She's coming."

* * *

When I joined Connie's Mothers-to-Be group, I certainly never expected to be involved in delivering a baby, other than my own. Wade did most of the work. Thank goodness the sheriff's department trains its deputies on what to do. Wade said, even though he'd never had to help deliver a baby before, he knew the basics.

I wasn't much help. Mostly I held Anna's hand and told her everything was going to be all right. Madeline Welkum did more. She went upstairs and got towels and water as well as a blanket to put over Anna. When the paramedics arrived, she quickly ushered them downstairs. I heard her yell at her daughter the first time she went upstairs, but I couldn't tell what she said. I wanted to know what had happened in the last twenty-four hours but taking care of Anna was our first priority.

Once Anna and her baby were in the ambulance and on their way to the hospital, I went upstairs. Jason was seated on the couch in the reception area, so I joined him. I was exhausted.

"You okay?" he asked, patting my hand.

I nodded, then slid an arm around his shoulders and hugged him. Tears slid down my cheeks, and I wasn't sure why. Relief that I was still alive? Happiness that we'd found Anna and that she and her baby were all right? Whatever the reason, I couldn't seem to stop crying.

"It's okay," Jason kept saying. "It's okay."

Finally, I had to laugh. "Yes, it's fine. I'm okay. My friend's okay. And her baby's okay."

"And Daddy got the bad lady." Jason looked through the doorway, into the office area where Wade and an officer from the Kalamazoo Public Safety were talking to Madeline Welkum. They'd moved her daughter, Jewel, onto one of the chairs in the area, and as she fought against the handcuffs holding her in place, she looked as wild-eyed as when I first saw her.

"Yes, he did," I said, so glad Wade had arrived when he did.

"I told him something was going on," Jason said. "I saw you try to open the door and I told him you wanted him to come."

"You did?" I hugged him even closer. "You are my hero."

Wade motioned for me to join them in the other room, so I gave Jason one more hug and told him we'd be through soon and once we were, we'd go out to dinner. He nodded and sat back on the couch.

"I'm so sorry," Madeline Welkum said when I joined the others. She looked over at where her daughter sat. "A year ago Jewel came to me looking for a job. She swore she was off drugs and no longer drinking. I do think she was clean back then. I certainly wouldn't have given her the job of treasurer if I'd thought she was still addicted."

She sighed. "I began to suspect something was wrong around Christmastime. She seemed jittery. Hyper. I put it off to the holidays, but then last month, she came here smelling of liquor and rambling on about this and that. I confronted her and she confessed that she was again on drugs and drinking and that she'd been getting the money to pay for her habit from Homes4Homeless. I told her she had to check into a rehab facility or I was going to turn her into the police, so she did. I thought I could cover the loss, and everything would be fine, but then the damn board sends Anna to audit the books and you show up."

She pointed at me, and I nodded.

"Oh, poor you," Jewel sneered from where she sat. "My fancy mother who wants to take care of the homeless but never had time for her daughter. You pretend you're so perfect. Well, you aren't." She looked up at Wade. "Get me out of here. She makes me sick

Chapter Thirty-Nine

Since the office for Homes4Homeless was within the Kalamazoo city limits, it was the Kalamazoo Public Safety Officer who made the official arrest, not Wade. Wade, Jason, and I were allowed to leave with the promise that Wade and I would go to the station in the next twenty-four hours and give our statements. I think Madeline Welkum went to the station with the officer. I wasn't sure, and I really didn't care. I'd had enough drama for one day.

"You still want to go out to dinner?" Wade asked.

"Beats cooking at home," I said, but then I turned to Jason. "What about you? You've had quite a day."

"I'm hungry. Can we go to Louie's?" He looked at me. "Dad used to take me there. Mom didn't like it."

I had a feeling I was being tested. "Louie's sounds fine."

And it was fine. Over a century old, Louie's Trophy House Grill wasn't exactly a kids eating place, but the taxidermy heads on the walls were fascinating, the waitress was friendly, and Wade was able to enjoy a beer while Jason had a soda, and I had iced tea. We agreed on a pizza, and when Wade thanked Jason for warning him that I needed help and not to wait ten minutes before going into the Homes4Homeless house, Jason beamed. "I was a hero twice today."

"Yes, you were." I grabbed the hands of both of my heroes. "Thank you."

While at the restaurant I received a phone call and so did Wade. His was a report on Principal Singer's condition. "She's off the

253

critical list," he told us. My call was from Connie. She was with Anna in the hospital. "Mother and baby are doing fine," she relayed. "Both are going to spend the night. I'll let you know how they are in the morning."

Jason fell asleep on the drive home, and I had a difficult time keeping my eyes open. I knew it was going to be an early bedtime for me.

* * *

Wednesday I woke feeling slightly nauseated. I wasn't sure if it was the pizza from the night before—neither Jason nor Wade complained of indigestion—or from fighting with Jewel or from the combination of all the excitement of the day before. What I did know was I wasn't up to hosting the Mothers-to-Be group, even with just three of us. When Connie called to report on Anna's condition, I told her how I felt and asked her to call Maria and cancel. She said she would.

"They're keeping Anna and the baby one more day," Connie said. "Anna's dehydrated. I can't believe that woman kept her tied up in the basement from Monday afternoon until you rescued her."

"The baby's all right?"

"Seems to be fine. Cute little thing. They want to keep her in the hospital to make sure she doesn't get any infections. Anna said that basement was filthy."

I remembered how bad the room looked and smelled and my stomach turned over. "The woman was crazy."

"They showed her picture on TV. It's sad what drugs and alcohol can do to a person. Anyway, let me know if you don't start feeling better. You're close enough to your due date, this could be the start of labor. I don't have anything important scheduled for the day. Give me a call if you think it's time."

"I will." The idea that the discomfort I was feeling might be the start of labor made me take in a shaky breath.

For days I'd been saying I was ready, but was I?

I didn't have time to worry about it. Jason came clomping down the stairs, Baraka behind him. "Since there's no school today, can I go over to Howard's and pick out my kitten?"

"They're not old enough to leave their mother," I reminded him.

"I know, but I want to watch them play, see which one I want."

"Howard's probably busy." I didn't know what Howard did during the day, but I had a feeling entertaining a seven-year-old wasn't high on his list.

"Yesterday, when he was here, he said I could. He said just to call, and he'd come over and pick me up."

"Oh, he did, did he?"

I thought about refusing, then decided to say no would be silly. With Wade at work and Jason at Howard's, I could do my personal taxes undisturbed. "Sure. Give him a call. If he says it's all right, I can take you there. It's only a quarter of a mile. Baraka and I will walk with you. It will be good exercise." And I hoped the walk would help ease the queasiness in my stomach.

Ten minutes later, Jason and I, with Baraka between us, started for Howard's place. The snow and ice we'd had the week before had melted, the sky was blue, and the temperature was in the low forties. A perfect day for a walk.

It was also a good chance for me to reinforce Baraka's leash training. Most of the time when I took him into the woods, I let him run free. I wanted to see if he still remembered the command to heel and to sit when I stopped. As a result, the quarter mile walk to Howard's took a little longer than Jason wanted, but I was pleased that, for the most part, Baraka stayed by my side whether I walked slowly or fast, and sat the moment I stopped walking.

By the time we reached Howard's driveway, Jason was bouncing with excitement. "They're in the barn," he said, running ahead. "Come on, I'll show you."

Howard's hound, Jake, started barking as we walked down the drive by the house, and Howard came out the backdoor. "Want to see the kittens?" he called to me.

"Sure, but I'm not certain how Baraka will act."

"Well, let's find out."

I tightened my hold on Baraka's leash when we entered Howard's barn. The open door let in some light, but it took a few minutes before my eyes adjusted to the dim interior. "They're over here." Jason was already at a stack of straw on the far side of the building.

Head held high Baraka sniffed the air. I could smell dust, old timbers, and the lingering aroma of animal manure, but I knew my dog was picking up thousands more scents. "Haven't had a horse for years," Howard said, "but I bet he smells him, along with the goats I used to raise."

"I didn't know you raised goats." I hadn't known he'd had a horse, either.

He grinned. "Lots you don't know about me."

He was right.

Howard stopped beside Jason. "So, which one do you want?"

"I'm not sure."

Jason picked up a tiny gray ball of fur and held it up for me to see. The kitten squealed, and Baraka pulled toward Jason. The mother cat also rose up from where she'd been lying next to her other babies. The moment she saw Baraka, she arched her back and hissed. "Jason," I said, "you'd better put that kitten down."

I pulled Baraka back away from the straw and nest of kittens, no easy feat considering my dog's weight was primarily muscle while a third of mine was baby. The effort caused a tightening in my abdomen that I hadn't felt before, and I took in a quick breath. The feeling didn't go away, which made me nervous. "Guys, I think I'm going to let you two decide on which kitten is the cutest. Baraka and I are going to go back to the house."

"You okay?" Howard asked, his expression concerned.

"I think so."

"Want me to go with you?"

"No, I'll be all right. But I think it might be best if I'm home."

Jason didn't seem to care. He'd put the one kitten down and had picked up another. The mother cat kept watching Baraka, and I backed up farther. "Be gentle with them," I warned Jason. "They're still very little."

His "I will" was automatic, and Howard chuckled. "He'll be careful."

Howard walked with me to the door. "If you need anything . . ."

"I'll call," I assure him. "And when you get tired of Jason, bring him home."

Baraka by my side, I slowly walked back to my house. The slight sensation of nausea hadn't gone away, and I felt edgy. The edginess grew stronger when I realized there was an unfamiliar car parked next to mine. It wasn't until I reached my driveway that I saw the gate to my front yard was open and Maria was on my porch. "I cancelled," I said as I entered the yard and closed the gate behind me. "Connie was supposed to call and tell you. I'm not feeling well."

"She call." Maria came down the steps to meet me halfway. "Where is Miguel?"

"Miguel?" I didn't understand.

"Saturday, I hear you say Miguel's name, that he was here. Now nobody hear from him."

"Miguel? The Miguel who worked at Patterson's Furniture store?"

"*Sí.*" She glared at me. "He is my cousin. New to this country. He work hard, but he come see you, now no one hear from him. Where is he?"

"Oh my." Wade had told me they didn't find Miguel's body with the truck, but I hadn't heard anything since. "I don't really know where he is."

"He was here Saturday. Yes?"

"That's what I heard." I unsnapped Baraka's leash. "That's what a neighbor told my husband."

"Why Miguel here? Why he come see you?"

Either Maria was a very good actress, or she didn't know what was going on. I decided to see how she reacted to the truth. "He's been breaking into my house, that's why he's been here. He's been stealing my thumb drives, and I guess diamonds."

"No!" She shook her head violently. "Not my Miguel."

She took a step toward me, and Baraka growled. A low, threatening growl that caused her to stop and look down at him. Then she looked back at me. "Miguel not a thief. You wrong."

"I saw him," I said, my hand resting on Baraka's head, his presence giving me confidence. "Twice. I saw him come out of my house, and I saw him drive into my yard. And I think he was here once before that."

Maria continued shaking her head. "You wrong. Miguel not a thief."

"Oh yeah? Then why did he take my thumb drives? Why did he take something off the rocking chair I bought?" Her denial had fired my anger. "The DEA and CBP know what's going on at that furniture store. Brenda didn't need to be killed. Your husband's going down."

Mouth open, Maria stared at me, then squeezed her eyes shut and lowered her head. "Going down where? *Mi esposo* just find job. With *bebé* coming, he cannot go anywhere."

She sounded on the verge of tears, and her response wasn't what I'd expected. "Your husband just found a job? He isn't the boss?"

"Boss? No." She looked confused. "He work in factory. Run big machine."

"He doesn't work at Patterson's Furniture store? Isn't the boss there?"

"No. Is Miguel who work there, but he not there when I stop by to see him. That's why I come here. Where iz he?"

From the way she was acting and her expression, I was beginning to believe she didn't know anything about Miguel's actions or what went on at Patterson's Furniture. "I don't know where he is, Maria," I said. "All I know is they found his truck in a lake."

"He no own a truck."

"Okay, the truck he's been driving. They found it in a lake."

She shook her head. "I no understand. What lake?"

I named it, but I could tell she didn't recognize the name.

"And Miguel?"

"He wasn't in the truck."

"So maybe he be okay?"

"I don't know." She looked shaken, and I suddenly felt sorry for her. "Come on, let's go inside and talk. You look like you need to sit down." I knew I did. I still didn't feel right.

Maria looked back at my front door, then nodded. She led the way up the steps to the porch and stood to the side while I unlocked the door. I was proud of myself for at least remembering to lock up before taking Jason's to Howard's place.

Inside, Maria took the closest dining room chair, and Baraka sat facing her. He didn't growl or show any aggressive behavior, but he watched her closely. With him guarding her, I went into the kitchen and got two glasses, then went to the refrigerator for water. Finally, I sat across from her. "So, your husband doesn't work for Patterson's Furniture?"

"No. I tell you, no. Just Miguel."

"Hmm." I sipped my water, trying to remember why I thought Maria might be involved with Patterson's Furniture store. "Back a couple weeks ago, the day that woman was run down in front of the church, you said you were late to our Mothers-to-Be session because your husband called you."

"*Sí.* Yes. I remember."

"You were upset with him. You said he made a mistake."

She nodded. "*Sí.* I leave him at house to work on light switch. He not turn off electricity." She shrugged. "He iz idiot. Nearly kill himself."

"So that call had nothing to do with Brenda." In my mind, I'd worked it out that Maria had called and let her husband know Brenda was at the church and that was how they knew where she was and were able to set themselves up to run her down.

"I see your friend come out of the bathroom while I am talking to my husband. She go upstairs. Then, after while, you come out of bathroom and go to meeting room."

"I didn't even see you."

"Ask Tamara. She know. She see me, and she see your friend go upstairs." Maria sighed. "How I find out about Miguel?"

"I'll call my husband, see if he knows anything." I got my cell phone and tapped Wade's number. As it rang, it dawned on me what Maria had said. "You say Tamara saw Brenda go upstairs?"

"Sí. Then she make phone call."

Wade answered at that moment. "You okay?"

"Maybe feeling a few contractions."

"Do you want me to come home?"

"No, not yet. I'm calling because one of the other pregnant women in my group is a cousin of the guy that kept breaking in here. I told her you found his truck. I think she deserves to know if he's alive or dead."

I saw Maria blanch when I said "dead," but I knew I'd want to know.

"No body, so far. They've had divers looking for three days now, but the lake is full of debris. Hard to say if he's in there or not, but tell her, if he gets in touch with her, for him to turn himself in. He needs to do it for his own good."

"I'll tell her."

"And, for your peace of mind, your buddy Ken contacted me. He's due here this afternoon."

"He's all right?"

"He sounded a little shaken up, but otherwise, I think he's okay." Wade paused. "You call if you need me. Promise?"

I promised, and after I hung up, I relayed all I knew about Miguel to Maria. Her usual brusque manner was gone, and her sigh was a long one. "So, maybe he dead. His mama take me in when my mama kick me out. She tell me to keep eye on him. I fail her."

"He was really nice to me," I said, feeling sorry for her. "At the store he went and found an infant rocking chair for me. One I'd seen on the store's website. He even carried it out to my car for me." And now that was gone, too.

Another tightening sensation in my belly made me cringe.

"You all right?" Maria asked.

I took a deep breath. "I think I might be going to have a baby." I picked up my phone. "I need to call Connie."

"You want me stay?"

"No. No, you go." I punched Connie's number. "I'll be fine."

Maria stood but didn't step away from the table. "You're sure?"

I nodded yes, and when Connie answered, I said, "I think it's time."

Chapter Forty

After I told Connie how often I was feeling the contractions, she assured me that she would be at my house long before Paige Joy made her appearance. "Relax," she said. "Make sure you have everything ready in your bedroom, then relax. This is your first baby. They generally take their time arriving."

I called Wade to tell him it was time. I got his voicemail. "Connie says there's no rush," I said, "but, I don't know. It feels like she's ready, so if you want to see your daughter's entrance, you'd better come home soon. Also, I think I know relayed where Brenda was that day she was killed."

That message delivered, I headed for the bathroom.

I'd just flushed the toilet and was washing my hands when I heard Baraka growl. A low, throaty, warning growl.

"Nice doggy," I heard someone say. "It's okay."

The woman's voice sounded familiar, but she was talking so softly, I wasn't sure who was in my dining room. I did know it wasn't Maria. No accent.

"Where's your mistress? Where's P.J.?"

Ah, I did know who it was, and after what Maria had said earlier, that realization put me on edge. Cautiously, I opened the bathroom door.

"Tamara," I said, hoping my expression didn't relay my concern. "What a surprise."

Tamara Trulain stood only a few feet from the front door, Baraka between her and where I stood, his body tense. The hairs on the back of his neck and over his shoulder blade were raised making it look like his ridge extended from the top of his head to his tail.

Tamara's gaze never left Baraka. "I don't think your dog likes me."

I stepped out of the bathroom. This was the second time in one day that Baraka had growled at a woman. Usually he was aloof with strangers, not defensive. His attitude toward Maria had surprised me, but with Tamara, I was glad he was acting the protector. "You shouldn't have come into the house without me inviting you."

I stepped closer and placed a hand on his back. "Good boy," I said.

He looked at me, then back at her. His posture relaxed a little, the hairs on his neck laying back down, but he didn't move.

My attention stayed on Tamara. "I'm afraid you made the drive out here for nothing. I'm not feeling well, so we cancelled the meeting. I think I'm going to have my baby today, and—" I stopped myself. "Oh, I'm so sorry, Tamara. Connie said you—"

"Had another miscarriage," she finished for me. " 'For the best,' the doctor said. 'Deformed. Wouldn't have survived even if I had gone to term.' " She glared at me. "Dammit, nothing's gone right in my life. I can't have babies, my husband's gotten us involved with a drug cartel, and you have to go into that bathroom at exactly the same time she's in there."

"By 'She' you mean Brenda?"

"Of course I mean Brenda," Tamara snapped and looked toward the living room. "Is that your office down there?"

I ignored her question. "Last week when we were talking about Brenda, you didn't tell us everything, did you? You didn't mention seeing Brenda come out of the bathroom and go upstairs."

Tamara looked back at me.

"Maria said she saw you make a phone call after that."

"Oh she did, did she?"

"You called your husband, didn't you? You told him where Brenda was. And when she came out of the church, he ran her down."

"And all would have been fine if she hadn't given you the pen." Tamara headed for my office.

"Pen?" I followed her, Baraka by my side. "If you're looking for a pen, why has Miguel been taking my thumb drives?"

"Because my husband hires idiots."

Tamara stopped just inside my little office area. I stayed on the living room side of the doorway. For a moment she simply looked at my desk and computer, then she reached over and dumped the pens and pencils I had in the plastic cup so they were spread out over my desktop.

I remembered finding a couple extra pens in my purse. Pens that simply looked like pens.

Tamara began pulling caps off the ones on my desk, dropping each on the floor after looking at it.

"If it looks like a pen, she could have left it anywhere."

"Maybe so, but we looked everywhere. In her purse and in that church." Tamara paused and glanced at me. "She had to have given it to you when you two were in the bathroom."

I thought back to that day. Me overhearing Brenda on the phone, seeing her, and telling her to call for help. Brenda hugging me, saying she would see me soon.

Hugging me.

"Got it." Tamara held up a black and silver ballpoint pen so I could see it. "I'm not exactly sure how it works, but this is it."

With the cap off the top of the pen, I could see where the micro end of a USB cable could be inserted.

"We didn't realize Miguel was looking for the wrong thing," she said, "until last Wednesday when you mentioned your thumb drives were being taken. Alan hadn't told Miguel this needed a cable for it to act like a thumb drive, that it looked like a pen. Miguel would have found this Saturday if your neighbor hadn't stopped him."

"Alan?"

"My husband."

The one with a different last name, which, at the moment I couldn't remember. "When I first met you," I said, "you never mentioned you had any connection to Patterson's Furniture store."

She shrugged. "No reason to. Alan runs a private equity group. He owns a variety of stores: a florist, the jewelry store downtown that features my pieces, a card shop, and Patterson's, which seemed like a great buy since furniture is an excellent way of bringing contraband across the border. Contraband like the diamonds I use in my jewelry." With her free hand she touched the diamond hoop hanging from her left earlobe.

"Getting the diamonds has been great; however, we didn't realize that Patterson's Furniture came with strings attached. Strings that are held by a very powerful drug cartel. You met Juan, I believe, when you visited the store." I guess I nodded because she went on. "Juan is the younger son of the cartel's drug lord. Personally, I like him. He's come up with some great ideas on ways to hide the diamonds. Problem is, he hasn't always been careful about who he hires. I have no idea why he put that doper Jerry something-or-other on the payroll. And it looks like Miguel was a mistake."

She sighed. "Juan's biggest mistake was telling Alan that keeping Brenda on as the bookkeeper would work. He said Blacks are accustomed to whites cheating in business, that she wouldn't be bothered by a few inconsistencies in deliveries. Boy, was he wrong."

Tamara laughed. "Last week you asked if Brenda said anything to me about being followed. I told you no, but that was a lie. Since I've

265

never gone into Patterson's when she's been there, she didn't know I had any connection to the store. As we went downstairs, she told me how she'd barely gotten away from the store's owner and that she had to get some pictures to her contact."

"So, after talking to Brenda, you called your husband and told him where she was."

"I don't think he would have found her if I hadn't." She twirled the pen between her fingers. "Poor Alan was a nervous wreck waiting for her to come out of the church."

"Your husband ran her down." Simply saying the words sent a chill through me.

"He had no choice. We couldn't let her turn this over to the authorities." Her voice lacked emotion and her eyes showed no feeling. "Problem was she didn't have the pen on her or in her purse."

"And it wasn't in the church." I remembered how calmly Tamara had told me about the break-in.

"Which meant she had to have given it to you."

"And so, you sent Miguel to break in here."

"Actually, it was Juan the first time. He had Miguel go after that. I think your dog scared Juan. Now I understand why. He is a big dog."

I hoped having him by my side scared Tamara, but the way she smiled at me, I wasn't sure. "Now what?"

"I get rid of this—" She held up the pen. "You tell me where the diamonds are, and then I leave."

I doubted she'd simply leave, and she'd said one thing that surprised me. "What diamonds?"

"The ones that were shipped with that rocking chair you took from the store."

"So, there were diamonds packed around that music box." I shook my head. "Sorry, I think your man Miguel got those."

"He said he didn't."

"He must have lied. There were no diamonds on or near the chair after I saw Miguel here. No wrapping around the music box. He had to have taken them."

"Then he died lying."

"You killed him?" I cringed at the thought of Miguel dead. Poor Maria.

"He went for a swim." She eyed me suspiciously. "Where's the rocking chair?"

"My husband took it. It's at the Sheriff's office."

"But you didn't find any diamonds." Tamara sighed. "Damn. Those diamonds cost a fortune. Alan said smuggling diamonds would be dangerous, that they're called Blood Diamonds for a reason." She pointed the pen toward me. "Question now is what do I do with you? Maybe—"

Perhaps the pen projecting from her fist looked like a rawhide twist to Baraka. Or maybe he thought she was going to poke me. Whatever the reason, he lunged forward and grabbed the end of the pen.

She gave a squeal of surprise and let go.

And so did he.

The pen dropped to the floor.

She stooped to pick it up.

Baraka also tried to pick it up.

I heard the crack of bone against bone when their heads met. A full-grown Rhodesian Ridgeback's head is hard as a rock, and the contact was enough to put Tamara off balance. As she stumbled backwards, her body hit the side of the doorjamb. Arms flailing, she tried to catch herself, but couldn't stop her downward motion. Her rear hit the floor, her shoulders the side of my computer chair.

For a second I stared at her, but only for a second. "Move," I yelled at Baraka, and as he moved, I reached down for the pen.

"No!" Tamara cried, twisting to the side to get back on her feet.

Pen in hand, I headed for my front door. I heard Baraka growl, but I didn't look back. I'm not sure if Tamara ran into Baraka as she tried to get to me, or if he actually tackled her, but I did hear a thump, and when I reached my front door and looked back, she was again getting to her feet, and Baraka was now right behind me.

Once outside, I headed for the gate. I wasn't sure what to do next. Running to Howard's place wasn't an option, not in my condition. My car keys were in my purse in the house, so driving off wasn't possible. All I could hope was someone would drive by in the next few seconds, someone who would stop and give me a ride.

"Stop!" I heard Tamara yell. I also heard a whoosh and a loud bang. Something hit the dirt in front of me.

I stopped. I hadn't thought of her having a gun. Slowly, I turned back toward my front door. Tamara stood on the porch. She held a small automatic between her two hands, the gun aimed toward me.

As I looked at her, she lowered the barrel so the gun was aimed at Baraka. "Bring me the pen, or I'll shoot your dog."

That was when my water broke.

I felt the warmth as the liquid ran down my legs, soaking my jeans, and pooling in my boots. Stunned, I stood where I was.

"Didn't you hear what I said?" Tamara shouted. "Bring me the pen."

"My water broke," I said, not moving.

"I don't give a damn about your water."

"My baby." She didn't understand. "My baby's coming."

Baraka understood something was happening. He came over and sniffed my pant leg, then looked up at me as if to say, "What's going on?"

I heard Tamara grumble. Still aiming the gun in my direction, she came down the steps and started toward me. I don't know what would have happened next if a blue Ford hadn't come roaring down the road just then. Tamara stopped midway between the house and me. She lowered her gun to her side so it wouldn't be noticed and watched as the car drove by. My legs started shaking, my heart racing. I knew the car. She didn't.

She started toward me again, then paused at the sound of brakes squealing. I watched Howard's car stop, make a hundred-and-eighty-degree reverse turn, and start forward, now facing the opposite direction. She frowned as the Ford slowly came back toward us on the wrong side of the road and close to the fencing I'd put up. The driver's side window was rolled down.

Howard stopped the car parallel to her. "What's up?"

"Nothing," she said. "We're just talking."

"Good." He smiled. "In that case, you can drop that pea shooter you're trying to hide."

I thought, for a moment, she would try to use her gun, either to shoot Howard or me, but then she saw the revolver he had aimed at her

Chapter Forty-One

I don't know what Tamara might have done if Wade hadn't pulled his Jeep up behind Howard's car right then. With a sigh she dropped her gun and raised her hands. I let the men deal with her. Now that the danger had passed, I convinced my legs to move, and though my wet jeans clung to my legs and I heard a squishing sound with each step I took, I made it back into the house.

By the time Wade came inside, I'd changed my underwear and pulled on a loose pair of maternity slacks. The first thing he did was hug me, then he asked, "What happened?"

"Her husband owns Patterson's Furniture. She came after this."

I showed Wade the camera pen and explained, as best I could, what I thought had happened the day I ran into Brenda. "Tamara said Brenda had never seen her at the store, so when they met at the church, Brenda told Tamara she was being followed and had to hide out to make a phone call. She had no idea that Tamara would tell her husband where to find her. And I had no idea, Brenda dropped this pen into my purse." I handed it to him. "You need to get this to Agent Tailor."

"Will do." He looked down at the wet clothes on the floor. "Are you all right?"

"Yes. That is—" A contraction started—a strong one—and I tried to breathe as Connie had taught us. Wade, I think, held his breath until I relaxed.

Finally, I could talk again. "Connie's on her way." I glanced at the clock on my dresser. The contractions were getting closer. I wanted Wade to stay, but I also wanted Tamara arrested. "What are you going to do about Tamara?"

"I called Dario. He'll take her in and book her."

"Good. Tell Lieutenant Gespardo she either killed or had Miguel killed."

Wade nodded.

"And tell Howard thank you." I started to lean over to pick up my wet clothes, but a sharp pain changed my mind. "I think I'll sit down for a while."

* * *

Connie arrived and took my blood pressure, listened to Paige Joy's heartbeat, and checked how much I'd dilated. "Oh my gosh," she said, stepping back and shaking her head. "P.J., don't you do anything the usual way?"

Maybe first babies took hours to deliver; mine was impatient. I was already in the second stage of labor, cervix fully dilated. Paige Joy was on the move. Together we set up the bed the way Connie wanted, and I stretched out, ready to "pop out" my baby.

But then Paige Joy changed her mind.

"This isn't unusual," Connie assured me. "Just relax and breathe with each contraction. You don't need to lie on your back. Find a position that's comfortable."

The next three hours became a blur of people coming and going and Connie checking my blood pressure and Paige Joy's heartbeat. Jason came in and held my hand for a while. Connie even let him hold the stethoscope against my abdomen and listen to the baby's heartbeat. When he grew restless, Connie sent him on an errand and promised she'd call him when the baby was closer to being born.

Wade came and went also. Between contractions, he massaged my back and told me what was going on regarding Tamara and the pen Brenda had given me. "Agent Tailor is here," he said at one point. "She's using your computer to look at what's on the pen. Your friend Brenda captured enough evidence to put Patterson's Furniture out of business and a lot of people in prison, including Tamara and her husband."

At the moment, I didn't care.

The contractions were coming closer and closer, the urge to push dominating my energy. "She's crowning," Connie finally said, and I pushed harder.

Wade was with me when Paige Joy was born. She came out screaming. Only after Connie placed her against my chest and told me to hold her tight did my baby stop crying. She felt so tiny, her skin so smooth. Connie placed a baby blanket over her and told me, if I wanted, to try to get her to nurse. I concentrated on that procedure and was barely aware of Connie clamping Paige Joy's umbilical cord or delivering the afterbirth.

It took a while before Paige Joy discovered what a nipple was for, but once she did, she took to the idea eagerly. Connie had me decently covered by the time Jason returned. He'd missed the delivery but didn't seem to care. Eyes wide, he stared at his little sister. "She's so tiny."

"She'll need your protection," Wade told him.

It was dark by the time Connie left. Paige Joy had been bathed, measured, and weighed and was wearing her first diaper and sleeper. I reluctantly placed her in the bassinet. As much as I wanted to keep holding her, I knew keeping her in bed with me was not a good idea. I was exhausted. I certainly didn't want to fall asleep and roll over on my little girl.

Chapter Forty-Two

Paige Joy Kingsley was five weeks old when Grandma Carter decided it was time to hold a post-partum welcome party for her great-granddaughter. "We'll have it at your place," she said and smiled. "A smoke-free environment. But I'll provide the food."

I certainly wasn't going to object. Both Connie and Wade had been right, new babies led to sleep deprivation. Paige—by the end of the first week, we'd stopped adding her middle name when talking about her—wanted to be fed every two to three hours, day or night. Connie said not to worry about it. Paige was growing and gaining weight, and most breast-fed babies demanded frequent feedings at first. "As her stomach matures, she'll start sleeping through the night."

I couldn't wait until that time came. My baby was doing fine; I was a walking zombie.

Grandma did the inviting to the party and took the RSVPs, so I had no idea who might show up. For the party, she purchased a cute little three-piece short set for Paige that had strawberries on the top. It was made by Carter. "Of course," she'd said when she gave it to me. "A Carter outfit from Grandma Carter."

I was able to squeeze into my pre-pregnancy jeans, but I needed to work on my abs if I wanted my girlish figure back. A turquoise smock-like top helped cover the fat I hadn't lost. Wade said I looked wonderful.

I do love that man.

His parents showed up first. They didn't stay long. They had a meeting to attend, they said, but wouldn't miss a chance to see their granddaughter again. They had come twice right after she was born, but then had been on a cruise for the last two weeks. "She looks like you," Joy Kingsley said, holding Paige. "She's going to have the same curly hair and brown eyes, but she's got Wade's smile."

"And temper," I added when Paige began to fuss.

Wade's mother handed Paige back to me. "You've made him very happy, P.J. Thank you."

Ginny dropped by just as her folks were leaving. She also didn't stay long, but I wasn't surprised. Ginny had been coming by two and three times a week ever since Paige was born. "Just to give you a break," she said, and she did, sometimes watching Paige so I could get a nap, sometimes taking Jason somewhere so he didn't feel neglected.

Other guests came and went—neighbors, former co-workers, clients—some bringing gifts. Paige was going to have more clothes than she would ever wear, but it was fun to open the packages and see the cute little outfits. I remembered playing with dolls as a child and the fun of dressing them. When I reached an age where I realized getting pregnant and giving birth might bring on schizophrenia, I banished the idea of having a child of my own. Now I held Paige in my arms, and so far I hadn't shown any symptoms of the disease.

Mom and Ben arrived with a huge bunch of helium-filled pink balloons, crazy party hats, and party horns. When Mom blew her horn, Paige started screaming, showing everyone what a strong set of lungs she had. Thank goodness Grandma Carter shooed Mom into the kitchen and put her to work, and Ben helped Wade set up extra chairs.

I'd quieted Paige down by the time Anna came with her baby. "She's adorable," I told her as we traded infants for a few minutes. "A mini you."

"If it hadn't been for you showing up when you did . . ." Anna gazed at her child. "I still have nightmares about that woman."

"What have you heard about her or Mrs. Welkum?"

"That Jewel has been charged with kidnapping and assault and battery and the judge refused bond. She'll be in jail until her trial, and long after that, I hope. As for Madeline, the board has agreed not to pursue embezzlement charges as long as she pays back everything her daughter stole."

"I guess that's fair," I said as Anna and I reclaimed our daughters.

"I think so," Anna said, hugging her little girl. "I've gotten to know Madeline since our ordeal in that cellar. She keeps apologizing for what her daughter did and for not turning her in as soon as she realized Jewel was stealing money from the charity. But, now that I have a daughter, I understand the desire to do anything possible to protect your child. One good thing that came out of the whole ordeal is the other day Madeline called and offered me a job decorating two of the houses Homes4Homeless is refurbishing. She also said she'd recommend me to all of her friends."

"And all's well that ends well." I gave Anna a hug. One of the positives of the Mothers-to-Be group was I'd made a new friend.

Ken showed up next. He brought a good-looking, middle-aged woman with him. "Adele Rose," he said, introducing her. "My next-door neighbor."

"I met your husband a few weeks ago," Adele said, "when he came looking for Ken. That was a scary time."

"Wade said you were very helpful that day." I looked around for him, and saw he was helping Grandma set food on the table.

"I'm just glad everything worked out all right."

Adele snuggled close to Ken and smiled up at him, and I knew they were more than simply neighbors.

"Brought something for your baby," Ken said and handed me a medium size, colorful gift bag.

I shifted Paige to the side and extracted a cloth doll almost the same size as Paige, dressed in pink pajamas. Paige reached a hand toward the doll, and Ken grinned. "A pajama girl for Pajama Girl's little girl."

Connie arrived next. Her gift was information. Maria had had her baby. A little boy they'd named Miguel in honor of her deceased cousin. Divers had found Maria's cousin's body five days after discovering the truck. Once Maria's baby was old enough, they were taking her cousin's body back to Mexico to be properly buried. She wasn't sure if she, her husband, and the baby would return to the United States or not.

Sarah and her baby were doing fine, the only problem was the boyfriend, Tommy, had decided fatherhood was not for him. That relationship had ended, but Sarah's family had stepped in, and Connie felt all was going to work out well.

"I'm starting another Mothers-to-Be group," Connie said. "I hope you and Anna will drop by sometime and talk to these women about your experiences."

I looked at Anna and we both laughed. "Are you sure you want us telling them about *our* birthing experiences?"

Howard brought the best gift that afternoon and it wasn't for me or Paige. In his arms he held a little gray kitten, the one Jason had finally decided he liked the most. "She's not quite eight weeks old, but I think she's ready to leave her mother," he told Jason. "Do you remember what we talked about, how to care for her?"

Jason nodded and took the kitten.

He cuddled his baby and I cuddled mine and all was fine until Baraka came over to sniff the kitten and the kitten swatted Baraka, her sharp little kitten claws hitting his nose. With a yelp, he bounced back, the noise scaring Paige, who began to cry, and Grandma came out of the kitchen wanting to know what was wrong.

It took a good fifteen minutes of nursing before Paige was again happy and the two of us rejoined the party. Jason was still playing with his new kitten, and Baraka had been confined to his crate, at least until the party was over. Lieutenant Dario Gespardo arrived then, carrying a gift I hadn't thought I'd see again. "As far as we can tell," he said, "there's nothing about this rocking chair to connect it to the drug or diamond smuggling going on at Patterson's Furniture store." He set the rocker in front of me. "Therefore, you paid for it, it's yours."

"Thank you," I said, and gave it a small push so the music box played its tinny rendition of "Rock-a-bye baby."

"Not sure I'm going to want to hear that over and over," Wade said.

That was when I noticed Jason's downturned head and look of shame. "I'm sorry," he said. "I didn't mean to break it. I just wanted to see what was under the paper."

Both Wade and I frowned. "What do you mean?"

"The glass covering it." He still wouldn't look at us. "When I pulled it down off the shelf, it broke."

"What glass?"

"The one around the music box." Jason looked up at me, as if I should understand.

"There was a piece of glass under the paper?" Wade asked.

"Yeah. It broke into lumpy pieces." Again, Jason lowered his head. "I didn't mean to break it. Really."

Wade looked at me, then at Gespardo before he asked Jason, "What did you do with those lumpy pieces?"

"I, ah . . . I kinda hid them," he admitted.

"Hid them where?"

"Under the wood in the shed."

"Show me where."

The kitten was handed back to Howard, and Jason slowly led Wade and Lieutenant Gespardo out the back door.

I was pretty sure I knew what they would find in the woodshed. Maria's cousin had been telling the truth. He hadn't taken the diamonds. Torturing him hadn't given Tamara any answers because Miguel didn't know where the diamonds were.

Wade nodded when he came back into the house, Jason by his side. I figured Gespardo would once again take the rocking chair away, but Wade said no. "We have a record of the rocking chair, when it was purchased, and from what store. There's no need to keep it in evidence as long as we have the diamonds. These, along with the ones Ken found and the video your friend Brenda took should be all the evidence the court needs to put Tamara and her husband away for a long time."

"Diamond," Jason said, taking his kitten back from Howard. "That's what I'll call her. Diamond. See our new kitty," he said, holding the kitten toward Paige.

To my surprise, she reached out to the kitten, and Wade chuckled. "I guess we're now the perfect family. A boy, a girl, a dog, and a cat."

And a lot of love, I thought as I looked up at him.

The End

WHAT'S NEXT

Now that you've finished *Something to Crow About*, I would really appreciate it if you would take the time to write a review on Amazon or Goodreads.

Reviews help authors and readers. If there was something you didn't like a review lets the author know what didn't work for you. If you liked the story, it helps readers know that they may also enjoy the story.

If this is the first book you've read featuring P.J. Benson and Wade Kingsley, you might enjoy the others in the series.

The Crows
As the Crow Flies
Eat Crow and Die

There's also a short story (e-book) titled *Eye of the Crow* that takes place the day P.J. and Wade marry. See the teaser I posted a few pages from here.

And, if Wade's Slow Baked Ribs sounded interesting to you, turn the page.

WADE'S SLOW BAKED RIBS
They are quite simple to make

What you need:

- A conventional oven
- Baking dish and aluminum foil
- A rack of ribs (Wade prefers pork, but beef ribs can be used.)
- Seasoning.
    - Sometimes he uses a rub he makes himself, other times it's a store-bought seasoning
    - Salt and pepper
- Barbeque sauce

Directions:

- Preheat oven to 225 degrees
- Season ribs with salt, pepper, and if you like a homemade rub (he uses 1/2 cup brown sugar,1 tbsp garlic powder, 1 tbsp onion powder, tsp salt, 1 tbsp chili powder, 2 tsp cumin, 2 tbsp smoked paprika, 1 tsp cayenne pepper) or a store bought rub
- Place ribs meat side down on aluminum foil, wrap so the meat is enclosed, and set in baking dish
- Bake for 3 ½ to 4 hours
- Open aluminum foil and drain drippings.
- Carefully flip ribs over and cover with barbeque sauce
- Return to oven (uncovered) for 20 – 30 minutes.
- Remove and serve.

They are yummy.
P.J. Benson Kingsley

ACKNOWLEDGMENTS

I am so glad I joined a critique group in Venice, Florida. Their encouragement, along with having to produce new chapters, finally spurred me on to finish this book. In addition to correcting my punctuation and grammar errors, the group became my "first readers." If something wasn't clear to them, I knew I needed to work on it. Thank you, Pat Averbach, Monicka Becker, Kate Borduas, Amy Susan Brown, and Judy Rousseau.

Also, my thanks to my nephew, Eric Tobin, for the information he sent about embezzlers. I am amazed by the number of embezzlement cases that have been uncovered in our local county and city governments. Most involve credit cards, but some embezzlers simply write checks to themselves.

And many thanks to my neighbor's daughter, Anna Nieboer, CNM, MSN, who is a midwife. Anna not only took time to answer my questions about what she does as a midwife, she showed me the kit she takes to deliveries.

Attending the **Writers' Police Academy** back in 2018 helped me with the information about an oxycodone overdose. The video I watched while there showed a man who had taken an overdose of oxycodone, how he acted and how he responded once the NARCAN was administered. Over the years, I've attended three WPAs, and I always return home filled with knowledge. Thank you Lee Lofland for putting these on.

Finally, many thanks to Gayle Gordon, Donna Johnson, Marie Latta, and Julie McMullen for being my Beta Readers. They corrected my spelling errors, punctuation, typos, and content gaffes. I even appreciate Gordon Aalborg, who proved that my eyesight (at least when it comes to catching errors in my manuscript) is far from perfect. And thank you, Chris Wait, from www.HighPinesCreative.com for another wonderful cover.

ABOUT THE AUTHOR

Maris Soule has had thirty books traditionally published, ranging from romance and romantic suspense to mystery and thriller. Over the years, her books have been translated into more than 18 languages, sold in more than 25 countries, and won and placed in more than a dozen contests. Born and raised in California, she was working on a master's degree in art history when she met and married her husband. She taught high school art and math for eight years before turning to writing full time. The Soules, who have two grown children and two granddaughters, now live in Michigan in the summer and Florida in the winter.

Visit her at:

https://www.marissoule.com
https://www.facebook.com/MarisSouleAuthor/
http://twitter.com/marisSouthHaven
https://www.goodreads.com/author/show/305476.Maris_Soule
https://www.pinterest.com/marissoule/

Here's a glimpse of

Eye of the Crow
A Short Story

SATURDAY

With a sigh of relief, I pulled up in front of the bank and parked directly behind a dark-blue car with a broken taillight. The clock on my car's dashboard showed five to twelve. I'd timed it close, but I'd made it before the bank closed.

I grabbed the endorsed checks, cash, and deposit slip I'd put together before leaving my house. I didn't bother locking my car door. Here in Zenith, with the population less than seven hundred, it's never been necessary.

A brisk wind scattered a flurry of leaves across the walkway leading to the bank, but as I hurried toward the door, I barely noticed. My mind was on all I had to do before my wedding. In four more hours I would be P.J. Kingsley, wife of Kalamazoo County Deputy Sheriff, Wade Kingsley.

A wife . . . and in five more months, a mother.

I'm sure I was grinning when I opened the door and stepped into the bank. I think I've been grinning ever since Wade proposed.

To my surprise, neither of the two tellers said "Hi." One or the other usually gives a greeting whenever anyone steps into the bank. Anne, the older of the two did give me a quick glance, but her expression didn't look welcoming, and she immediately looked back at the short, chubby man standing on my side of the counter.

He had on some kind of hat that from the back appeared to have ears . . . but not Mickey Mouse ears. I was in the process of trying to figure out what kind of hat it was when he turned toward me.

It wasn't a hat.

Halloween wasn't for another two weeks, but what I was looking at was a mask: a panda bear mask that covered his entire head except for eye holes and a couple smaller holes where his nostrils would be. I was so surprised by the mask that it took me a second to notice that Panda was pointing a gun at me.

"You," he growled, "over here."

He motioned to a spot closer to the tellers' counter. I hesitated, dozens of thoughts racing through my head. I was only two or three steps from the front door. Could I get back outside before he pulled that trigger? Was that bulletproof glass in the door? If I got outside, would I be safe? If I…?

"Now!" Panda demanded, ending those thoughts.

It was a good thing I didn't try to run outside. My legs were shaking so much I could barely manage to walk over to the spot he indicated. It had been over a month since I'd suffered morning sickness, but the knot forming in my stomach threatened to bring up my breakfast. I wanted to look calm, but I could feel my heartbeat in my throat, its erratic rhythm taking my breath away.

I glanced at Anne and then at Betty, the other bank teller. Both looked as scared as I felt.

"Put the money in the bag," Panda demanded. The mask made his voice sound weird.

For the rest of

Eye of the Crow

Go to Amazon.com

Made in the USA
Columbia, SC
11 March 2021

34353559R00176